DECEIVED
By DESIRE

Books by Marie Force

The Gilded Series
Duchess by Deception
Deceived by Desire

The Gansett Island Series
Gansett Island Boxed Set,
　Books 1–3
Gansett Island Boxed Set,
　Books 4–6
Gansett Island Boxed Set,
　Books 7–9
Gansett Island Boxed Set,
　Books 1–10.5
Book 1: Maid for Love
　(*Maddie & Mac*)
Book 2: Fool for Love
　(*Joe & Janey*)
Book 3: Ready for Love
　(*Luke & Sydney*)
Book 4: Falling for Love
　(*Grant & Stephanie*)
Book 5: Hoping for Love
　(*Evan & Grace*)
Book 6: Season for Love
　(*Owen & Laura*)
Book 7: Longing for Love
　(*Blaine & Tiffany*)
Book 8: Waiting for Love
　(*Adam & Abby*)

Book 9: Time for Love
　(*David & Daisy*)
Book 10: Meant for Love
　(*Jenny & Alex*)
Book 10.5: Chance for Love,
　A Gansett Island Novella
　(*Jared & Lizzie*)
Book 11: Gansett After Dark
　(*Owen & Laura*)
Book 12: Kisses After Dark
　(*Shane & Katie*)
Book 13: Love After Dark
　(*Paul & Hope*)
Book 14: Celebration After Dark
　(*Big Mac & Linda*)
Book 15: Desire After Dark
　(*Slim & Erin*)
Book 16: Light After Dark
　(*Mallory & Quinn*)
Book 17: Episode 1:
　Victoria & Shannon
Book 18: Episode 2:
　Kevin & Chelsea
Book 19: Desire After Dark
　(*Riley & Nikki*)
Book 20: Yours After Dark
　(*Finn & Chloe*)
Book 21: Trouble After Dark
　(*Deacon & Julia*)

DECEIVED *By* DESIRE

MARIE
FORCE

ZEBRA BOOKS
KENSINGTON PUBLISHING CORP.
www.kensingtonbooks.com

ZEBRA BOOKS are published by

Kensington Publishing Corp.
119 West 40th Street
New York, NY 10018

All Kensington titles, imprints, and distributed lines are available at special quantity discounts for bulk purchases for sales promotion, premiums, fund-raising, educational, or institutional use.

Special book excerpts or customized printings can also be created to fit specific needs. For details, write or phone the office of the Kensington Sales Manager: Attn.: Sales Department. Kensington Publishing Corp., 119 West 40th Street, New York, NY 10018. Phone: 1-800-221-2647.

First Printing: September 2019
ISBN-13: 978-1-4201-4787-2
ISBN-10: 1-4201-4787-0

ISBN-13: 978-1-4201-4788-9 (eBook)
ISBN-10: 1-4201-4788-9 (eBook)

10 9 8 7 6 5 4 3 2 1

Printed in the United States of America

Chapter One

June 1903
Newport, Rhode Island

He first noticed the alluring curve of her neck. The delicate stretch of pale skin suggested elegance, a sweetness that begged to be explored and an aura of strength that intrigued him. Aubrey stood in the doorway to the drawing room for the longest time, riveted by a woman's neck for the first time in his life, before clearing his throat to let her know he was there.

Startled, she whirled around, letting out a gasp of surprise as the oversized feather duster she'd been using fell to the dirty marble floor with a loud clatter. She would need a hundred feather dusters, perhaps a thousand of them, to wipe the layers of grime from every room in the house. How had it gotten so filthy over the winter?

That was one of many mysteries confronting him since his arrival thirty minutes prior at Paradis Trouvé, his family's summer home on Newport's Bellevue Avenue. The name meant "paradise found" in French. It had been bestowed upon the home by a previous owner, and unfortunately, his parents had embraced the pretentious name when they acquired the property.

Aubrey cursed himself for scaring the young woman as he entered yet another room in complete disarray. What the hell had happened to their "cottage" since the family left last September? "Pardon me."

The woman took a step back, immediately on guard. Her reddish-brown hair had been gathered into a neat bun, and her drab olive-colored shirtwaist dress—muslin if he wasn't mistaken—was serviceable at best but showcased interesting curves. However, her face was the showstopper. Her alabaster complexion reminded him of the cameo his grandmother had worn—ivory perfection with a dusting of freckles across her nose and brown eyes that were at once shrewd and suspicious.

"Wh-who are you?" The lilt of an Irish brogue danced through the dusty air like music.

Captivated, Aubrey had to remind himself that she expected a reply. "I apologize for frightening you."

"Are you the new butler? It's about time you showed up." All business now that the fright had passed, she bustled across the room toward him, removing work gloves as she went.

He ought to set her straight but decided in a prescient flash to let her think he was the butler. At least until he had a chance to find out more about her. His dusty, wrinkled travel clothing and hair damp with sweat from the unusually warm weather wouldn't give him away as a member of the family that owned the forty-room seaside monstrosity. His father had bought it six years ago from a member of the Astor family. Under normal circumstances, the Italian Renaissance–style palazzo was all gold and glitter and ostentatious excess, but Aubrey had been shocked by the filth and disrepair. He'd been sent by his mother to oversee the preparations for his illustrious guests, the Duke and

Duchess of Westwood, who would arrive in three weeks, along with the other friends Aubrey had invited.

"I'm Maeve Brown, the housekeeper. I have no earthly idea what's become of the rest of the staff, but Mrs. Nelson will be arriving in two short weeks, and as you can see, the house is in complete disarray. Did the agency inform you that the Duke and Duchess of Westwood will be visiting this summer? Apparently, they're friends of the Nelsons' son, Mr. Aubrey. Mrs. Nelson is the daughter of a British earl, so needless to say, she has exacting expectations, especially when entertaining a duke and duchess." Maeve bit her deliciously full bottom lip as she seemed to debate whether she should say more.

Aubrey wanted to beg her to continue, just so he could listen to her melodic voice that spoke of culture and breeding far above a housekeeper's station.

"From what I was told, the previous staff quit in protest of Mrs. Nelson's treatment of them. In this day and age, there are plenty of other homes that treat their employees with respect and dignity. I was told a new staff had been hired, but no one has come."

"If Mrs. Nelson is such an ogre, why are you here?"

Maeve's cheeks flushed with a rosy glow that enchanted him. "By the time I arrived in New York, this was the only housekeeper position remaining for the Season. However, Mrs. Nelson's reputation is well known, which is probably why the rest of the staff never arrived. Unless we both want to find ourselves out of work and without references, we'll need every minute until she arrives to prepare for her guests."

"I'm not afraid of hard work. Are you?"

"Certainly not."

He'd known her for two minutes and already wished he could sit and talk to her for hours, until he knew everything there was to know about Miss Maeve Brown, formerly of Ireland. His mother would have an apoplexy over the thoughts he was having about the housekeeper, which was all the more reason to have them. After both of his older brothers had sworn off marriage, it had fallen to Aubrey to continue the Nelson name, a predicament his mother took far more seriously now that the family had become ridiculously wealthy. Prior to that, she hadn't given a fig about the family name. Defying his mother had been one of his favorite activities as a child and younger man. With her pressuring him relentlessly to make an "appropriate marriage," admiring the curve of the Irish housekeeper's neck would be the last thing she'd want him doing.

But it was a splendid neck, perhaps the most delightful neck he'd ever beheld, and he'd seen some truly excellent female necks in his day, most recently last year in London where he'd endured a second Season to placate his mother. She'd positively salivated at the thought of him marrying into the British aristocracy. Alas, it was not to be, and he was through with that charade. The only thing that had kept it from being completely unbearable had been his friendship with Derek Eagan, the Duke of Westwood, as well as Derek's cousin Simon and their mutual friend Justin Enderly, who was the second son of an earl. With Derek and Simon now married, and Justin avoiding the social scene, Aubrey had flat-out refused to return to London this spring. His mother had been furious, but he'd stood his ground.

Now with a summer in residence with his mother about to transpire, Aubrey fully expected another charade to unfold that would have to be endured rather than enjoyed. However, the Newport house was his favorite place in the world, and there was nowhere he'd rather be, even with his mother and her many charades to endure.

"Sir?"

Aubrey realized Miss Brown was talking to him.

"I asked if you'd like me to show you to your quarters before you get to work."

"Yes, please." Aubrey knew he ought to end this misunderstanding immediately, but something stopped him. He couldn't say what, but rather than confess to not being the new butler, he followed her through familiar hallways thick with dust and spiderwebs to one of the back corridors and the stairs that led to the servants' quarters on the third floor. As they went up the stairs, Aubrey tried not to notice the gentle sway of her backside. He failed utterly as her backside was almost as intriguing as the curve of her neck.

"I cleaned this room yesterday after we received word of your impending arrival. There're fresh towels in the wardrobe and a bathroom down the hall. Mr. Nelson had plumbing put in the house two years ago, and it's quite delightful."

Aubrey agreed. Indoor plumbing was delightful, and so was she. "How did the house get so filthy?"

"I was told by one of the other housekeepers in town that after Mrs. Nelson left at the end of last summer, the remaining staff opened the windows and left them that way. When I arrived a week ago, the house was filled with rodents and seagulls. I almost didn't stay."

Horrified, Aubrey didn't know what to say. She'd had to contend with that alone? He was also ashamed that he'd stopped paying attention to his mother's high-handed behavior years ago. That she mistreated her staff to the point they'd leave the windows open for the harsh New England winter came as a shock to him and was something that would have to be addressed as soon as she arrived. At least he had a couple of weeks to dread that conversation.

"Didn't the pipes freeze?"

"Apparently they were spared because the water had been shut off. For that we can be thankful."

"Indeed. Why did you stay?"

She hooked her fingers together and looked down. "I need the position."

Her quiet dignity touched him deeply. He wanted to know her story, where she came from, what had brought her to America. "We'll see about getting you some more help."

"It's going to take a miracle to have this house ready for the arrival of the duke and duchess."

"You needn't worry about them. They don't stand on formality."

Her brows knitted adorably. "And you know this how?"

Damn. Aubrey realized he'd spoken as their friend and not as the new butler. "People speak of them in New York. The duke is well regarded in social circles in London, and his duchess is said to be very down to earth."

"Who were your employers in New York?"

He had to think quickly to come up with a name she'd recognize. "The Smiths." Thankfully, he'd gone to Choate with Adam Smith and knew the family.

Her eyes widened with amazement. "They're one of the wealthiest families in America."

"Yes, they are."

"So why are you now employed by the Nelsons?"

"I wanted to come to Newport, and the Smiths don't summer here. Mrs. Smith has an aversion to the sea. Her father drowned while rescuing her from a rogue wave when she was a child."

"How awful!"

"She's never forgotten it."

"How could anyone forget such a thing?"

"It's very tragic indeed."

She gave him a look that had him wishing his hair was clean and his face shaved. "You're very . . ."

Aubrey held his breath, waiting to hear what she would say.

". . . *young* for a butler."

He was young for a butler—by decades, in fact. "While I was with the Smiths, their butler and under-butler succumbed to typhoid, and I was the head footman. The family promoted me to butler." *Where was this nonsense coming from?* He told himself to stop it, to tell her the truth, to end this ridiculous farce.

"I see. Would you like something to eat before you begin work?"

"Yes, please. I'd appreciate that after the long journey." He left his bag in the room she'd assigned him and followed her down the backstairs, where his sisters' children hid from their governesses.

They went down three flights to the kitchen and the servants' dining room in the basement.

"This is the new cook, Mrs. Allston. Mrs. Allston, this is the new butler . . ." Maeve turned to him, her face flushing with a pleasing shade of pink. "I'm sorry, I didn't get your name."

"It's Jack. Jack Bancroft." The name of the duke's estate manager popped into Aubrey's head.

"A pleasure to meet you, Mr. Bancroft." A stout, sturdy woman with ruddy cheeks and neat gray hair, Mrs. Allston stood watch over a pot of something that smelled delicious.

Aubrey's stomach growled loudly.

Maeve laughed, and the delicate sound traveled through him the way a bolt of lightning might. He wanted to hear that laugh again and again. He wanted to hear it in his dreams and in his every waking hour. As a man who'd relished his freedom and independence, the feelings she evoked in him were frightening and unprecedented, to say the least.

Aubrey glanced at her. "I beg your pardon. I'm apparently hungrier than I thought." He'd taken the overnight steamship from New York and had been served an elaborate breakfast several hours before the boat docked at Newport's Long Wharf.

Mrs. Allston ladled soup into two bowls and set them on the rough-hewn wooden table along with a basket of freshly baked bread. "There you are then."

He waited for Maeve to be seated before he slid onto the bench across from her. The huge table would easily accommodate thirty people. When the house was fully staffed, there would easily be that many in service, if not more.

They ate the delicious split-pea soup and bread in silence, but he was aware of her every move, her every breath. In all his thirty-two years, through hundreds of hours spent in London ballrooms and New York social clubs, in music halls, opera houses and at countless society dinners, picnics and house parties, he had never once responded to a woman the way he had to her.

His reaction to her defied explanation.

It defied belief.

It would *infuriate* his mother.

Aubrey smiled to himself, imagining her reaction to hearing that he'd finally found the woman he wanted, and she was the new Irish housekeeper at their Newport estate.

Once the epicenter of the cotton, rum and slave trades, Newport had become the place to see and be seen in the months of July and August when most of New York society relocated to their cottages by the coast. The social climbers came to make their annual impression on the hostesses who determined whether one was in or out—and if you were out, there was little chance of ever getting in.

His mother, the ultimate social climber, had made a blood sport out of climbing the rungs in Newport. Imagining her reaction to learning he'd developed a sweet spot for the Irish housekeeper had Aubrey picturing her exploding into a rage the likes of which would be talked about for years to come. He'd seen her rages before, most of them directed at others, including his siblings, but had never been the reason for one.

Compared to his far more rebellious siblings, Aubrey had been her good boy, her golden child as his siblings liked to say chidingly. Perhaps it was time for him to take his turn in stirring her ire. He had a feeling that Miss Maeve Brown, formerly of Ireland, would be worth the hell his mother would rain down upon him.

As he surreptitiously watched Maeve eat her soup, he noted the way her lips closed around the spoon and how her throat moved when she swallowed.

How was it possible that the pedestrian act of eating soup could be so impossibly erotic? A surge of heat to his groin had him holding back a groan.

"Are you quite all right, Mr. Bancroft?"

That voice. Dear God, the sound of her words was the sweetest music he'd ever heard. He could listen to her speak all day without ever tiring of the sound. It wouldn't even matter so much what she said, as long as she never stopped talking to him. Aubrey summoned his composure, which had deserted him the second he first laid eyes on the appealing curve of her neck. He nodded in response to her question. "I'm quite well, thank you."

"And the soup is to your liking?"

"It's delicious."

"I agree. Mrs. Allston is a wonderful cook. We're lucky to have her, especially in light of the reputation this house has with those in service."

Aubrey wiped his mouth on the cloth napkin, made of much coarser cotton than the linen he was accustomed to upstairs. "So there're exactly three of us then?"

"I'm afraid so, at least until the others turn up. *If* they turn up."

"And the task before us is . . ."

"Monumental. Wait until you see the wreckage that is Mrs. Nelson's room." She shuddered. "It's a travesty."

"If we were to take it a room at a time, focusing on the public spaces and the bedrooms required by the Nelson family and their guests, we might be able to get it done in time."

"We have two weeks until Mrs. Nelson, her daughters and grandchildren are due to arrive and three until the duke and duchess are expected."

"I'll see what I can do about getting some more help. Surely there have to be more people seeking positions for the summer."

"I certainly hope so, because without more help, I can't envision how we'll ever be ready for the duke and duchess. I quite fear Mrs. Nelson's infamous rages."

"Don't you worry about her. We'll have everything in place for her and her guests."

"Thank goodness you're here." She took a sip of the hot tea she had steeped for them both. "I have felt quite like I was climbing a mountain all by myself with no possible way to reach the summit in time."

"We will get there together." As he said the words, he considered the double meaning of the two of them reaching the summit together. A shiver rippled through him, making him shudder from the desire that gripped him. He thanked goodness for the table that hid his obvious reaction from her.

"Are you sure you're well? You seem rather . . . flummoxed."

That was a good word for how he'd felt since first laying eyes on her. Flummoxed indeed.

He was about to respond to her when another man came into the kitchen, looking as road weary and dusty as Aubrey imagined he did, too. This man was older, with silver strands mixed in to his dark hair, his face craggy with age and wisdom, his eyes red with fatigue but friendly.

"May I help you?" Maeve asked.

"I'm Joseph Plumber, the new butler. The agency indicated I should report today."

Maeve's shocked gaze shifted to Aubrey. "If Mr. Plumber is the new butler, then who, pray tell, are you?"

Chapter Two

Caught in the crosshairs, Aubrey smiled and decided the only honorable thing he could do was come clean. "You've found me out."

Maeve stood, hands on her hips, eyes flashing with fury. *Dear God*, she was *spectacular*. "What is that supposed to mean?"

"I'm Aubrey Nelson."

She recoiled in horror, which was the only word that could possibly be used to describe the expression on her face. Then she turned and walked swiftly from the room, shoulders set and head held high on that magnificent neck.

Aubrey cursed under his breath, feeling like an absolute heel for upsetting her.

Holding his hat in his hands, Mr. Plumber bowed his head. "It's an honor to meet you, sir."

Aubrey went around the table to shake the man's hand. "Thank you, and I apologize for the confusion. That was entirely my fault. Miss Brown has done an excellent job since she's joined the staff."

"I couldn't help but notice the house and grounds appear to be in a state of . . ."

"Disarray?"

Mr. Plumber seemed relieved that Aubrey had stated the obvious so he wouldn't have to. "Yes, sir."

"Apparently, there was a problem with the former staff at the end of last Season. Windows and doors were left open, the caretaker walked off the job and the gardener is apparently long gone, as well."

Mr. Plumber's eyes bugged. "They left the windows *open* all winter?"

"I'm afraid so. When Miss Brown arrived, there were rodents, seagulls and all the accompanying mess."

"My goodness! And this was done deliberately?"

"From what I'm told, yes."

"The pipes! Does the house have indoor plumbing?"

"It does, but the water is shut off at the end of the Season, which is why the pipes didn't freeze and burst."

"Well, that is a relief then. Why would they allow the house to be vandalized?"

Aubrey ran his fingers through his hair, wishing now that he'd taken the time to bathe. But he hadn't wanted to miss the chance to dine with Miss Brown. "My mother . . . She's a bit of an . . ." He was going to say "ogre" but thought better of it. "She's rather exacting, and from what I'm told by Miss Brown, the staff quit in protest after last Season." Fearing the man would think better of his plans to spend the summer running the household, Aubrey quickly continued. "But that won't happen this year. The staff will answer to me and only me. I'll see to it that you're not bothered in any way by my mother."

Mr. Plumber exhaled a sigh of relief. "That is very good of you, sir. However, I can't help but notice there doesn't appear to be any staff other than Miss Brown."

"And Mrs. Allston, the cook."

"We need housemaids, footmen, gardeners, stable men, kitchen help. . . We need, well, everything. A house of this size and prominence won't run itself without a size-able staff."

"I understand, and I plan to see what we can do about hiring more help."

"Very well then. I shall endeavor to help in any way I can. I understand the family is hosting the Duke and Duchess of Westwood for the Season?"

"That is correct. They're close personal friends of mine, and I invited them and several other friends from England to summer with us." Aubrey glanced at the doorway Maeve had fled through, anxious to go to her, to apologize, to grovel, if need be. "If you'd please excuse me, I need to find Miss Brown and clear up a misunderstanding."

"Of course. I'll ask Mrs. Allston to show me to my quarters and then get to work after I've had a chance to clean up and change my clothing."

"Thank you very much. Please, have something to eat as well."

"I'll do that. Thank you, sir."

Aubrey left the room and headed for the backstairs because they were closer, taking them two at a time until he reached the second floor and began a search for her. He quickly realized that she could be anywhere, and if she didn't want to be found, she could hide out very effectively in a house of this size.

His heart beat fast from exertion and dismay. He'd hurt her, and he hated himself for that. What had he been thinking? Why hadn't he told her the truth from the outset? He didn't know anything other than he'd been caught off guard by an unprecedented reaction to her and hadn't wanted to ruin any chance he had to get to know her by telling her he was a member of the family she worked for.

Instead, he'd ruined everything by lying to her. He should've learned from the mess Derek had made for himself. Derek had taken on the identity of Jack Bancroft, his estate manager, after Derek met Catherine and discovered she disdained the aristocracy. After they were married, she'd learned he was actually the Duke of Westwood. He'd faced the formidable task of making his wife fall in love with him all over again—this time as the duke. It had worked out well for them in the end, but not before they'd both suffered significant—and unnecessary—heartbreak.

And what exactly was Aubrey hoping for with the delightful Miss Brown, he asked himself as he methodically searched the house, finding each room filthier than the last. So many damned rooms. What family needed that many rooms anyway? The first time he'd seen the home his father had acquired in Newport, Aubrey had cringed. Nothing screamed "new money" quite like a forty-room cottage on the coast, filled with gold and glitter and priceless antiques that had conveyed with the house.

Though the Nelsons had always been comfortably upper crust, Aubrey hadn't been raised with the kind of wealth his family now enjoyed since his father's company cornered the market on component parts for railway cars. Nelson Industrial had made its fortune manufacturing the wheels, couplings and other parts that had been in massive demand as the railway system rapidly expanded.

The family's fortunes had truly exploded when the company began competing with Pullman by also producing high-end cars for first-class travel along with baggage cars, mail cars, stock cars and its latest addition—refrigerator cars. The demand was so intense, the company could barely keep up and had expanded as rapidly as the railway system itself. Last year, when the company adopted the revolutionary assembly line process Ransom Olds had first used in 1901 to mass produce automobiles, the Nelson company's production capabilities had quadrupled along with their fortune.

That fortune fueled a lavish lifestyle that now included

this monstrosity of a house in fashionable Newport. Despite the ostentatiousness of the house, however, Aubrey adored Newport, the shore, the summer parties, the sloop he kept at anchor in the harbor and the general sense of harmony that came from being near the ocean.

"Where in the hell could she be?" He was running out of doors to open on the second floor when he entered the ball-room, which had clearly been a favorite spot for the seagulls that'd wintered there. Almost every surface was covered with white, sticky bird refuse and more feathers than he'd ever seen in a ballroom, and that was saying something after spending two Seasons in London.

Strolling to the far end of the vast ballroom, he threw open the doors that led to an expansive veranda that looked out on the ocean, which today was calm and sparkling in the late spring sunshine. Standing at the rail, arms wrapped around herself and head bent, was Maeve Brown. Her posture and the heaving of her shoulders indicated that she was crying. He was gutted to know he'd caused that.

"Miss Brown." Aubrey spoke softly so as not to startle her and managed to startle her anyway.

She whirled around, her face red and ravaged by tears.

"I'm so very sorry for misleading you."

"How *could* you? I spoke freely to you *about your own mother*!" She hiccupped on a sob and then covered her mouth, as if trying to contain future sobs.

"Everything you said about my mother is true."

Her eyes flashed with fury that he richly deserved. "She is my *employer*. I was under the impression I was speaking to a fellow member of the staff, *not* a member of the family that employs me."

"I realize that, and I apologize profusely for mislead-ing you."

"Why did you?" Her fury had abated somewhat, leaving

a small voice that he already knew was unlike her. The Maeve he had met earlier didn't suffer fools—and he'd indeed been a fool to deceive her.

"I . . . I liked you." He swallowed hard. "And I wanted to know you. When you mistook me for the butler, I saw an opportunity to relate to you as peers. It was wrong of me, and I'm truly sorry to have misled and upset you. I've never done anything like that before, and I shouldn't have done it to you. I hope you will accept my sincere apology."

She stared at him for a long, charged moment before she spoke again. "What do you mean you *liked* me?"

He took a step closer to her. "I meant that I *liked* you."

She recoiled, which wasn't exactly the reaction he'd hoped for. "How can you *like* me? You don't even *know* me."

"I want to know you."

She shook her head. "I don't know what kind of game you're playing here, Mr. Nelson—"

He took another step. "Aubrey."

If there'd been anywhere for her to go, she would've moved farther away from him. "—but I'm not interested in playing that game. I'm here to work. I'm a housekeeper. I do not associate with men of your social strata."

"I understand that, and I respect it. But I still like you."

Her face flushed with the rosy color that made him breathless. "Stop it. Don't look at me that way. I'm not that kind of woman."

"I know you're not, and I'm sorry again. I don't mean to make you uncomfortable. It's just that from the first second I saw you, I just . . ." He rubbed a hand over his stomach, which churned with nerves, another thing he'd never experienced when speaking to a woman.

"Whatever you're going to say, please don't. You know as well as I do the way things work in the world in which we live. I'm here to do a job. That is all I'm here to do."

Keep talking to me. It didn't matter what she said, even words he didn't want to hear, as long as she kept speaking.

"Mr. Nelson! Are you listening to me?"

"Yes, Miss Brown. I'm most definitely listening to you."

"If you respect me, as you said you do, you'll stop this at once and see to the hiring of additional staff, so we might make the house ready for Mrs. Nelson and her guests." She gasped as she seemed to realize something. "They're *your* guests."

"Yes, they are, and despite their lofty social standing, they're kind, generous, wonderful people. You'll like them very much."

"Whether or not I like them is of no consequence. My duty is to prepare for their arrival, to make the house ready to receive them." She gestured to the bird refuse decorating the room. "And as you can plainly see, we're a very long way from ready."

"Yes, we are, but I'll help you and Mr. Plumber and whatever staff we are able to hire. We'll work together until the house is standing tall and fully restored to its former glory."

Her expression went flat with shock. "We will work *together*?"

"Yes."

"That's not done. You *own* the house."

"Technically, my father does."

"Which means you do as well."

"Despite what you might believe, I'm not a pampered prince who's incapable of the kind of work that'll be required to clean up this mess and make the house ready for occupancy. I assure you I'm more than capable of pitching in and doing my share."

She shook her head. "It wouldn't be right for you to do that."

"Who says?"

"*Everyone* who is *anyone*. It's simply not done."

"Who would know if I help? The two of us, Mr. Plumber and Mrs. Allston. Somehow, I think between the four of us we can manage to contain the scandal."

"It's bad enough that you lied to me, but don't make it worse by mocking me."

She was magnificent. There was, simply, no other word that would do her justice.

"Why are you smiling like a loon?"

"Am I?"

"You know you are. There's nothing funny about this. You lied to me, allowed me to disparage your mother, who's also my employer, in front of you—"

"Nothing you said about my mother is untrue. Her reputation as an exacting, difficult woman is well known here and in New York. That her former staff would stoop to leaving the doors and windows open for the winter says a lot about her treatment of them. Perhaps we should leave her bedroom untouched, so she can see what you walked in on because of her bad behavior."

Maeve recoiled in shock. "I will *not* leave her bedroom untouched, and if I have my way, she will *never* know what I walked in on. I'll work tirelessly to make sure there's not a single particle of dust left in this house by the time she arrives."

Tipping his head to the side, he studied her intently. "Why?"

"Why what?" She squirmed ever so slightly, as if his attention overwhelmed her.

He hoped it did. He wanted nothing more than to overwhelm her in the best possible way, even as he realized that thought was highly inappropriate. He prided himself on being a gentleman in all his dealings with women and would continue that tradition with her no matter how inappropriate his thoughts might be. "Why do you care so much about making things right for a woman who obviously mistreated her staff?"

"She hasn't mistreated me, and I was hired to do a job—a job that I fully intend to do. Now, if you wouldn't mind letting me by, I'd like to get back to work."

"I do mind."

"Pardon me?"

"I'll step aside when you agree to let me help. I'm strong and able-bodied and willing to work. You need me, Maeve." He took a risk calling her by her given name, but he couldn't stop himself from seeking something more with her, something deeper. All the reasons it was wrong for him to feel this way couldn't drown out the need to know her, to understand her.

Her cheeks flushed with the rosy glow that made her even more appealing to him. "You take liberties you have no right to, Mr. Nelson."

"My name is Aubrey, and I wish I could say I was sorry, but I'm not. Let me help you get the house ready. You need my help. Why not accept it?"

She eyed him suspiciously. "What's in it for you if I allow you to assist?"

"Nothing other than the satisfaction of helping someone who needs it."

"That's it?"

"What else would there be?" The slow lift of her left brow would go down in Aubrey's personal history as one of the most erotic things he'd ever seen. "Why, Miss Brown, I'm shocked."

"I highly doubt that. But since I'm rather desperate for help, I shall accept your kind offer with the caveat that it shall be *only* help preparing the house. Nothing more."

Her final two words touched him profoundly, because he sensed pain, betrayal and something infinitely sad in them. He desperately wanted to know more about her, and he vowed to use the time they would spend working together to find out who or what had hurt her so deeply. "Where shall we begin?"

"Since you can't very well sleep in the butler's quarters, we shall begin by preparing a bedroom for you to use."

Aubrey bit his tongue so he wouldn't be tempted to comment on the fact that he'd have her to himself in his bedroom. The thought amused him, especially when he considered her potential reaction to him saying such a thing.

She swept past him, head held high, leading the way. "Which room is yours?"

"Third door on the right."

With a growing feeling of trepidation, he followed her out of the ballroom, down the hallway to the closed door. What level of disaster awaited them inside the room?

"I haven't been in this room yet, so I don't know what to expect." Maeve rested her hand on the door and glanced at him, her expression indicating that she shared his concern about what they might find.

"Let's get it over with."

She opened the door and stepped inside.

Aubrey went in after her to find the room exactly as he'd left it.

"This is one of the only rooms on the back side of the house that wasn't damaged." She glanced at him. "That must mean the former staff held you in high regard."

"I should hope so. I was never anything other than kind to them."

Maeve went to open the windows, pulling the curtains back to let in the cool spring air.

Other than a light layer of dust, the room was in good condition. Aubrey rolled up his shirtsleeves and tossed his coat on one of the fussy Louis XIV chairs that had come with the house. His mother adored those chairs. He and his siblings often joked that she seemed to love her furniture more than her children, which she hadn't denied. "What can I do?"

Maeve bit her lip as if trying to decide.

"I'm quite capable of anything you need done. It may surprise you to learn that I wasn't raised as a pampered, privileged son of fabulously wealthy parents. The big money came later."

"It does surprise me."

Aubrey realized she was teasing and laughed, delighted to discover that she could be quite witty. "Touché. My father made his fortune with the advent of the railroad. Prior to that, his company manufactured church bells. There's far more demand for railroad components than there was for church bells."

"I imagine there is." She pulled on work gloves and handed him a feather duster that she produced from a closet in the adjoining bathroom.

He accepted it from her with a feeling of victory that she had decided to allow him to assist her.

"Isn't your mother the daughter of a British earl?"

"She is indeed, but my grandfather had squandered most of the estate's resources by the time she was of marriage-able age. Because she had no dowry to speak of, she had to settle for an uncouth American who had more in the way of potential than he did resources."

"Theirs is not a love match, then?"

"Oh God, no." Aubrey snorted with laughter. "Not at all. They can barely stand to be in the same room with each other, but it's been a very effective partnership. Luckily, when Father stumbled into a disgusting fortune, Mother knew how to navigate the social aspects of their newfound wealth. Thus the house in Newport where people of quality and disgusting riches gather for the summer. Apparently, she has much to learn about how to properly manage a staff."

"Wait until you see the carnage in her room."

Aubrey grimaced. "I can hardly wait."

Chapter Three

Maeve didn't want to be fascinated by the handsome, down-to-earth son of her famously difficult employer. She didn't want to be charmed by his willingness to help prepare the house for his illustrious guests or be drawn in by his stories of humble beginnings.

As she led him into the wreckage of his mother's suite of rooms, she didn't want any of those things and yet, she was charmed, intrigued and alarmed.

He'd walked into the house a mere hour ago and had completely upended her plan to remain aloof and disengaged from everything and everyone having to do with her new position. She was here to do a job, not become involved in any way. Becoming involved hadn't worked out well for her in the past, and she'd like to think she'd learned her lesson.

But the handsome, charming son of her employer had her hanging on his every word, wanting to know more about him despite her fervent desire to remain uninvolved. The man was too handsome for his own good, with silky dark hair and warm brown eyes that crinkled in the corners when he smiled. And he smiled often.

She opened the door to hell and moved aside to let him go in ahead of her.

He stepped inside and stopped short at the sight of disaster. "Dear God."

His whispered words summed up the destruction she had found in his mother's room on her first day at the house. She hadn't been back in here since that day as the sheer madness of it had daunted her to the point of nightmares.

Maeve had learned everything she knew about keeping a home from her mother and her family's beloved house-keeper, Bridie, which was short for Bridget. Maeve's earliest memories included Bridie. Watching her mother and Bridie manage a much smaller home had prepared Maeve well enough to pretend she had the skills necessary to run a grand house. The only reason she had landed the job was because no one else wanted to work for Mrs. Nelson. However, no amount of formal training could've prepared her to contend with the nightmare in Mrs. Nelson's bedroom.

Maeve covered her face with a lavender-scented hand-kerchief that she'd been carrying since that first day. "It's my belief that the former staff left food in here to encour-age the rodents to take up residence."

Mr. Nelson took a long look around, his expression one of shock and revulsion.

"Thankfully," she continued, "once the food was gone so too were the rodents, but as you can see, they left their mark."

"I would say so. Where do we even begin?"

"If I may make a suggestion . . ."

"By all means."

"I would dispose of everything that can be removed and acquire new furnishings. Nothing here can be salvaged."

"I tend to agree." He withdrew his own handkerchief and covered his nose and mouth. "The smell is . . ."

"Revolting."

"Indeed." Glancing at her, his eyes conveyed boundless

empathy. "I'm so very sorry that you've had to contend with such filth."

"I'd like to say I've seen worse, but I can't say that in this case. If you wish to rescind your previous offer of assistance, I would certainly understand."

"I would never leave you or anyone to contend with this on their own." He crossed the room to the windows and peered down to the yard below. "We will toss everything out the window and burn it."

Maeve admired the plan and the determination she heard in his tone. She hadn't thought of tossing the contents of the room out the window or the possibility of burning everything. "That would be the best course of action."

"I'll do it."

"I'll help you."

"That's not necessary."

"I *will* help you." She gave him the mulish look that had gotten her into trouble with her mother as a girl—and later as a woman with her husband. But she couldn't think of that, wouldn't think of it. Not ever again. She had left the past where it belonged when she stepped onto the ship that brought her to America, giving her a fresh start in a new country where no one knew her. She prayed every night that she wouldn't be found. They had to be looking for her.

Maeve realized Mr. Nelson was watching her closely and shook off the unsettling thoughts.

"It'll go quicker if we work together."

"If you insist," she said.

"I do."

Maeve went to the far side of the bed and opened the other set of windows. The fresh air couldn't compete with the rank odor, but it made it possible for her to tuck the scented handkerchief into the sleeve of her dress, freeing her hands to begin stripping the soiled linens from the bed.

Wincing from the now-familiar pain coming from the palm of her right hand, she rolled the linens into a large ball that Mr. Nelson hoisted and tossed from the window.

"The mattress must go, too," he said.

Maeve choked back a gag at the stains and the smell that emanated from the fouled mattress. "Agreed."

Working together, they lifted the mattress, dragged it to the window and pushed it out. She tried not to think about what she might be touching.

It took more than an hour to haul everything that could be removed from the room to the window and drop it to the yard below. When they were finished, only the bed frame, antique dresser and vanity remained. With a good cleaning, they could possibly be salvaged. The scent of the room had improved vastly as the soiled items were removed.

"I wouldn't have thought it possible to save this room," Maeve said, "but we're well on our way to restoring it to rights."

"The walls will need to be scrubbed, and we'll need to order new bedding immediately to have it here in time for my mother's arrival."

"I'll see to that. The household has accounts with several local merchants who can provide the quality required."

"Thank you for taking care of that."

"Will you tell your mother about what happened?"

"I suppose I'll have to when she notices that everything is new."

"I must confess that I was concerned about her getting here before I could clean the mess."

"She would've been here in my stead, but my father has taken ill. They're visiting various doctors trying to determine what's wrong with him."

"I'm sorry to hear that. Is he seriously ill?"

"He may be." Mr. Nelson's grim expression indicated

his concern. "He's had a terrible cough for a number of months now."

"Is it consumption?"

"They don't think it's that, but they don't know what it is. It's very concerning. Since she couldn't be here, my mother sent me to make sure the house is ready for my friends from England."

"What took you to England?"

"The Season." He seemed almost embarrassed. "My mother had the idea that I might marry into the British aristocracy."

"Oh, I see." She went into the adjoining bathroom, returned with a bucket of soapy water and turned her attention to the crusty surface of a priceless dresser, scrubbing it with determination to think about anything other than the handsome Mr. Nelson flitting about with British debutantes. He must've been very popular.

"No, you don't see. That was *her* plan for me, not mine for myself. I indulged her with two spectacularly unsuccessful efforts."

Maeve told herself it was none of her business but knowing that had never stopped her before. "Are you not past the point where you can choose your own wife?"

"You would think so, but you haven't met my mother."

She glanced around the destroyed room. "And yet I feel as though I have."

He unleashed that potent smile that made her feel warm and tingly. The last time she'd felt that way about a man, she'd ended up running for her life from the only home she'd ever known. Shame and misery overwhelmed her as she recalled the terrifying last day that had changed her life forever and forced her to vow that no man would ever again have power over her.

Maeve trembled, shook her head and forced those troubling thoughts from her mind. She'd put an entire ocean between herself and the nightmare she'd left behind, but the fear had followed her.

"Miss Brown." Mr. Nelson's voice cut through the silence, startling her from her troubling thoughts.

She turned to face him, forcing a smile.

He looked at her with concern that she didn't want. Not from him. Not from anyone. "Are you quite all right?"

"Of course."

"Your hands are trembling, and your face has gone pale."

He saw too much, and that made him the greatest threat yet to her new life. "This time of year," she said haltingly, "I suffer from congestion when the trees begin to bloom."

"I have a sister who suffers similarly."

"Do you have many siblings?" Maeve asked, taking the focus off herself.

"I have four older sisters, all of whom are married with children, and two older brothers, neither of whom is married. They work for my father's company as do I when I'm not being paraded through the London and Newport social circus."

"You're the baby of your family then."

"Yes, and they never let me forget it. They say I'm my mother's favorite, but I think my brother Anderson is her favorite."

"Do you all have names that begin with the letter *A*?"

He cringed. "Unfortunately, we do: Anderson, Alfie, Aurora, Audrey, Adele, Alora and yours truly." He ended with a dramatic bow. "Aubrey."

"They're lovely names."

"I'm glad you think so. We took some teasing about the

A names when we were children. What about you? Do you have siblings?"

"I have three sisters, all of them younger." A pang of sadness struck in the vicinity of her heart. Leaving them had been excruciating, but she'd had no choice. She hoped they knew that but had no way to know for certain. Cutting off all contact with her family had been necessary to ensuring her safety.

If Mr. Nelson ever found out what she'd done . . .

No. He wouldn't find out. No one knew her here or knew about her past. Her stomach ached at the thought of him finding out. That couldn't happen.

"Miss Brown?"

She realized he'd said something that she had missed. "I beg your pardon?"

"I asked what your sisters' names are."

"Bridget, Aoife and Niamh."

"They are beautiful names, as is Maeve."

"Thank you."

"What does Maeve mean in Gaelic?"

Her face heated with a flush. "It means 'she who intoxicates.'"

Mr. Nelson cleared his throat. "Well, the name certainly suits you."

She couldn't bring herself to look at him, even though she desperately wanted to. Instead, she moved on to scrub the bird refuse from the silk wallpaper. That was easier than confronting the yearning Mr. Nelson inspired in her. Not for the first time, Maeve suspected something was wrong with her. Why did she feel things so intensely? Why did her body betray her by wanting things that were bad or wrong or destined to cause trouble that she didn't need?

It had always been that way, from the time she was a

young girl and the careless slights of other children would sear her heart. Children could be awful to each other, and while others let the painful moments roll off their backs, Maeve carried those scars with her to this day. Her propensity to feel everything had the potential to ruin this new life she'd made for herself, and she couldn't let that happen. She was here to work and only to work.

If she kept telling herself that again and again, perhaps she could reverse the downhill slide into the kind of emotional upheaval that had been the hallmark of her troubled existence. She simply didn't have the fortitude to go through that again, not when she'd risked everything to start a new life in America, far away from the pain of the past.

"Miss Brown?"

Jolted again from her thoughts, she looked up to find Mr. Nelson looking at her with concern etched into his handsome features. Tingles ran up and down her spine. This was not good. Not good at all. "Yes?" Her voice wavered.

"You're scrubbing a hole in the wallpaper."

She shifted her gaze to the spot she'd been scrubbing while thinking about all the reasons she could not—*would not*—be taken in by the charming son of her employer. Sure enough, the bird refuse was long gone, and she'd nearly succeeded in creating a hole in the priceless wall covering. "My apologies."

"No need to apologize. I admire your dedication to your duties."

She tried to ignore the charming smile that accompanied the compliment, but she couldn't ignore the tingles or the flutters. "I can finish in here if you'd like to tackle your father's rooms. They didn't fare much better than your mother's."

"I'll take care of removing the items that need to be added

to the bonfire we shall have later. And then I'll venture into town to see what I can do about finding us some more help."

"Very good. Thank you for your assistance."

"I'm happy to help you, Miss Brown."

The formal way he said her name sent new tingles down her spine.

This wasn't good at all.

After clearing the fouled bedding and furniture from his father's rooms and hurling it out the window to the growing pile below, Aubrey went into his own room to bathe and change his clothing. The tepid water in the tub went a long way toward cooling his overheated body. Cleaning was hard work, especially when dealing with the kind of mess that had befallen Paradis Trouvé. That name . . . Aubrey and his siblings had tried to compel their parents to give the house a less pretentious name, something like Sea Swept, which had been his suggestion.

But his parents had loved the French name given to the home by the preeminent architect Richard Morris Hunt and had rejected all their children's suggestions in favor of keeping the home's pedigree intact. Hunt had designed and built most of the palatial cottages that lined Bellevue Avenue, nearly all of them fashioned after a European home of similar distinction.

The Nelson house, like the others in the neighborhood, was filled with Aubusson rugs, priceless artifacts shipped from France and Italy, paintings by the Old Masters and Louis XIV chairs so fragile that one risked one's own life by sitting on them. A guest last summer had chosen to sit on the hearth rather than take a chance on destroying the priceless piece.

Aubrey leaned his head back against the cast-iron tub. So much had changed since his father's company had begun working for the railroad. He barely recognized his life anymore and knew his siblings felt the same way. They'd gone from the relative anonymity of the upper class to the expectations that accompanied enormous wealth. So many demands, customs and rules—and the socializing! *Dear God*, the balls, soirees, house parties, lawn parties, parlor games, clubs. It never ended. The best part had been the new friends he'd made, particularly those in London. He was eager to see Derek, Catherine, Simon, Madeleine and Justin again and looked forward to their arrival.

As long as he thought about his friends and his social obligations, he could avoid stewing over his unprecedented reaction to Miss Maeve Brown.

His mother would have an apoplexy if she had the first inkling of his attraction to the housekeeper. She'd go out of her way to make sure he never saw the delightful Miss Brown again, so he could never, ever, *ever* let on that he fancied her. His mother would ship her off to Siberia so fast his head—and Maeve's—would spin.

No, he would have to be very careful indeed. He'd disappointed his parents by not making an aristocratic match in London. Aubrey was fully aware that they'd begun to despair of what would become of him and the Nelson family legacy with none of their three sons inclined to marry and ensure the continuation of the Nelson name. His older brothers seemed to have no interest whatsoever in marrying, so all his parents' focus had turned to Aubrey. Despite that enormous pressure, he had made it clear that he would only marry for love—nothing less. His father had accused him of being a fool. "Marriage isn't about love," he'd said disdainfully. "It's about power."

Aubrey had no interest in acquiring power or a wife he didn't love or even like. He had held out hope for all this time that he might meet someone who would make him feel . . . *something*. He'd seen Derek and his cousin Simon fall madly in love with Catherine and Madeleine McCabe. His own sisters were happily married to men they seemed to truly like and love. Surely it wasn't too much to hope for such a match for himself. However, in thirty-two years, he'd only ever felt "something" for two women, including the one he'd met earlier that day, and she was completely and totally off-limits to him for more reasons than he had time to list.

For starters, the scandal would be epic.

Men of his ilk didn't take up with the Irish housekeeper, no matter how delectable her neck might be. It would be better to chalk this odd morning up to travel weariness and the shock of finding the household in such disarray. That had to be it. He got out of the tub, ran a towel over his body and dressed in clothing more befitting his stature—gray twill trousers, a matching vest, a crisp white shirt that had been ironed by his valet in New York, a necktie and a gray pinstripe frock coat that would make him roast in the heat. No matter. He needed to look the part when he went searching for the help they desperately needed.

Since the day had become cloudy and overcast, Aubrey decided to walk the short distance into town where his first stop would be at the Newport Casino, an exclusive club founded by James Gordon Bennett Jr., the notorious publisher of the *New York Herald*. As the story went, after Bennett's friend Captain Henry Augustus "Sugar" Candy rode a horse into the rarified confines of the Newport Reading Room—on a dare from Bennett—Candy was thrown out and Bennett, in his outrage, had founded the

Casino as an alternative club. This was the same man who'd once, while drunk, urinated into a fireplace during a party at the Fifth Avenue home of his fiancée's parents, thereby ending his engagement along with his welcome in high society.

The stories about Bennett were the thing of legend, and Aubrey hoped to get the chance to meet the man one of these summers. Aubrey related to Bennett, who'd refused to be constrained by the expectations laid out by society, choosing instead to follow his own path no matter where it might lead. While Aubrey couldn't imagine himself urinating into a fireplace at one of the massive society homes he frequented, he wished he had a fraction of Bennett's legendary moxie.

He also wished he was the kind of man who could finally meet a woman who interested him and act on the attraction without a care as to the scandal that would ensue. Perhaps if he spent some time with men like Bennett, their bravado might rub off on him and give him the courage to once and for all stand up to his family's rigid expectations for him. How many times had he wanted to remind his mother that he needed to lead his *own* life, not the life she envisioned for him?

Here he was now at thirty-two years of age and still worried about what his mother might say or do. Well, things were going to be different after the nightmare the former staff had perpetrated, due to his mother's mistreatment of them. It was time to put a stop to her iron rule over everything and everyone around her, including him.

Fueled by outrage and determination, Aubrey removed his hat and entered the club inside the shingle-styled building that had begun a trend of other such buildings. Since he hadn't been there in a while, he fully expected to have to produce his membership card. However, that proved unnecessary when an attendant greeted him by name.

"Welcome back, Mr. Nelson. It's wonderful to see you again."

Aubrey handed over his hat. "Thank you, Frederick. It's great to be back in Newport."

"May I offer you some refreshments?"

"I'd love a bourbon and water with a twist of lemon."

"I'll have that brought to you immediately. I believe you'll find friends in the billiard room."

"Thank you very much."

Aubrey made his way through the space that had been designed by preeminent architect Stanford White to offer secluded areas for private conversation as well as open space for larger gatherings. During the Season, the Casino hosted a wide variety of events, including daily tennis matches on the grass courts, and served as a social hub for the Bellevue Avenue set.

In the billiard room, Aubrey recognized several familiar faces, including Matthew "Mutt" Jarvis, who'd been in his class at Yale, earning the name Mutt after a stray dog on campus took a liking to him. The dog had gazed at him with blatant adoration and followed him around until "Mutt" finally adopted the mutt.

Aubrey shook hands with his old friend.

"Look at what the cat dragged in." Mutt had put on twenty pounds since their college days and had the red, ruddy face of a man who overindulged in spirits on the regular.

"Good to see you, Mutt."

His brows furrowed. "I go by Matthew here."

"Of course. My apologies. How's the other mutt?"

Matthew's expression immediately turned tender. "She

passed a year ago, rest her soul. The old girl had to be close to twenty years old. Broke my heart to lose her."

"I imagine so. I'm sorry for the loss."

"Thank you. Heard you invited some lofty guests to join you for the Season."

"That's right, but the only thing lofty about them is their titles. They are just like you and me. You'll like them."

"Hopefully, they're more like you than me."

Aubrey laughed. "Are you keeping busy then?"

"Eh, as busy as one can be as the son of a local solicitor father who expects me to take over the business one day whether that's what I want or not. I hadn't expected to spend my whole life in Newport, which is nowhere near as exciting in the off season as it is in the summer. It's down-right boring, in fact."

"Ah, Matty," one of the other men said, "don't we keep you entertained?"

Matthew scowled at the man. "You're not the kind of entertainment I'm looking for." To Aubrey he added, "Any single sisters left in the Nelson stable?"

"Not a one. They're all married and producing nieces and nephews at an alarming rate."

"Pity. As I recall, the twins were quite the lookers."

Aubrey wanted to smack the lusty look off his friend's face but chose instead to redirect the conversation. "May I buy you a drink?"

Matthew handed his pool cue to another man and asked him to finish his game. "I never say no to a drink."

Frederick came into the room with a tray bearing Aubrey's drink.

"I'll have the same," Matthew said as they went into an adjoining room in search of a place to sit.

They found an unoccupied space and settled into the plush leather easy chairs.

Matthew stretched his legs out and helped himself to Aubrey's drink, downing half of it before Aubrey could protest.

Frederick returned a minute later with the second drink, which he handed to Aubrey when he saw Matthew drinking the other one.

"Thank you, Frederick," Aubrey said.

"My pleasure."

When they were alone, Aubrey fixed his gaze on Matthew, wishing he had the right to express concern about Matthew's obvious drinking problem, but people didn't discuss such things in polite society, and the Newport Casino was most definitely polite society. "I need a favor."

"What can I do for you?"

"I need to immediately hire some help to get Paradis Trouvé ready for the arrival of the duke and duchess."

"So it's true then that the staff quit at the end of last Season?"

"It's true," Aubrey said with a sigh, "and they didn't go quietly." He described the disaster he'd walked into earlier.

Matthew stared at him, agog. "They left the windows *open*? All winter?"

"That they did, and the mess is . . . well, it defies description. My father is ill, so my mother sent me to make sure the house is ready, and I find myself with a catastrophe on my hands and no chance of being ready for guests unless we can bring in some more help posthaste. And let me add—anyone who comes to work at the house will answer only to me. My mother will no longer have any responsibility for the staff."

Matthew's brows lifted. "And you've informed your mother of this?"

"Hell no."

His friend laughed so hard he had tears in his eyes. "Good for you. I'll put out the word that you're in need of help. I'll have them report to the servants' entrance if they're interested. Will that do?"

"That'd be excellent. Thank you."

"I'm happy to help in exchange for hearing how your dear mother reacts to learning you've relieved her of her duties."

"You, my friend, have got yourself a deal."

Chapter Four

After dinner and with Mr. Plumber's help, Aubrey dragged the items he and Maeve had tossed out the windows far enough from the house that there would be no risk of stray sparks causing an even bigger disaster than the one they had to contend with inside. The 1892 fire that had destroyed the Vanderbilts' original Breakers mansion remained fresh in the minds of everyone who spent time in Newport.

Mr. Plumber was horrified by the condition of the bedding and furniture. "The former staff should be prosecuted for allowing this to happen."

"Perhaps," Aubrey said, "but that would require a public airing of the grievances that led to their actions."

"If you don't mind my asking, sir, what could've led to them doing such a thing?"

"My mother has a volatile personality. She is easily riled, and often doesn't think before she speaks. I'm ashamed to confess that I hadn't noticed any difficulties with the staff last summer, but then again, I was only here on the weekends and didn't pay close attention."

"Ah, I see." Plumber paused. "If I may be blunt, sir."

"By all means. Please speak freely."

"Under the current circumstances, I fear there's no chance we'll be ready to entertain a duke and duchess."

"They're my close friends, and I can assure you, they don't stand on pretense. They'll be satisfied with a clean bed and three meals a day."

"They are *royalty*, Mr. Nelson."

"I'm aware of their standing, but I'm not concerned about trying to impress them. If need be, I'll tell them what transpired and explain that we made every effort to ensure the house was ready for their arrival, but if we missed something, I'll ask them not to look."

Mr. Plumber seemed more horrified by that notion than he was by the fouled bedding. "They are a *duke* and *duchess*."

"They are regular people. In fact, Derek puts his pants on one leg at a time, just as you and I do."

"Be that as it may, he's still a *duke*, and as such he'll expect certain amenities."

Aubrey realized there would be no convincing Mr. Plumber that Derek didn't stand on formality or expect to be fawned over simply because of his title. He'd have to meet Derek and see with his own eyes what kind of man he was. "I think we're ready to light."

He'd found some kerosene in the basement that he sprinkled liberally over the more flammable items. As he looked around to make sure Mr. Plumber was far enough back, he noticed Miss Brown had come outside to watch. She stood on the stone patio, arms wrapped around her body as if protecting herself from impending doom.

Aubrey had no idea why he reached that deduction, but that was the thought he had when he saw her. "Here we go." He struck a match and tossed it on the pile, stepping back when it immediately caught. As the flames billowed high into the air, he watched Miss Brown, captivated by the wistful expression on her face, which was lit by the rosy glow of the fire. What was she thinking as she watched the fire burn through the items they'd removed from his parents' rooms?

He could only wonder.

"I believe I'm going to call it a night," Mr. Plumber said when the fire had burned down somewhat.

"Please do. I'll stay to make sure the flames are fully extinguished."

"Good night, Mr. Nelson."

"Good night."

Aubrey heard Mr. Plumber say good night to Miss Brown as he went by her. When Aubrey was sure they were alone, he gestured for Miss Brown to join him. To his surprise, she came over to him when he'd expected her to decline.

"It was a good idea you had to burn everything."

"It was the only option. None of it was salvageable."

"True."

"You seem pensive tonight. Are you all right?"

"We used to have bonfires at home. My father would spend months adding to the pile and then invite extended family and friends over to enjoy the fire."

"You must miss them very much."

"I do." All at once she seemed to realize she had shared something with him that she hadn't intended to reveal. "It's late. I must get to bed. The sun will rise early on another busy day."

"Before you go, I just want to say thank you again for your hard work since you've been here."

"I haven't done nearly enough."

"You've done much more than most would have, and it's appreciated."

She offered a small smile and a nod. "Good night then."

"Good night, Miss Brown. I'll see you in the morning." As he watched her walk away, Aubrey wished—for the first time ever—to have been born to a lower-class family, one that would support and understand his affection for a woman like Miss Brown. He wished he had the right to ask her to stay a while and talk to him.

But because he didn't have the right, he let her go and was left to watch the waning embers, feeling lonelier than he'd been in a very long time.

Late the next morning, Aubrey went looking for Miss Brown and was horrified to find her at the top of a very tall ladder, teetering precariously as she attempted to remove spiderwebs from the massive chandelier in the ballroom.

"Miss Brown!"

His shout startled her, and she faltered, grasping the ladder to try and stop her inevitable fall.

Aubrey didn't think. He acted, running toward her at full speed, arriving in the middle of the vast room in time to neatly catch her and stop what would've been a terrible fall.

She landed in his arms with an *oomph*.

He took two steps backward to try and keep himself from falling but couldn't stop the momentum that landed them in a heap of tangled limbs on the floor. She ended up sprawled on top of him, breasts pressed against his chest, his legs tangled in her full skirt. It took her a second to recover her wits, and then she began to thrash, catching him square in the groin with a well-placed knee.

Aubrey gasped from the pain.

"Oh dear, Mr. Nelson. Are you all right?"

Aubrey couldn't speak or breathe or do anything other than try not to cast up his accounts all over the parquet floor.

She crawled off him and sat on the floor next to him as

he writhed in agony. "Whatever were you thinking startling me that way?"

Through gritted teeth, he said, "I was thinking to save you from a bad fall."

"Instead you caused one!"

He hoped he would still be able to father children some-day. A surge of bile burned his throat. He swallowed hard, hoping he wouldn't be sick in front of her. The last thing either of them needed was another mess to clean up. "Pardon me for trying to save you from serious injury. What were you thinking climbing that ladder?"

"I was thinking to remove the cobwebs from the chan-delier."

"You shouldn't have done that alone."

"You shouldn't have startled me. I was doing fine until you showed up."

He had never met anyone quite like her—fiery and passionate and outspoken. She was nothing like the sim-pering, demure women he'd grown up with in New York or those he'd met in the ballrooms of London. Those women sought only to please him, hoping he might be interested in marrying them. This one vexed him, and he found that he far preferred vexing to simpering.

Aubrey forced himself to sit up, to breathe through the pain and to take control of this out-of-control situation. "I apologize for startling you, but I stand by my belief that you had no business being atop that ladder without some-one to catch you if you fell."

"Mr. Nelson, if I waited around for a *man* to catch me, I'd never get anything accomplished."

Magnificent. Especially when her color was up like it was now, her cheeks flushed with embarrassment and pique. "Why're you staring at me that way?"

"Because I find you quite pleasing to look at, especially when you're annoyed with me."

"Then I must be pleasing to look at most of the time."

Laughing, Aubrey fell back on his elbows, wishing they had nothing better to do but take a picnic down to the shore and enjoy the warm spring sunshine. Alas, there was no time for such frivolity on this day, but he vowed to invite her on a picnic as soon as possible.

She rose to her feet and tugged off the cotton gloves she wore while working. "I thought you'd gone to town yesterday to hire more help."

"I did. I've put out the word to anyone seeking work, asking them to report to the servants' entrance."

"Good lord. How are we to know if we should hire the people who come to the door?"

"If they have two working arms and two working legs, they're hired."

"That's hardly the standard we should apply to hiring staff for a home as grand as this."

"It's the only standard we have as we're desperate."

Maeve chewed on her thumbnail, something she seemed to do when anxious.

"It'll all be fine. I'm sure of it."

She gave him a withering look. "You have no way to know that."

"I can see that the pressure is starting to get to you. Let's take a break and have a picnic at the shore." Why put off until later that which could be done today?

She stared at him as if he had two—or maybe three— heads. "I don't have time for a picnic at the shore nor should I be doing such things with you."

"I'm your employer, and I'm offering you the free time as well as the pleasure of my company if you would do me the honor of granting me the pleasure of yours."

She wanted to. He could see that as plainly as the button nose on her face.

"I'm afraid I must insist that you take a well-deserved break so you don't fall ill from the strain of the monumental task before it's completed in the short time we have left."

"That makes no sense. You admit the task is monumental and the time is short, but you think I ought to take time away from work. Are you completely daft?"

He was beginning to think so, for watching her rage made him happy to be alive at that moment in time. It made him happy for the twists of fate that had brought him to Newport early, even if he wasn't happy about his father's illness.

"Mr. Nelson? Whatever are you staring at?"

Her face flushed with color that almost hid the light dusting of freckles across the bridge of her nose. Was it possible to love someone's nose? If so, he loved hers. "Yes, a picnic would be just the thing. I'll get with Mrs. Allston and meet you on the back veranda in thirty minutes. Don't be late."

He was gone before Maeve could push a protest past the shock of his invitation or order or whatever it was. The man was clearly insane if he thought nothing of inviting his housekeeper on a picnic by the shore. Who did that? And why had her heart soared with nostalgia for how her life had been before it all went so very wrong?

She was no longer a woman who had time for picnics or other things that wasted valuable time that could be spent working to survive. But her employer had given her a directive, so how could she disregard that directive? She could choose not to show up at the appointed meeting place, but he would find her—that much she knew for certain. He was nothing if not persistent.

Resigned to attending his ridiculous picnic, Maeve stomped up the backstairs to her third-floor room to retrieve a hat and gloves to protect her fair skin from the sun, still in a pique from Mr. Nelson's foolishness. The spiderwebs hanging from the chandeliers weren't going to clean themselves, and that was one of a hundred tasks that needed to be completed before his mother arrived a week from Friday.

If they worked day and night between now and then, they'd barely get it done, and he wanted to have a *picnic*?

She would give his silly picnic a few minutes of her valuable time, but only because she needed to eat. Other than the spiderwebs, the ballroom was taking shape. She would move on next to the family's sitting room, where they would spend most of their time when in residence. Thinking about her plan of attack made her feel better about taking even a brief break from her duties as she went back downstairs to the veranda.

Stepping out into the warm, sunny day, her heart gave a happy jolt at the fragrant scent of the air, the sound of the sea crashing against the rocks below and the dazzling sight of the trees in full bloom. How long had it been since she was outdoors? She had arrived to a nightmare seven days ago and had been working ever since, having hardly made a dent, and hadn't been out of doors except the night before for the bonfire.

Mr. Nelson stood on the path that led to the shore, wicker picnic basket in hand and a plaid blanket tossed casually over his arm as if he had all the time in the world to while away with her.

A feeling of unease crept up her back. Were the cook and butler watching her leave with him and coming to their

own conclusions about what kind of woman she was? That
would never do. "Mr. Nelson, I'm unable to accompany
you, but I do hope you enjoy your picnic."

His handsome face fell with disappointment that made
her feel badly for being so disagreeable when he'd tried to
do something nice for her. "Mrs. Allston packed the basket
full after I told her I was taking you for a much-needed
outing after days of hard work."

Maeve stared at him, stunned and furious. "You *told her*
you were taking me on a picnic?"

"Yes, of course I did. How else was I to get her to pack
enough for two?"

"What she must think!"

"She thought it was a capital idea as you haven't been
out of the house in all the days since you arrived."

"She . . . she said that?"

"She did indeed. Feel free to go ask her yourself if you
don't believe me. I'll wait for you."

Torn between wanting to know the cook approved and
not wanting to appear to disbelieve him, she glanced at
the house and then back at him, finding him waiting ex-
pectantly for her to make up her mind. "That won't be
necessary." She'd find out soon enough if the cook thought
less of her for accompanying Mr. Nelson on his picnic.

"Let us be off then." He extended his arm.

Maeve shook her head.

His arm fell to his side, and he began to walk along the
well-worn path that led to the shore, glancing back to make
sure she was following.

She linked her fingers and walked with her head down,
determined to get through this as quickly as possible so she
could return to where she was supposed to be. The time
when she could run away for a picnic in the middle of the

day with a handsome man was long behind her. Now her days were about work, work and more work. That was a small price to pay for the freedom and safety she'd found in America, and not even the charming Mr. Nelson could make her forget about how far she'd traveled to find a new life. She would do nothing to jeopardize that precious new life.

Mr. Nelson insisted on taking her hand to help her down the flight of stairs that delivered them onto the sandy beach.

Maeve tried not to overreact to his courtesy. He was doing for her what he'd do for any woman.

"This looks like a nice spot." Releasing her hand, he spread the blanket on the sand and placed the basket on one of the corners. "I don't know about you, but I could eat a horse. Let's see what Mrs. Allston prepared for us." He unloaded containers wrapped in cloth towels she recognized from the kitchen. "Fried chicken, potato salad, fruit salad, bread, cheese and cake."

Maeve's mouth watered. She'd had breakfast before dawn and had been busy ever since. The smell of the fried chicken had her taking the seat he offered her on the blanket and accepting the plate he prepared for her.

"This is wrong."

"What's wrong?"

"You waiting on me. It should be the other way around."

"Says who?"

She gave him a withering look. "I'm employed by your family. I should be tending to you."

"For this short interlude, can we not be employer and employee but rather two friends enjoying a lovely day with a delicious lunch and this incredible view of the ocean?"

"Two *friends*? You're indeed daft if you think that is what we are."

"Miss Brown, are we not two human beings who both need to eat around this time of day and who have earned a break from the drudgery of cleaning cobwebs from chandeliers?"

"We are two human beings. I'll give you that."

He flashed a grin at her, as if he was enjoying her commentary. "Eat your lunch."

She took a delicate bite from the chicken leg.

Mr. Nelson got comfortable on the blanket and devoured two legs in the time it took her to eat most of one. "Where're you from in Ireland?"

"Dingle, a tiny fishing village on the west coast."

"What's it like there?"

"A lot like Newport, actually. That's why I wanted to come here. It reminds me of home."

"Do your sisters still live there?"

Nodding, she looked down at her plate where most of the food he'd served her remained.

"Are they married?"

"Two are. The other is still in school."

"Nieces? Nephews?"

"Two adorable nephews. Jack and Hughie. They're three and four with another baby on the way." Would she ever know if she'd had a niece or nephew? The possibility that she might never know pained her.

"Do you write to them?"

With her lips tightly set, she shook her head.

"Do you have photos of your family?"

"I have one."

"May I see it sometime?"

She gave him her "you must be daft" look. "Why would you want to see it?"

"Because they're special to you, and as I mentioned before, I'd like to know you better."

"*Why?*"

He released a deep sigh. "I wish I knew the answer to that, but all I can tell you is from the time I first met you, I wanted to know you."

"Mr. Nelson, please forgive me for being rude, but I'm not sure what kind of game it is you're playing. A man of your means and stature could have his pick of the debutantes in New York or London. Surely you're not unable to attract the interest of someone from your own world."

He flashed a delighted grin. "Indeed, you're right. They quite like me."

"Then *what* is the problem?"

"*I* don't like *them*, not enough anyway. They're often silly and sometimes desperate and shockingly forward at times. They have no *substance* to them."

"You just haven't met the right one yet. I'm sure you'll have the opportunity to meet many lovely young ladies this summer."

"It'll just be more of the same."

"If you think that way, you'll never find anyone."

"I want someone like you, someone with fire and passion and the ability to handle whatever life throws at you with grace and aplomb."

She stared at him in disbelief. "That is *not* me. I'm none of those things."

"You are *all* of those things. I saw those qualities in you from the very beginning when I walked into a calamity to find you trying to fix it all by yourself. The women I've met in New York and London ballrooms would've sooner set the place on fire before they would've tried to fix it."

"You barely know me." Her words were hardly a whisper. "I certainly don't know you."

"I would tell you anything you wanted to know."

"Mr. Nelson—"

"Aubrey."

"Mr. Nelson, I appreciate that you think you see something special in me. That's the nicest compliment I've received in a very long time. However, if you continue to pursue the ridiculous notion that we will ever be more than employer and employee, then I shall be forced to seek employment elsewhere."

"Please don't do that. I would never do anything to endanger you or your position."

"You already have by inviting me on a picnic at the shore. Imagine the conversation Mr. Plumber is having with Mrs. Allston as they enjoy their midday meal in the servants' dining room, which is where I should be."

"I apologize. I only wanted to give you the opportunity to enjoy some fresh air and for us to have the chance to get to know each other better." He began to pack up the picnic and seemed shocked when her hand on his arm stopped him.

"The damage is done at this point. I suppose it won't do any further harm to finish our meal. I believe you said Mrs. Allston sent cake?"

She watched him try to hide his shock—and delight. "That she did." He served her a large piece of the coconut cake with the rich vanilla icing and then cut a piece for himself. "This is the most delicious thing I've eaten since I left home. Perhaps there could be an advantage to having a 'friend' with connections in the kitchen."

"Have you a sweet tooth, Ms. Brown?"

"A terrible, awful sweet tooth that's going to be the very death of me."

When she finished her cake, he cut her another smaller

piece and put it on her plate so quickly she never saw it coming.

"I couldn't possibly! I'll burst."

"Have it so it doesn't go to waste."

"That would be a terrible shame."

He smiled widely at her. "Indeed, it would."

As she took delicate bites of the cake, clearly trying to make it last, she felt him watching her.

"I can't help but notice that you have the bearing of a well-educated, upper-class woman."

She swallowed her bite and blotted her lips with a napkin. "I'm well educated. My father is a banker and ensured that we were properly raised."

"Then how did you end up a housekeeper in Newport?"

His question brought her right back to reality. "That's a story for another day, Mr. Nelson."

"I'd love to hear that story—and any others you'd like to tell me. Despite our different stations, Miss Brown, I think you'd find that if given the opportunity, I could be a very good friend to have."

Chapter Five

He flummoxed her, and Maeve hated that. The last man who had flummoxed her had ruined her once beautiful life, and she needed to remember that as she sat across from the charming, handsome Mr. Nelson, who seemed nothing at all like the man she'd known at home. But he'd been wonderful at first, too.

No, she couldn't be wooed by a picnic at the shore or sweet cakes or kind words. She had left the past behind and had only herself to depend upon now, and she could not—and *would not*—do anything to endanger her position. The only reason she'd landed the position in the first place was because no one else wanted to work for the dragon lady, as they called Mrs. Nelson in servant circles.

Mr. Nelson had promised to run interference for her with his mother, but she would believe that when she saw it. His first loyalty would always be to his family over a lowly housekeeper.

She blotted her lips with the creamy linen napkin and then folded it, brushed the crumbs off her skirt and stood. "I must get back to work."

"But you haven't even taken an hour for yourself."

"I'm not paid to take time for myself in the midst of a workday, Mr. Nelson."

"Aubrey. You can call me Aubrey."

"I prefer to call you Mr. Nelson."

He sighed deeply as he seemed to realize his picnic hadn't changed anything between them. He was still her employer and she a member of the household staff.

"Thank you for the picnic. I enjoyed it very much." With that, she left him and headed up the stairs and back along the path they had taken. It would take some time for him to clean up, so she anticipated a clean getaway. Pounding footsteps behind her disabused her of that notion. Maeve kept her head down and continued to walk briskly toward the house.

"Miss Brown! Wait. Please wait."

She shouldn't stop. She knew it, but stopped anyway, turning to face him. "Yes, Mr. Nelson?"

"I wanted to share something with you. Something personal that I haven't spoken of in years."

Tell him it's not appropriate for him to share personal things with you. Walk away. Though her inner voice urged the opposite, she stayed put, intrigued and curious despite the many reasons she shouldn't be.

"I was to be married." He cleared his throat. "Her name was Annabelle, and we were best friends from childhood. We wrote to each other while I was in school at Choate and then at Yale, and during the Christmas break of my final year of school, I asked her to marry me. The wedding was planned for spring. It would've been ten years today, in fact."

Maeve gasped when she realized the import of the date. She didn't want to be interested but was nonetheless. "Wh-what happened?"

"Four days before the wedding, she went to sleep with a headache and never woke up. The doctor said it was a vessel in her brain that had probably always been defunct."

"I'm so sorry, Mr. Nelson." Her heart broke for him and the grief that was readily apparent, now that she looked more closely, even after all this time.

"Thank you." He looked down before again bringing his gaze up to meet hers. "I haven't spoken of her in many years. Not even to my dear friends in London."

The significance of his statement wasn't lost on Maeve. He'd told her but not his close friends. "Why did you tell me this?"

He took hold of her hand.

She let him.

"Because when you have been through something so painful, you recognize that pain when you see it in others. I see it in you. And I want you to know that if you need someone to share it with, I'm here, and I understand."

Maeve could only stare at him. If he had stripped her bare, she couldn't have felt more *seen*. Sometimes she felt that no one ever saw her. They usually looked right through her. Mr. Nelson, this man she had only just met, saw the very heart of her, and she simply couldn't have that. She pulled her hand free, turned and walked away, keeping her head down and her eyes peeled for hazards along the path.

As the house came into view, she began to run, desperate to escape the fierce longing he'd inspired in her for things she could not have.

He'd looked so sad telling her about the woman he'd loved and lost and the wedding that should've happened ten years ago today. She'd wanted to hug him, to pat his back and tell him everything would be okay, even if she had no way to know if that was true. She wanted to offer comfort she had no right to give to a man who was so far off-limits to her he may as well have lived in a different world.

The world she lived in required her to work in order to

stay alive. She entered the house through the kitchen and encountered Mrs. Allston tending a huge pot on the stove.

"How was the picnic?" she asked, her smile friendly and free of judgment. Or so it seemed, anyway.

"The luncheon was delicious. Thank you for preparing it."

"I'm glad you got a spot of fresh air. It can't be healthy to breathe in so much dust and refuse."

Maeve studied the other woman, looking for some sign of disapproval, but couldn't detect anything but genuine concern. "Yes, I suppose you're right. Well, I must get back to work." She went upstairs and picked up where she'd left off, atop the ladder cleaning the spiderwebs from the chandeliers in the ballroom and thinking about a handsome man with warm brown eyes who saw far too much.

She worked until she was so tired she couldn't see straight, ate a solitary dinner in the staff dining room and passed an all-but-sleepless night, tossing and turning and wishing for things that could never be. Perhaps she could find a way to avoid him completely, but that didn't seem feasible with only four people in the house and more work to do than could be completed in a month of twenty-four-hour days.

Awaking from a restless doze when the sunrise filtered into her room, she rose to wash and dress for another day of scrubbing. Her hands ached from the days of hard work, and the harsh soap that seeped through the thin gloves, leaving her skin red and raw. She had badly burned her right hand in the incident that resulted in her fleeing Ireland, and two months later, the new skin on her palm was still pink and tender. She worried all the time about contracting an infection where the burn had been, which is why she wore the gloves while working. In addition, her back ached and she had an odd crick in her neck, probably from hours of looking up at the chandeliers the day before.

She hadn't seen Mr. Nelson since she left him at the shore yesterday and hoped she could get through this day without having to encounter him.

A soft knock on her door had her hoping it wasn't him, coming to tempt her some more with that face and those eyes and the lips that made her want things she had no right to. Not anymore.

She opened the door to Mr. Plumber.

"Pardon the interruption, Ms. Brown, but there are men at the kitchen door, claiming to have been hired by Mr. Nelson to assist in preparing the house for the Season."

"Ah, yes. I'll be right down."

"I, um, would be remiss if I did not inform you that they seem rather . . . rough."

"I'm sure they are, Mr. Plumber, but in these desperate circumstances, I'm afraid we can't afford to be fussy about whom we hire."

"As you wish, ma'am." He nodded and departed, but his concerns stayed with her as she headed downstairs to see what the cat had dragged in.

Aubrey woke with a sore head, a dry mouth and a stiff neck. The copious amounts of whiskey he'd consumed the night before had gotten him through the difficult day and torturous night full of memories of a young woman who'd been lost far too soon. Per his tradition, he allowed himself to wallow in the grief on one of the two dates that arrived four days apart every year with maddening regularity. He couldn't bear to mourn the day she died, so he instead descended into the pits of despair on what should have been their wedding day.

After all this time, his memories of Annabelle had grown fuzzy. Sometimes, he couldn't remember the sound of her voice or recall specifics about her. It all ran together in a stream of disconnected thoughts that showed up to torture him this time every year. He'd grown accustomed to it by now, but knowing it was coming didn't make enduring it any easier.

He felt like death itself as he dragged himself out of the chair he'd slept in, picked up the empty bottle from the floor and placed it on a sideboard before pouring himself a glass of water that he downed in greedy gulps.

Where would they be now, he wondered, if Annabelle had lived? Would they have remained in New York to raise their family or perhaps headed west in search of new adventures? She had been an adventurous sort who'd craved travel and experiences and new people. They would've had a jolly good time, for sure.

But in the last few days, something else had nagged at him, something dark and disturbing and altogether disrespectful of Annabelle's memory. It had started the first moment he caught sight of Miss Brown's delightful neck and had continued unabated every time he'd been in her presence—desire. Hot, desperate desire, the likes of which he had never once felt for his beloved Annabelle.

Shame had his stomach turning with disgust at the direction his thoughts had taken. How could he admit such a thing to anyone, even himself? In the desperate hours, days, weeks, months and now years since Annabelle's sudden and tragic death, he'd vowed to protect her memory and to love her always. How was he to do that if he was forced to admit that what he'd felt for Annabelle paled in comparison to the fiery passion the lovely housekeeper had inspired in him over the course of two short days?

It was because he'd gone without a woman for far too

long. He and Annabelle had been creative about finding ways to be alone with each other and had been having relations for years when she died. Since he lost her, he'd been with a few women, here and there, but only out of desperation, not because he actually wanted them.

His reactions toward Miss Brown surpassed pedestrian feelings such as want or need and went straight to craving. He *craved* her, and he had no idea what to do with such inappropriate feelings that she most certainly did not welcome. There had been a moment, at the shore yesterday, when he told her about Annabelle, when he'd felt her soften toward him.

But that had been out of pity. She felt sorry for him, for what he'd lost. Sympathy did not equate to desire, and it would do him good to remember that and not make it into more than it had been.

The sound of voices in the hallway had him running his fingers through his hair, straightening his clothing and heading for the door to see what was going on.

He opened the door to bedlam. A dozen men in ragged clothes, many without a full set of teeth and one with an eye patch, followed Miss Brown up the stairs like a ragtag army under the command of the most magnificent general who'd ever lived.

"We have just over a week to put this house to rights, and we're willing to pay for a hard day's work. Anyone who isn't pulling his weight will be dismissed immediately and paid only for the time worked. You'll be provided with a meal at midday, and if you should happen to do exemplary work, you'll be considered for a permanent position."

The men were rapt, their gazes fixed to the gentle swell of her backside as she went up the stairs, hanging on her every word.

That would not do.

"Gentlemen."

The brigade halted halfway up the stairs and turned to face him.

"I'm Aubrey Nelson. This house belongs to my family, and I'm appreciative of your willingness to work."

Was it his imagination or was Miss Brown refusing to look at him?

"Miss Brown is in charge. You will do whatever she asks of you, and you'll behave as gentlemen in her presence, or you'll deal with me. That means you will not leer at her, speak to her unless spoken to, or in any way make her feel uncomfortable. Am I clear?"

Muttered responses of "yes, sir," and "whatever you say, gov'na," echoed through the vast front hall.

"Very well. Carry on."

Maeve turned and continued up the stairs, leading her ragtag army into battle.

In need of food and coffee, Aubrey headed for the kitchen where Mr. Plumber was discussing the men with Mrs. Allston.

"It's *unheard of* to allow ruffians to work in a house of this caliber," Plumber said, sounding every bit the upper-crust butler.

"If it's them or no one," Mrs. Allston said, "I suppose we have to take what we can get."

"We'll be the talk of the town," Plumber said. "Surely Mr. and Mrs. Nelson wouldn't approve of such people working in their home."

"I can assure you they would most definitely *not* approve," Aubrey said when he joined them.

Mr. Plumber sputtered with mortification. "I apologize, sir. I was merely expressing my concerns."

"Your concerns are valid, Mr. Plumber, but alas, the ruffians are the best we can do on short notice, and perhaps under your tutelage they could be whipped into a staff in time for the arrival of my family and guests."

Plumber stared at him as if he were speaking in tongues. "You can't be serious, sir. If I had a lifetime to spend on the effort, I couldn't turn that group of misfits into anything more than what they are—street urchins."

"I wouldn't be so certain. They're men, just like you and me, who have perhaps fallen on hard times. With the right incentive and training, who's to say they couldn't become first-rate footmen, drivers, stable men and gardeners?"

"And you expect me to bring about this miracle of which you speak?"

Aubrey held the butler's gaze, refusing to blink until the other man did. "I expect you to try."

"Mr. Nelson, with all due respect, what you're asking is not only impossible, it's . . . well, it's ridiculous."

"Be that as it may, they are the staff we have to work with. Do what you can with them, and I'll take the blame for anything that goes wrong."

Before Plumber could respond, Aubrey turned to the cook. "Good morning, Mrs. Allston. I'll take my usual in the dining room, if you wouldn't mind."

"Of course, sir. I'll be right up."

If she wondered why he was still wearing yesterday's clothing, she didn't let on. Rather, she got busy preparing his breakfast.

He would've moved toward the dining room, but Mr. Plumber's hulking presence blocked the way. "Was there something else, Mr. Plumber?"

After a long pause, Plumber shook his head. "No, sir."

"Very well. Please keep a close eye on the goings on

upstairs. If anyone steps out of line, let me know, and we'll remove the perpetrator from the premises."

"As you wish, sir." Plumber spun on his heel and left the room.

"Well, that went well, wouldn't you say?"

Mrs. Allston snorted out a laugh. "You've shocked poor Mr. Plumber into a near apoplexy." Like Maeve, she spoke in the lilt of Ireland, but her speech wasn't as refined as Maeve's.

"I suspect he'll survive. What else are we to do with so much to accomplish and so little time in which to do it?"

"What else, indeed?"

"Will we really be the talk of the town?"

"Yes, you will, but I suspect you'll survive the scandal, which will promptly be forgotten when your illustrious guests arrive."

"True," he said, chuckling.

"If I may say one thing, however . . ."

"Of course. Please speak freely."

"I can't help but notice a spark between yourself and Miss Brown."

Aubrey opened his mouth to deny it, but he couldn't lie to the woman's face, so he closed his mouth.

"She's a very special young lady, and I only ask that you be careful with her. Men of your social standing have the power to ruin the life of someone like her while you go about your merry way." She quickly added, "I mean no disrespect."

"I know you don't, and I appreciate your concern for her."

"I've been where she is, and it's not easy to be a woman alone. Before I married my dear Mr. Allston, I was like Miss Brown, on my own and trying to make ends meet, at the mercy of an often merciless world."

The thought of Miss Brown alone and frightened and at anyone's mercy filled him with fear and despair.

"I understand what you're saying, and I promise to be careful with her. Always."

"Thank you, Mr. Nelson. You're a decent sort of man. I could tell that about you right away."

"I've always tried to be."

"I have a feeling our Miss Brown is working below her station in life. It's nothing I can say for certain, but the way she carries herself, her manner of speaking . . . I could be very wrong."

"I don't think you are. I had suspected the same thing. She told me her father was a banker and saw to it that she and her sisters were educated."

"That would make sense. At any rate, it's none of our business. I'll bring your breakfast right up."

"Thank you, Mrs. Allston."

"A pleasure, sir."

After Aubrey ate the eggs, potatoes and sausage Mrs. Allston had prepared for him and drank two cups of the strong coffee she brewed just the way he liked it, he began to feel somewhat human again. He went upstairs, intending to bathe, change his clothes and make himself useful. At the top of the stairs he followed the sound of voices in the drawing room and went to see how Miss Brown was making out with her new workers.

They had wrought a miracle in the drawing room. In one hour, they had cleared away the cobwebs, removed the soiled dust covers from the furniture and had attacked the dust. The room actually smelled clean, which was a miracle in and of itself.

In the middle of it all, amid the raggedy workforce she commanded, Maeve shone like a jewel sparkling in the sunlight.

Aubrey stood in the doorway, unable to look away, barely able to breathe as he watched her. In that moment he understood that he would never tire of being in her presence, of hearing what she had to say, of watching the confident, graceful way in which she moved.

Her gaze connected with his, and when she realized he was staring at her, she faltered, albeit briefly, before recovering herself to continue directing the workers. The only reaction she had to his attention, that he could see, was the flush that overtook her porcelain complexion.

Aubrey shook off the stupor she caused whenever she was nearby and rolled up his sleeves to help the men move furniture so they could clean under it. He could bathe and change later.

When they had the drawing room returned to its original splendor, they moved on to his mother's room where he broke a sweat moving furniture, sweeping, mopping and dusting along with the rest of the men. It took the remainder of the day, but by the time they sent the men home with full stomachs and a day's wages, the room was ready for occupancy.

Throughout the day, Miss Brown never again looked his way or said so much as a word to him. After the men left, she disappeared and he didn't see her again until he went downstairs to join her and Mr. Plumber for dinner.

"I'd be happy to serve you in the dining room, Mr. Nelson," Mrs. Allston said.

"This is fine, thank you." Eating alone in the dining room had been fine for breakfast, but now he found himself in need of some company. "No need to be formal when it's only the four of us in residence. However, we will need to hire you some kitchen help before the others arrive at the end of next week."

"I have several nieces I could hire with your permission."

"That would be fine."

She served a pot roast with potatoes, carrots and baby onions that was so delicious that Aubrey happily accepted a second serving.

His mouth went dry and his heart skipped a beat as Maeve's eyes lit up with delight when Mrs. Allston served hot apple crisp with vanilla ice cream for dessert. He wanted to see her eyes light up with every kind of delight, but he kept that thought to himself.

Their days fell into a predictable pattern of long, fruitful workdays followed by quiet dinners in the basement. After dinner, he spent long nights alone in the library where he drank away his frustrations. As the house was returned to its former splendor, Aubrey slipped deeper into a state of frustration and pervasive loneliness at knowing the woman he desired was close by but so far out of his reach. If he pursued her the way he wanted to, he ran the risk of ruining her reputation and endangering her livelihood. He would never do either of those things, so he kept his distance out of respect, reliving their picnic to the shore over and over again until even that memory could no longer bring solace.

This must be what it was like, he thought, to slowly go mad from wanting something you could not have. The feeling reminded him far too much of the dark days and familiar despair that had followed Annabelle's sudden death.

More than once, he considered leaving, but he couldn't do that. He couldn't leave Miss Brown, Mrs. Allston or Mr. Plumber to his mother to terrorize, nor could he abandon the guests he'd invited to join them for the summer. But he wanted to get on a horse and get the hell out of there before he did something that couldn't be undone.

He went into the kitchen, looking for more of the chocolate cake Mrs. Allston had served for dessert that evening, cut himself a healthy piece and then cut another one and placed it on a second plate.

What is your plan?

I don't have a plan.

He had the conversation with himself as he carried the two plates up the backstairs to the third floor, which was deserted. Mr. Plumber's room was at the other end of the long hallway, and Mrs. Allston didn't live there. She went home to her own house in Newport's Fifth Ward at the end of every day.

Aubrey tapped lightly on Miss Brown's door.

He could barely bring himself to breathe as he waited for her to answer.

The door opened, and he nearly dropped the plates when he saw her glorious hair down around her shoulders and the subtle hint of curves under her robe.

"What're you doing?" she said in a whisper that more resembled a hiss.

"I brought you cake." *You sound like an idiot.*

She looked around him to make sure no one else was nearby to witness the conversation. "I already had cake. After dinner."

"Does that mean you can't have more?"

"It's inappropriate for you to be here."

"I know, but there was one piece of cake left, and I wanted you to have it." He held out the plate to her.

She took it from him. "Thank you."

"Good night."

"Good night, Mr. Nelson."

"Aubrey."

"Good night, Mr. Nelson."

He smiled at her and forced himself to walk away before he did something stupid like reach out to touch her glorious hair to see if it was as soft as it looked.

Chapter Six

He'd brought her cake.

Maeve closed the door, leaned against it and looked down upon the plate, trying to understand why he had taken such a risk, knowing full well that Mr. Plumber might see him visiting her room at night.

She took a bite of the cake and closed her eyes.

So moist and sweet.

Mrs. Allston was a wonderful cook.

And Mr. Nelson was a wonderful employer to bring her something he knew she'd enjoy.

She sat on her bed, curling her legs beneath her, intent on enjoying every bite of her second piece of the delicious cake.

He had kept his distance since the day they'd picnicked at the shore, and though she appreciated that he had heeded her concerns, she found herself missing him, which was ridiculous. How could she miss someone she barely knew whom she saw every day? She caught him watching her at least once a day, often more than once, but they hadn't spoken about anything other than the house in days.

She missed the conversations they'd had, about their families and their homes. And yes, she missed his obvious interest in her as a woman.

There. She'd admitted it. As much as she'd feared what his attentions could lead to, she'd also been flattered to have gained the favor of such a handsome, kind man.

She took the last bite of cake, put the plate on the bedside table and released a deep breath full of regret. Why couldn't she have met him under different circumstances? Because life wasn't fair. She'd known that for some time now, but that didn't stop her from wishing things could be different.

Maeve eyed the dirty plate on the table and decided to take it downstairs to the kitchen, lest she attract vermin. Or that's what she told herself anyway. What she really wanted was another chance to see him, to speak to him, to breathe the same air as him.

Foolish thoughts, perhaps, but the need was too great to resist. Tightening the belt of her robe and wearing slippers, she left her room, started down the two flights of stairs and landed in the kitchen, which was dark except for one small light burning over the stove. Her home in Ireland had also had electricity. In fact, it had been among the first homes in Ireland to have electricity and indoor plumbing, so she'd been accustomed to both before she came to live in this house.

As she entered the kitchen, she stopped short at the sight of Mr. Nelson sitting alone at the table eating his cake. A bottle of amber liquid and a glass were also on the table.

He seemed equally surprised to see her, his fork freezing in midair.

For the longest time, neither of them moved until he cleared his throat and put down his fork.

"I'm sorry for disturbing you," she said.

"You're not. How was the cake?"

"Delicious. Thank you."

"My pleasure." As he said those words, his gaze traveled

from her face to her chest and below, while his jaw clenched with tension.

She felt as if she'd been set on fire, and all he'd done was look at her. Forcing herself to move, she went to the sink and washed the plate and fork, placing them on the rack that contained several clean pots and pans. Using the towel that had hung over the sink, she wiped her hands and spread the towel out to dry.

With nothing else to do, she summoned the core of inner strength that had guided her to this place, far from her home, and turned to find him watching her with those eyes that saw her so clearly.

"Can you sit for a minute?"

"I really shouldn't."

"Who will know?"

"Mr. Plumber could come downstairs."

"And what would he see? Two people sitting across from each other at a table."

Using his foot under the table, he pushed a chair toward her.

She eyed the chair, wondering what she was thinking as she perched gingerly on the seat.

He got up, fetched a second glass and returned to the table to pour several fingers of the amber liquid into the glass, pushing it across the table to her.

Maeve licked her lips and reached for the glass, glancing at him to find him watching her with fire in his eyes. No one had ever looked at her the way Mr. Nelson did, and while it was unsettling and concerning, it was also deeply flattering to fully understand the depth of his desire for her.

"Your hair is so very lovely."

"Thank you." She took a sip of the familiar liquid and felt the whiskey burn its way through her, warming her from the inside.

"The color defies description. Calling it red or brown wouldn't be adequate."

"My mother used to call it liquid fire."

"Yes," he said gruffly. "That's it exactly. I've never seen that particular color before."

"I used to hate it when I was younger, but I've grown used to it."

"You must never hate something so beautiful."

"You flatter me, Mr. Nelson."

"You occupy my every thought, Miss Brown."

She choked on the sip of whiskey she was taking when he said the provocative words.

He jumped up and came around the table to pat her back while she coughed and wheezed until she finally regained her breath.

"Are you all right?"

Mortified, she nodded and wiped the tears from her eyes. "You mustn't say such things."

Keeping his hand on her shoulder, he sat in the chair next to hers. "I only speak the truth."

"It cannot be," she said softly.

"We're both consenting adults who find ourselves in a difficult situation, but I've never been one to back down from difficulties. If anything, they bring out my competitive spirit."

"You have nothing to lose. I have everything to lose."

"I would make sure you lost nothing." He took her hand and brought it to his lips. "I would take care of you always if you would only let me."

She shook her head. "You can't promise such things."

"I can."

"No, you can't. Your family—"

"Is very important to me, but they don't dictate how I live my life."

She knew she ought to withdraw her hand from his but couldn't bring herself to do it. "They would never understand this."

"They don't have to. The only ones who need to understand are the two of us."

"You say that now, but when you're ostracized from polite society—"

"You'd be doing me a favor. I *abhor* polite society."

"Your friends, the duke and duchess—"

"Will adore you. They are so very, very happy together, and one of the last things Her Grace said to me before I departed London was that she hoped I one day found someone who made me as happy as her husband has made her."

Maeve looked down at the floor, wishing she had the fortitude to resist the overpowering desire he aroused in her.

"Tell me what you're thinking."

"You make me feel weak."

Taken aback by that, he said, "I do?"

She nodded. "I like to think I'm a strong, independent woman, but when you look at me the way you do, I'm no longer strong. I'm weak and powerless."

"You, my dear, have all the power here."

"No, sir. You do. I'm nothing but a lowly housekeeper."

"You're so much more than that to me." His gaze fixated on her mouth, and she knew that if she stayed there, he would kiss her, and she would let him.

She stood abruptly, withdrawing her hand and wrapping her arms around herself. "Good night, Mr. Nelson."

"Aubrey," he said with a small, sad smile that let her know he too wished things could be different.

"Mr. Nelson," she said firmly, leaving no room for negotiation.

She turned and left the room. Making her way upstairs, her legs felt wobbly and uncertain beneath her. It occurred to her halfway up the stairs that Mr. Nelson presented an even greater risk to her than the man she'd fled in Ireland. That man had been a danger to her physical self. Mr. Nelson had the power to break her heart into a million pieces that could never be put back together again.

In the morning, Aubrey received a telephone call from his mother. As the line crackled with static, he wished he couldn't hear her as clearly as he did.

"Yes, Mother, the house will be ready for your arrival and that of the duke and duchess. Miss Brown, the housekeeper, has done a spectacular job."

"That is a relief."

"How's Father?"

"He's had a difficult few days but seems better today. We're seeing another specialist tomorrow."

"Will he be strong enough to make the trip to Newport?"

"We're hoping so, but he'll need to rest."

"The salt air and sunshine will do him good."

"That is the hope. I won't keep you, Aubrey. I just wanted to check on you."

"There're things we must discuss when you arrive."

"What things?"

"It'll keep until you're here."

"Very well. I'll see you on Friday."

"Good-bye, Mother."

Aubrey ended the call with a sinking feeling. Four more days until his mother, sisters and their children would arrive and take over the house. He experienced a growing sense of desperation at the thought of so many people around to witness his tender feelings for Miss Brown.

After their late-night conversation, he had passed another

sleepless night trying to think of a solution to his "problem" with Miss Brown.

Maeve.

He liked to say her name out loud, to think about her, to imagine what might be possible if only they could find a way. If he hadn't invited Derek, Catherine and the others to spend the summer in Newport, he would've been tempted to run away in the night with her and never look back.

Thanks to the unprecedented success of the company, he had resources of his own that would keep them comfortable for the rest of their days. They could go west, maybe to California. He'd heard so many interesting things about the far western state and had wanted to visit for quite some time. They could find a home there where no one knew them and start a whole new life.

Even the idea of never seeing his beloved siblings, nieces and nephews again wouldn't stop Aubrey from stealing away with her. She would be enough. He knew it in the deepest part of him. But with his friends having already left on the transatlantic crossing, it was too late now to change the plans.

Not to mention, his mother would have an apoplexy if he suddenly uninvited the duke and duchess.

Since leaving London just over a year ago, he'd looked forward to this summer with his friends, and now . . . Now, he couldn't care less about their plans. He wanted only to find a way to be with the woman who had captivated him, body and soul. Perhaps Derek, Simon and Justin would have some advice that would help him to see a way forward with Maeve.

At the moment, he saw no such path, and despair overwhelmed him.

He was unaccustomed to problems that couldn't be solved in one way or another, and the pain of his dilemma had him eyeing the whiskey decanter before luncheon. While he despaired, she kept her distance, continuing to supervise the ragtag army that appeared in greater numbers every day, making it no longer necessary for Aubrey to lend a hand.

She didn't need his help and that only added to the growing ache inside him.

A knock on the door diverted his attention.

"Enter," he said, relieved to have the interruption. Anything to give him something else to think about.

Mr. Plumber stepped into the library where Aubrey had holed up. "There's a man at the front door demanding to speak with you, sir."

"What is his business?"

"He refused to say, sir."

"Show him in."

"Yes, sir."

Mr. Plumber left the room and Aubrey stood, came around the desk and prepared to meet his visitor.

The man, dressed all in black and sporting the muttonchops that had become fashionable in recent years, held his hat in hand as he came into the room, escorted by the butler.

"A Mr. Tornquist to see you, Mr. Nelson."

"Thank you, Mr. Plumber."

Mr. Plumber nodded and closed the door to leave the two men alone.

Aubrey shook the man's hand. "What can I do for you?"

"I'm looking for someone."

Right away, Aubrey noticed the man's Irish accent and felt his hackles go up.

"I have followed her trail to Newport but have been unable to locate her and wondered if you have any information about her whereabouts."

"Who is it you're seeking?"

"Her name is Maeve Sullivan, but we have reason to believe she may be living under an assumed name."

Aubrey forced himself to show no reaction. "Do you have a photograph?"

"I do." He withdrew the sepia-toned photo from the inside pocket of his jacket and handed it over to Aubrey.

He looked down at the image of a younger version of Miss Brown and took a perfunctory glance before handing it back to Mr. Tornquist. "I don't know this woman."

"If I asked the others in your employ if they know her, would their answers be the same as yours?"

"They would."

"Very well." Mr. Tornquist returned the photo to his inside pocket.

"Can you tell me why it is you're looking for her?"

"She is accused of a serious crime in Ireland, and I've been hired by the victim's family to bring her back to face charges."

Panic gripped his heart. "What serious crime is she accused of?"

"Murder."

Aubrey felt as if he'd been punched. Maeve had *murdered* someone? He couldn't for the life of him imagine that, no matter how hard he tried. But before he could do anything else, his first order of business was getting rid of Mr. Tornquist.

"I'm sorry that we're unable to assist in your search," Aubrey said, while praying to God that Miss Brown would remain upstairs and out of sight until the man was long gone.

"If you hear anything about her whereabouts, I would appreciate the information. I'm staying at the Marlborough Inn."

Aubrey nodded and showed Mr. Tornquist out of the library, holding his breath as they crossed the foyer to the main door. He didn't release the breath until the man was out the door and back on his horse heading down the driveway.

As soon as Mr. Tornquist exited the property through the front gates, Aubrey bolted for the stairs, taking them two at a time in his haste to get to her.

"Miss Brown!" Aubrey yelled at the top of his lungs, hoping to be heard over the din of workers talking as they carried out their duties. "Miss Brown!"

He encountered one of the ragtags, a Mr. Tanner. "Where is she?"

"Last I saw, she was in the water closet." The man had two teeth and a ruddy, sun-browned complexion.

Aubrey went to the water closet at the end of the hallway and pounded on the door. "Miss Brown!"

After a full minute had passed, the door opened to a visibly annoyed Maeve. "Whatever is it that has you bellowing, Mr. Nelson?"

What did it say about his state of mind that he found her extraordinary, even when she was annoyed with him and accused of murder? "Come." He took her by hand and half dragged her toward his bedroom where they could speak in private.

She fought back. "Mr. Nelson!"

"Not another word, Miss Brown." The harsh words shocked her into silence. He pushed her into the room and closed the door behind them.

"How could you do this? The men will talk."

"They won't say a word if they wish to continue working here."

"What's wrong?"

"I would like to ask you the same thing, and I would caution you to tell me the truth, Miss Brown, or is it Miss Sullivan?" Only because he was watching her so closely did he see the color leach from her face and her knees go liquid beneath her. He lunged for her and caught her when she would've fallen.

"Wh-why did you call me that?"

"Is it not your name?"

"H-how do you know that?"

Keeping his tight hold on her, he sat in one of the up- holstered chairs, setting her on his lap. That she didn't fight him in any way indicated her profound shock. "A man was here. A Mr. Tornquist. He was looking for a woman named Maeve Sullivan and had a photograph of you."

"Oh God. Oh no. Oh *no*."

To his great dismay, she began to cry. His magnificent Miss Brown didn't cry, and he couldn't bear to see her in such a state.

"Tell me." He gently brushed away her tears with his fingertips, delighted to discover her skin was as soft as it looked.

She shook her head. "I can't."

"You must. How am I to keep you safe if I don't know what's happened."

"It's not up to you to keep me safe." All at once she seemed to realize where she was sitting and started to get up. "I'll leave at once."

He stopped her by tightening his arms around her. "No, you'll stay right here with me, and we'll figure this out together."

"It's not your concern."

"I would like to make it my concern. Let me help you, Maeve. Please let me help."

"There's nothing you or anyone can do. I was a fool to think that I could escape."

Her hopelessness touched him deeply. "Escape what?" He tucked a strand of hair that had come loose from her bun behind her ear and took the opportunity to trace the fragile shell of her ear with his fingertip. "Tell me what you're running from. I can help."

She swallowed hard and blinked as two more tears slid down her cheeks. "I . . . I was married in Ireland, to the son of a very prominent family. He . . . he was sweet and lovely until after we were married when he changed. He became a monster. He hurt me."

Filled with rage so potent it threatened to consume him, Aubrey forced himself to stay calm for her sake. "How did he hurt you?"

"He hit me. In my face, so hard that my eye was swollen shut for a week. He kicked me here." She flattened her hand on her belly. "And he tried to force me to do things." She shuddered.

Aubrey guided her head to his shoulder. "Shhh. He can't hurt you anymore. I won't let him."

"He's dead. I killed him." Her tone was flat, devoid of the usual animation that colored her words.

"Tell me what happened." He caressed her back in small circles that he hoped would soothe some of the tension from her muscles. He relished the chance to touch her and be close to her. Hearing she had killed the man who'd harmed her didn't change anything for him. If anything, it made him fiercely proud to know that she'd defended herself and only added to his determination to keep her close so he could protect her from ever being hurt again.

"He beat me. He hit me again and again, until I was certain he was going to kill me. I reached for the pot on the stove, burning my hand rather badly. I threw the hot soup at him and when he came at me, I hit him as hard as I could in the head with the cast-iron pan. When he fell to the floor, I noticed he wasn't breathing and realized what

I had done. I took the money he had hidden in one of his boots, and I ran."

"You were injured. How did you manage to get away?"

"We lived at the coast, so I was able to find a ship leaving for America. Because I had the money to pay for the passage, they didn't ask any questions about an injured woman traveling alone. The crossing was dreadful. Storms and high seas. I was sick the entire time, and by the time I arrived in New York, I was very ill. The ship's captain took mercy on me and brought me to his home to recover. His wife connected me with the employment agency that found the position here."

"So you only recently arrived in America?"

"Six weeks ago. And now they've found me." A sob erupted from her tightly clenched jaw. "They're going to take me back to be hung."

"No, they aren't."

"They will. His family is very powerful. His grandfather is a British viscount, and his family was scandalized when he insisted on marrying me, the lowly daughter of a banker, when he could've had an aristocratic wife. I was a fool. I thought it was a love match, but he had an unnatural fixation on me that I had mistaken for affection. Almost right away, I realized I'd made a dreadful error in marrying him. When his family threatened to cut off his allowance in retribution for marrying a lowly Irish whore, as they called me, he worked off his frustrations with his fists."

"I'm so very sorry that happened to you."

She hung her head. "I'm ashamed of what I did, taking the life of another. But had I not done it, he was going to kill me. I have no doubt of it. The local constable wouldn't have helped me. He was a friend of my husband's."

"You did the only thing you could do."

"I could've just run and not killed him, but he would've come after me." Her body trembled violently.

"Shhh, you're safe now."

"I'm never going to be safe as long as they know where I am. It took only two months for them to track me to Newport." She sat up abruptly. "I must leave at once."

"You're not going anywhere."

"But they've found me! They know I'm here. They'll take me back and hang me for killing him."

"No one is taking you anywhere. I'll send Mr. Plumber to fetch the local justice of the peace at once."

Her body went rigid with shock and horror. "You're going to turn me in?"

"No, my dear lady. I'm going to marry you."

Chapter Seven

Maeve's shock turned to disbelief. "Whatever do you mean?"

"You heard me. I'm going to marry you and put you under my protection."

"That's not possible."

"Why not? You're no longer married, and I've never been married. If you're married to me, you'll have the full weight of the Nelson family name and resources behind you."

"That's very kind of you, but I still can't marry you." She tugged on his arm, seeking her freedom. Thankfully, Mr. Nelson let her go, and she stood to get away from him and his warm brown eyes. It wasn't possible to have this conversation while seated on the man's lap, with the scent of his shaving soap filling her senses and making her want to lean in closer to him when that was the last thing she ought to be doing.

She ought to be packing and figuring out where to go next. Thankfully, she had the last of Mr. Farthington's money tucked away under one of the floor tiles in her room and was due wages from the Nelsons. It wasn't much but it would get her to Boston where she might be able to secure another housekeeping position. If Mr. Nelson gave her a recommendation, that is.

"Miss Brown?"

She realized he'd been speaking to her while she was busy making plans.

"Tell me why you can't marry me."

"Because after I fled my home in Ireland, I made a vow that I would never again shackle myself to a man and give him that kind of control over me."

Mr. Nelson stood and took a step toward her.

She took a step back.

He took another. "Stop." Placing his hands on her shoulders, he held her in place. While she would've been terrified of what was coming if her husband had done that, with Mr. Nelson she wasn't afraid. Not yet anyway. "I'm not looking to control you, Maeve. I want to take care of you and protect you from harm. You would never have anything to fear from me except, perhaps, an overabundance of affection."

His hands dropped to encircle her waist, bringing her in even closer to him, until their bodies were aligned. "For if I were lucky enough to convince you to marry me, I'd be the happiest husband who ever lived, and I'd want to hold you and kiss you and touch you as much and as often as you would allow. I would never, *ever* touch you in anger. You have my word as a man and a gentleman on that."

With his lips hovering a heartbeat above hers, she could neither breathe nor move nor do anything other than wait to see what he would do next. When his lips touched hers, she knew she should tell him to stop. She should pull free of him and run, but she couldn't seem to get that message from her muzzy brain to the feet that remained rooted in place as his lips moved persuasively.

"Kiss me back, Maeve." As he spoke, his lips continued to slide over hers, softly and sweetly, not at all the demanding, painful crush of lips and teeth and tongue she'd been subjected to by the beast she'd married. Nothing about this was anything like that. This was seduction, pure and simple.

"Kiss me back." He said the words more urgently this time, and when Maeve parted her lips to respond to him, he took that as invitation to deepen the kiss.

She had never been kissed like this or even known it was possible for a kiss to invoke so many emotions, more than she could possibly process all at once.

His tongue rubbed against hers, and her knees buckled. Only his arms around her kept her from stumbling.

Slowly, he withdrew from the kiss, but kept his lips close to hers. "If you marry me, I'll care for you and protect you every day for the rest of my life. I'll never touch you with anything but affection in mind. I swear to you on the lives of everyone I hold dear that you can trust me."

She looked away so she wouldn't be swayed by his beautiful eyes or handsome face. "Your family would never understand this."

"They don't have to. You wouldn't be marrying them. You'd be marrying me—and only me."

"We both know that's not the case."

"The only thing that matters is that you'd be safe from anyone who would try to harm you. All you have to do is agree to marry me, and I'll take care of everything."

Maeve's chest felt tight, as if someone were standing on it, the feeling reminiscent of how it had felt to flee in the night after killing her husband. If she said no to his proposal, would he allow her to leave? She had to know.

"If I decline your very kind offer," she said haltingly, "would I be permitted to leave?"

The only sign of his displeasure with her question was in the tightening of his jaw. "Only if you allow me to accompany you to ensure your safety."

Maeve took a deep breath, hoping to alleviate the

pressure in her chest. He had been kind to her from the beginning, and other than the farce about being the new butler, he'd never been deceitful. His family was obscenely wealthy, and he had the resources to untangle her from the mess she'd left behind in Ireland. And his interest in her, though wildly inappropriate, had seemed genuine from the outset.

She licked her lips and looked up at him, feeling uncertain but knowing the question must be asked. "What about our religious differences?"

"What about them?"

"I'm Roman Catholic. I assume you're not."

"You assume correctly. I'm a lapsed Protestant."

"It would be important to me to be allowed to continue to attend mass as I do every Sunday and to practice my faith."

"I would never forbid such a thing."

"It would be another reason for your family to dislike me."

"I've already told you their opinions don't matter to me."

As the debate raged on, he surprised her when he dropped to his knees, took her hand and kissed the back of it. "Beautiful Maeve, if you would please do me the enormous honor of being my wife, I'll care for you until my dying day. Will you marry me?"

Looking down at him looking up at her with his heart in his eyes and his desire for her visibly apparent, Maeve's resistance crumbled. If she was wrong about him, too, she would know for certain that her judgment was faulty. "Yes," she said softly. "I'll marry you."

He stood slowly, almost as if he was afraid she'd change her mind in the time it took for him to get up. "You will?"

She nodded. "I will. Thank you, Mr. Nelson, for your kindness."

"I should be thanking you."

"What did I do?"

"You agreed to be my wife." He kissed the back of her hand once more and then gazed into her eyes. "I swear on my life you'll never regret it."

Months' worth of panic, uncertainty and fear slipped away as she realized she was no longer alone.

He released her hand. "Don't move. I'll be right back." He went to the door, opened it and stepped out into the hallway where the low vibration of male voices could be heard.

As she waited for him, Maeve hoped that her band of ruffians was seeing to the work she had assigned them. She wanted to go and check on them, but he had told her to stay put. So she stayed put. But she vibrated from the effort required to remain still, to take this day one minute at a time rather than jumping ahead to what came next. She would find out soon enough if he was a man of his word. And if he wasn't? She had run away once before and would do so again, if it came to that.

But she hoped it wouldn't come to that.

Today, her greatest fears had come to fruition. Farthington's family was looking for her and would probably stop at nothing to see her pay for taking his life. It wouldn't matter to them that she'd been defending herself against yet another ruthless attack at his hands.

The pervasive, sickening fear of what would happen if they found her had haunted her days and nights. She'd been plagued by nightmares that had them tearing her from her bed to take her home to be hung. On many a night, she had awoken in a cold sweat after dreaming about the hangman's noose.

They'd hated her before she took his life. She could only imagine how they felt about her now.

Mr. Nelson returned. "What is it? Why are you pale as a ghost and trembling?"

She thought about dissembling but found she couldn't be dishonest with him after everything he was doing to help keep her safe. "I'm afraid of them finding me."

"They'll have to go through me to get to you, and that's not going to happen."

"You can't possibly know that."

"I do know that. No one will get into this house unless we allow it, and we'll not allow Mr. Tornquist in again. We told him you weren't here."

"People know I'm here. The ragtag army . . . If one of them were to confirm it . . ."

"I'll speak to them and ask for their discretion."

"That doesn't mean we will get it."

"Maeve, sweetheart, please take a breath and settle yourself. You're safe now. I'll see to it personally."

"It'll take some time for me to stop being afraid."

His warm smile lit up his beautiful eyes. "Take all the time you need. I'll be right here by your side any time you're frightened."

"I worry mostly that you're too good to be true." She'd no sooner said the words than she wanted to recall them out of fear of offending him.

"I'm exactly what I appear to be—a man who has convinced the woman he wants above all others to spend the rest of her life with him. I've never been more elated in all my life."

She wanted so badly to believe him but her many concerns about marrying him couldn't be pushed aside like the piles of dust in the hallways. For one thing, his parents would be incensed when they learned he'd married the Irish housekeeper. She'd already begun one marriage under similar circumstances and that had ended in disaster. Mr. Nelson's mother had hoped for an aristocratic marriage for him. Marriage to the Irish housekeeper was as far from an aristocratic marriage as one could get.

"What are you thinking now?" He went to the sideboard to pour amber liquid into a glass that he handed to her.

Even though it was early in the day, her nerves needed the fortification the liquor could provide, so she took a healthy sip of the whiskey. "I'm thinking about your mother."

His brows furrowed adorably. "What about her?"

"She'll be furious when she discovers that you married the housekeeper."

"That'll be her problem, not ours."

She gave him a withering look. "Do you honestly believe that?"

"I do believe it. I care not what she or anyone else thinks of my choice of a bride."

"Not even your friends the duke and duchess?"

"Especially not them. They aren't the kind of people who judge someone unkindly simply because they're different or foreign. They will care for you because *I* care for you."

"You make it sound so simple when we both know it'll be anything but."

Aubrey took the glass from her and put it on a side table. He grasped the hands she had clenched tightly together, pried them apart and brought them to his waist while he placed his hands on her shoulders. "I'm more than up for the challenge. Are you?"

Her backbone stiffened. "I've never met a challenge anything less than head on."

He unleashed that potent smile. "There she is, my fierce Irish warrior. You should know that the norms of society mean nothing to me. I haven't the first concern about what anyone says about me or thinks of me, and you shouldn't either. I'm marrying the only woman who has captured my attention since I lost Annabelle ten long years ago. That should count for something with my family."

She feared he was being overly optimistic but refrained from saying so. They would find out soon enough. Glancing down at the drab, olive-colored dress she had donned for what she'd thought would be another long workday, Maeve had a thought. "Would you mind terribly if I went upstairs to change? I have a dress that my benefactor in New York gave me that would be more suitable for . . . To be married in." She tried not to stumble over the words, so he wouldn't know how terribly nervous she was about exchanging vows with him. Despite his sincere assurances, she still had her doubts that this was a good idea.

"Of course. Do you require assistance?"

"I don't think so."

"I'll wait for you right here."

"I'll hurry." Maeve rushed from the room and went up the main staircase, which was quicker than using the staff stairwell. She reached the third floor just as Mrs. Allston appeared on the far end of the hallway. "Is it true? You're to marry Mr. Nelson?"

The cook's scandalized expression only confirmed Maeve's greatest fears. No one would understand or accept this union. And why should they? Mr. Nelson could have any woman he wanted. Forcing herself to remember why she had accepted his proposal, she gave a tight nod.

"It's true."

"Are you with child?"

"No! Of course not."

"Then why?"

"He . . . I . . . He's helping me."

"With what?"

"I'm in a spot of trouble, and he's offering his protection."

"What sort of trouble?"

"I would prefer not to say." She glanced at the cook, who had been so nice to her from the beginning. Would that change now? "Could I ask a favor?"

"You may ask."

"I came up to change into a more appropriate dress but could use help with the buttons. Would you be willing to assist me?"

After a long pause, the cook made a sound that some-how managed to convey her reluctant willingness to help. She followed Maeve into the bedroom where she quickly removed her work dress, her face flaming with shame over the dingy state of her undergarments.

"Wherever did you acquire such a fine gown?" Mrs. Allston asked when she saw the pale blue confection that Maeve withdrew from the wardrobe.

"A friend gave it to me because it no longer fit her after having children."

"It's quite lovely."

"Thank you." Maeve moved quickly to don a corset that Mrs. Allston tied for her, and then the gown, hoping it still fit her. The first time she'd tried it on had been after being so dreadfully ill from the ocean crossing. It had been big on her then, but perhaps after a few weeks of regular meals, it would fit better. She could only hope, because she didn't have anything else to wear to be married.

Married.

To Mr. Nelson. *Aubrey.*

A flutter of excitement and anticipation had her cover-ing her abdomen with her hand as Mrs. Allston tended to the buttons down her back. When she was finished, Maeve put on the jacket that matched the skirt. "Does it look all right?"

"You look lovely."

"I do? Really?" She wanted to be lovely for him, for the lovely man who was risking so much to offer her protection. She wanted him to be proud of the woman he was marrying, regardless of the circumstances that had brought them to this moment.

"You do. But if I may say one thing . . ."

"Of course."

"People aren't going to understand this marriage, Miss Brown. They'll be swift in their condemnation of you and of Mr. Nelson."

"I tried to tell him that, but he said he didn't care what people say."

"Everyone cares what others think of them. When I married my Mr. Allston, his mother didn't approve because she had someone else picked out for him. She made our lives quite difficult for many years."

Maeve hung on to her every word. "How did you get through it?"

"By focusing on each other and the reason we wanted to be married in the first place. If you do that, if you focus on what brought you together and not on what could tear you apart, you'll find a way through the storm."

"Thank you, Mrs. Allston. I truly appreciate your advice."

"I have seen the way Mr. Nelson looks at you when he thinks no one is watching. I believe he truly cares for you."

"Yes, I think he does."

"That makes you a very lucky young lady."

"I've never been particularly lucky before."

"I think your luck may be about to change, my dear."

After a knock on the door, Mrs. Allston opened it to Mr. Plumber.

His eyes widened when he saw Maeve wearing the beautiful dress.

Mrs. Allston cleared her throat. "Mr. Plumber? Did you want something?"

"Mr. Nelson asked me to inform Miss Brown that the justice of the peace has arrived."

"Thank you." Maeve reached for the straw hat that matched her dress and placed it on her head, using the small mirror over the dresser to adjust it. She took comfort in knowing that while she had absolutely no business marrying a man of Mr. Nelson's ilk, at least she would look like a woman who deserved him, for a brief time anyway.

Before she left the room, she glanced at the photo of her family on the dresser and wished with all her heart they could be with her on this auspicious occasion, that she could ask their opinions of the man she was to marry, that they could stand by her side when she took this momentous step.

"Miss Brown? Are you ready?"

Mrs. Allston's query interrupted Maeve's thoughts before they could turn maudlin.

"I'm ready." As ready as she would ever be.

She followed Mr. Plumber and Mrs. Allston down the main stairs to find Mr. Nelson waiting for her at the bottom. A man with thick white hair and white muttonchops stood next to him.

Mr. Nelson stared at her for an uncomfortably long moment. He stepped forward, took her hand and helped her down the last of the stairs. "You are exquisite."

"Thank you." His reaction made her breathless.

He continued to stare at her as if they were the only people in the room.

"I take it this is the bride," the other man said.

"Yes, this is my bride. Maeve, this is Mr. Taylor, the justice of the peace."

"Pleased to meet you, sir."

"Likewise." If Mr. Taylor was shocked to hear an Irish accent coming from Mr. Nelson's bride, he did an admirable job of hiding it as he looked to the groom for guidance. "Where would you like to hold the ceremony?"

"In the library." Mr. Nelson tucked her hand into the crook of his arm and led her into the room that was one of her favorites in the grand house. "I trust this will suffice?"

"Yes," she said.

"You're trembling," he said softly so he couldn't be overheard.

"I'm nervous."

"Please don't be."

"You're not at all nervous?"

"Not one bit."

"How can that be?"

He shrugged. "If I were marrying anyone but you, I'd be in a panic. But because it's you, I'm calm and collected."

"I'm glad one of us is calm." She placed her hand over her upset stomach. "I'm afraid I may cast up my breakfast."

He put his arms around her and brought her into his embrace, not seeming to care that there were three other people watching them. "Everything will be fine. Leave it to me to take care of you."

Maeve felt both relieved and conflicted by his assurances. While it was a great relief to know she would have his help and protection, she'd been determined to take care of herself after fleeing her abusive marriage. Only knowing her former husband's family had managed to track her to Newport so quickly had her accepting Mr. Nelson's offer of help.

Well, that and the attraction that had simmered between

them from the first time they met. Would theirs be a marriage in name only or would he want to explore that simmering attraction in the privacy of their bedroom? They hadn't discussed that when they made their plans, so she had no way to know what he expected.

"Shall we go ahead and take care of the formalities?" he asked in a casual tone, as if those "formalities" wouldn't change both their lives forever.

If it didn't work out, she could obtain a divorce. Newport had become the place to go for society people looking to get out of marriages as Rhode Island had some of the country's least stringent laws regarding the dissolution of marriage.

"Yes, we shall," she said in response to his question as she swallowed hard, hoping she would not embarrass them both by losing her gorge during the ceremony.

Standing in front of the fireplace, she faced Mr. Nelson, forcing herself to really look at the man she was about to marry. He looked back at her with affection and perhaps satisfaction. He'd made it clear that he fancied her, so of course he was satisfied to be getting what he wanted. Although it would be unfair to accuse him of having nefarious ulterior motives. He'd offered help and protection that she desperately needed. If he got something he wanted, too, well that was only fair.

Possibly sensing the bride's disquiet, Mr. Taylor moved through the recitation of vows with all due haste, forgoing fancy or flowery words about marriage. For that, Maeve would always be thankful.

When Mr. Nelson slid a plain gold band on her finger, Maeve looked up at him, startled.

"It was my grandmother's. She told me to give it to the woman I married. I believe she would be pleased with my choice."

Maeve didn't believe that for a minute, but she wasn't about to argue the point. She had never met his grandmother, so who was she to say what the woman would've wanted for him?

"By the power vested in me by the state of Rhode Island and Providence Plantations, I now pronounce you husband and wife. Mr. Nelson, you may kiss your bride."

That detail hadn't been part of her first wedding, so Maeve found herself unprepared to kiss the man who was now her husband with three sets of curious eyes looking on.

Her husband, on the other hand, had no such concerns. He raised his hands to her face and placed a gentle, tender kiss on her lips and then flashed a huge, satisfied grin.

A trickle of unease traversed down her backbone as she wondered if this was the moment when he would reveal his true nature. She braced herself for blows that didn't materialize and then immediately felt guilty for anticipating such treatment from a man who had been nothing but kind to her.

Seeming puzzled by her tense posture, he extended his arm to her.

She tucked her hand into his elbow and allowed him to escort her toward the doorway, where Mr. Plumber and Mrs. Allston stood guard over her ragtags, who had gathered in the hallway to greet the newly married couple.

Denny, Padraic, Heine, Kaiser, Wiggie and Timmy, each of them smiling while seeming dumbfounded by the turn of events. Between the six of them, they could put together a full set of teeth, but their lack of teeth didn't stop them from cheering and clapping wildly.

A flush of embarrassment overtook Maeve's face when she imagined what they must be thinking. Yesterday she'd been the housekeeper. Today she was married to the son of the people who owned the house. As soon as the men went home for the night, she and Mr. Nelson would be the talk of Newport.

That thought turned her stomach. "Polite" society was anything but when one of their own stepped out of line. By marrying the Irish housekeeper, Mr. Nelson was so far out of line, he could never return to the status he'd enjoyed only that morning, before he bound himself to her and sealed both their fates.

Chapter Eight

"No frowning allowed on our wedding day." Aubrey's lips were close to her ear, his voice low enough to keep their conversation private. His nearness did funny things to her insides, or maybe it was the overabundance of nerves affecting her? It was hard to tell when her emotions were a jumbled mess of fear, relief, shame, foreboding and yes, desire for this man who was now her husband.

The justice of the peace had them sign the marriage papers with Mr. Plumber and Mrs. Allston signing as their witnesses.

"And with that," Mr. Taylor said, as he put the papers into a leather satchel, "it's official. Congratulations, Mr. Nelson, Mrs. Nelson."

Mrs. Nelson.

She was now his *wife*.

When her legs would've buckled under her, she settled into one of the many chairs that adorned the vast library.

Mr. Nelson went to see Mr. Taylor out and returned alone, closing the door to the prying eyes of the servants. "Are you all right?"

"I don't know what I am."

"I know one thing you are."

"What's that?"

He sat in the chair next to hers. "Married."

"Indeed I am." She forced herself to look at him. "I'm not sure I said thank you."

"There's no need to thank me."

"There is every need to thank you. You've saved me from certain death."

He took her hand and brought it to his lips. "By saving your life, I saved my own because if you had left, I never would've stopped looking for you." The combination of his heartfelt words and the brush of his lips against her skin set off a wildfire of need inside her the likes of which she had never before experienced.

"What will happen now?"

"I'll contact our family's legal counsel to determine how we should handle your former husband's family and the charges pending in Ireland. I'll move heaven and earth to free you from the horror of your past."

"If we do that, they'll know where I am." The thought of them finding her had filled her with stark terror even before they tracked her to Newport.

"They'll also know that you're under my protection."

"Wouldn't it be better to hope they never find me?"

"Perhaps, but I would rather you not have to live with that threat hanging over you."

"I'm afraid, Mr. Nelson. They're powerful people, and they'll want retribution for their brother and son."

"Their brother and son was a brute who beat his wife."

"That won't matter to them."

"Try not to worry. We have the truth on our side and the best legal minds money can buy working for us."

"And your family won't mind if you request their assistance on behalf of your new Irish wife who murdered her former husband?"

"My new wife defended herself against a violent attack. That's the only fact that matters."

"I wish I shared your confidence. Your family will not understand."

"I'm not concerned about what my family thinks. I married the woman I wanted to marry for reasons that're entirely my own. It's none of their concern."

She didn't believe it would be that simple, but she chose to keep that thought to herself.

"We must move your belongings from the third floor into my suite and enjoy the wedding luncheon I asked Mrs. Allston to prepare for us."

"But there's work to be done."

"That work is no longer your concern."

"Of course it's my concern! Your family will be here at the end of the week and the duke and duchess a week later. The house is in no way ready for occupancy."

"I'll see about hiring a new housekeeper tomorrow to oversee the final preparations."

"There won't be time to hire someone and get her here. I'm already here and well aware of what needs to be done. I insist that you allow me to finish what I've started." She no sooner used the word "insist" than she recoiled from the pervasive fear that he would react badly.

"Please don't do that," he said softly. "Don't think that I'll strike you if you speak your mind to me."

"I apologize."

"Don't do that either."

"It's apt to take a while for me to believe you won't treat me the way he did."

"Take all the time you need." He stood and gave a gentle tug on the hand he continued to hold. "Let me assist you in moving your belongings."

"There isn't much to move. I could do it myself."

"Tomorrow, I'll invite one of the local dressmakers to come measure you for a new wardrobe."

"That's not necessary."

"Ah, but it is, my dear. I'm going to want to show off my beautiful wife at the many parties and gatherings this summer, and you'll want to be properly attired."

"The local hostesses won't welcome me."

"If they wish to entertain our friends, the duke and duchess, they will absolutely welcome you. And let me assure you, they *all* want to entertain the duke and duchess."

"So you'll blackmail them into accepting me?"

"Blackmail is such an ugly word."

Maeve released an inelegant snort of laughter.

Mr. Nelson stopped and turned to her, his face a study of shock and longing.

"What's wrong?"

"Absolutely nothing. It is just that you so rarely laugh, and I do love the sound."

"I haven't had much reason to laugh in recent months."

"I hope to hear more of that delightful sound now that you're safe and protected." He tucked her hand into the crook of his elbow and escorted her upstairs to the third floor.

"You never said if you'll allow me to continue to oversee the preparations for your family and guests."

"It's no longer necessary for you to work."

"It may not be financially necessary, but I like to finish what I start, and the only way this house is going to be ready in time is if I continue to oversee the work."

"It's important to you then?"

"It is. I want your family and guests to be comfortable."

"I'll make you a deal. You may continue to oversee the work on the house if you allow me to provide you with a new wardrobe."

She thought about that for a minute and decided the deal was fair enough. "I agree to that."

"All right then. But I'll do my best to hire another housekeeper to assist you. I'm going to want to spend time with my new wife, and that won't be possible if she's busy working from sunup to sundown."

Hearing that he wanted to spend time with her set off that fluttering sensation inside her that occurred whenever he looked at her in that special, proprietary way.

Maeve opened the door to the room that contained a bed, a bedside table and a wardrobe. Its most redeeming feature was the breathtaking view of the ocean from the one small window. It took a matter of minutes to fold and pack her three work dresses, undergarments, two nightgowns, robe and slippers into the carpetbag she had brought from New York.

Aware of him watching her every move, she bent to retrieve the stash of money she had taken from Mr. Farthington and tucked it into the carpetbag, deciding it was good for him to know that she had the means to flee, should it become necessary.

The only other item she owned was the silver-framed photo of her family that she had grabbed in her panic after the altercation with her husband.

Former husband.

"May I?" Mr. Nelson said of the photo.

Maeve handed it over to him.

He studied the photo of her parents and sisters that had become her most precious and prized possession. "I'll take you to see them the minute it's safe for you to return to Ireland."

Maeve stared at him, hoping she hadn't misheard him. She had left Ireland expecting to never return, to never see her family again. And now he was offering her the possibility of someday returning home. It was almost too much to take in.

He relieved her of the bag containing her meager possessions and once again offered her his arm to escort her from the room. The sound of the door closing behind them symbolized the end of one life and the beginning of another.

A spark of hope ignited inside her. Mr. Nelson had lit that spark and continued to fan the flame with everything he said and did.

A mere flight of stairs separated the third-floor servants' quarters from the palatial rooms occupied by the Nelson family. As they descended the stairs, Maeve vowed to maintain perspective. Mr. Nelson had done her a favor by marrying her. When his family, friends and society rejected his wife, he would, too. It was only a matter of time before he realized he'd made a huge mistake in marrying her. So it would behoove her to keep her emotions out of this farce of marriage. Under no circumstances could she allow herself to fall in love with him.

As Aubrey escorted his new wife into the suite of rooms that they would share, he felt lighter than air. The beautiful, mysterious, capable Miss Brown was now his wife, and he could honestly say that since he lost Annabelle, he'd never been as happy as he was right in that moment.

The surreal aspects of the day made him feel as if he were living a dream and that at any moment he might wake to find that his fertile imagination had conjured the threat Mr. Tornquist had brought to his door as well as the solution that had made her his wife.

Aubrey's stomach took a nasty dip when he thought about what his mother would have to say about him marrying the Irish housekeeper. He'd told his new wife that he didn't care what his mother thought, and he didn't. But he didn't relish the unpleasantness that would surely ensue when she learned what'd transpired after she sent him to Newport to make the house ready for the family and their guests.

He could only hope any ugliness would occur out of earshot of his bride, who certainly didn't need to hear his mother's thoughts on the matter.

Pushing aside those concerns, Aubrey chose to focus entirely on his wife. Perhaps by the time they were joined by his family, they would be on more level footing with each other and could convince the others that their marriage was legitimate. If he could get his sisters on board, Aubrey stood a slim chance of avoiding a protracted dispute with his mother.

But that was a big "if." Though his older sisters adored and doted on him, they had taken to their new position in society with unexpected zeal, and if Aubrey's marriage to the Irish housekeeper caused them to be shunned by Newport's most influential hostesses, his sisters would be unforgiving.

Thank goodness Derek and Catherine were coming, Aubrey thought for the umpteenth time. The presence of the duke and duchess would help to alleviate whatever enmity his sisters and mother might feel toward him at this perilous moment in his fragile new union with Maeve.

"You can put your things in the wardrobe next to mine."

"Thank you."

"In New York, we'll have separate accommodations, but here we must share a room when the entire family is in residence."

"Th-that is fine."

"Maeve." He waited for her to look at him. "Nothing

will ever happen between us unless you wish it to. I'll never touch you with anything other than respect and reverence."

"I'm deeply grateful for your many kindnesses, Mr. Nelson."

"Aubrey."

She looked directly at him, causing his heart to skip a beat. "Aubrey," she said softly, seeming to test the way the word felt on her lips and tongue.

"Say it again, Maeve."

"Aubrey."

"I like the way you say my name." He kissed her gently, because she was his wife and he could, but carefully so as not to scare her by letting her see the powerful way in which he wanted her.

She glanced at the door. "I should see to the workers. To make sure they're on task."

"And I have several cables to draft. After that, please join me in the dining room for our wedding luncheon."

She nodded in agreement, even though he could see she was still uncomfortable with the fact that she had moved from servant to family member in the course of one unforgettable morning. He only wished he knew her true feelings on the matter. Yes, she was relieved to have his protection and the resources that would allow her to fight off her former husband's family. Was relief all that she felt? He'd sensed desire for him in the way she had kissed him earlier, but again, was that fueled by the relief or did she genuinely desire him? Perhaps one day she would share her true feelings with him. He could only hope so as he'd like to know everything about her.

That fascination with another person was entirely new to him. He hadn't experienced that with Annabelle because they'd grown up together and knew each other inside and out. With Maeve, everything was new, and he looked forward to each and every discovery he would make.

Leaving her to get settled in his bedchamber, he went downstairs to use the room where his father conducted business while in residence. Despite the house having a telephone, it was not possible to make outgoing long-distance calls without an appointment at a specially outfitted, soundproofed phone booth. There was one at the post office, but it could take days to get an appointment, especially this time of year when the summer residents were arriving. As he sat to draft a cable, detailing Maeve's dilemma to the family's solicitor, Mr. Charles Nightingale, he began to question the wisdom of involving the family's legal counsel in his personal business.

Mr. Nightingale would convey the information directly to Aubrey's father and brothers, for whom he worked. No, that wouldn't do. Rather than reach out to his family's employee, he wrote a quick note to Matthew and asked him to come by the house at his earliest convenience to discuss a matter of extreme urgency. Knowing Matthew, the "extreme urgency" would get him there sooner rather than later.

Aubrey asked Mr. Plumber to get one of the men to deliver the note to Matthew as soon as possible.

"Yes, sir," Mr. Plumber said. "And may I say, sir, the local men are proving to be a hardworking group. I do believe we may be able to turn some of them into footmen, stable men and gardeners."

"That's excellent news. Encourage them to recruit their friends and family members as we're still in need of housemaids as well as a new housekeeper. Before long we'll have a full staff."

"I will do that, sir."

Aubrey was relieved to realize that at some point, Mr. Plumber had come around to embracing the challenge of turning the ragtag army into a household staff.

"And may I also add my felicitations on your marriage."

"Thank you kindly."

"Miss Brown, or I should say, *Mrs. Nelson*, is a delightful young woman."

"I agree."

"I hope I'm not speaking out of turn by asking if Mr. Tornquist brought news that led to your nuptials."

"He did."

"And as such, your marriage is intended to protect Mrs. Nelson?"

"It is." Mr. Plumber didn't need to know that Aubrey also had feelings for the woman who was now his wife. That was no one's concern but theirs.

"Ah." Plumber seemed relieved to have discovered the reason for the hasty marriage.

"If Mr. Tornquist returns for any reason, he's to be turned away and I'm to be notified immediately."

"Yes, sir. Is Miss Brown . . . er, Mrs. Nelson, in danger?"

"Not anymore." Aubrey needed to believe that because the alternative was too frightening to be borne. "My note to Mr. Jarvis is intended to address the danger."

"I will see to it that it's delivered immediately."

"Thank you, and will you also contact the better dressmakers in town and ask them to come tomorrow to outfit Mrs. Nelson with a wardrobe for the Season?"

"Consider it done. Mrs. Allston is ready to serve the wedding luncheon whenever you and Mrs. Nelson are ready to dine."

"I'll see if she is ready."

"Very good, sir." Mr. Plumber took his leave.

Aubrey hoped that Matthew would be by soon to help him figure out how he ought to proceed with the situation. Matthew's father was a well-regarded local solicitor and Matthew was also a solicitor, but would he know how to handle an international situation such as the one Maeve found herself in? Aubrey could only hope he was doing the right thing by circumventing the family's legal counsel.

If nothing else, he would hopefully postpone the inevitable airing of his family's opinions about his new marriage. He'd postpone that forever if he could.

Chapter Nine

As he headed for the stairs to see what was keeping Maeve, she descended the grand staircase.

Aubrey stopped to watch her come toward him, noting the regal curve of the neck that had first entranced him. He held out his hand to help her down the last few stairs, not that she needed his help. Her independence and courage were two of the things he found most attractive about her.

Tucking her hand into the crook of his elbow, he escorted her into the dining room and held the chair to the right of his for her.

Once they were settled, Mrs. Allston came in to serve bowls of steaming fish stew, pickled herring, boiled potatoes and asparagus in a delicious cream sauce.

Aubrey opened the chilled bottle of champagne he'd procured from the wine cellar and popped the cork, sending a stream of fizzy bubbly into the two flutes that had been placed on the table. Mrs. Allston had seen to every detail, and he would express his gratitude in the form of a handsome tip at the end of the summer.

"A toast to you, Mrs. Nelson," Aubrey said when they were alone in the enormous dining room that sat thirty people comfortably. His voice echoed off the ceiling and the tall walls that boasted a series of paintings depicting seaside activities—a woman holding a parasol on her shoulder as she walked along the shore, a sleek sailing vessel heeling in the wind and a young child collecting shells into a pail. "Thank you for doing me the honor of becoming my wife."

She touched her glass to his. "I should be thanking you. Without your grand gesture, I would still be running from the past."

"I would've had no choice but to chase after you, so thank you for agreeing to my plan."

"It wasn't exactly a hardship to marry a wealthy, influential man who also happens to be kind, thoughtful and exceedingly handsome."

Aubrey wished for a way to capture that sentence in some format that would allow him to hear it back any time he wished to be reminded of what she'd said and how she'd said it in that melodic sound of Ireland. "You find me exceedingly handsome?"

He was delighted when she rolled her eyes dramatically. "Don't pretend that I'm the first to tell you so."

"You're the first since Annabelle whose opinion mattered to me."

If they lived together for the next fifty years, he would never tire of the way her cheeks flushed with color whenever she was embarrassed or aroused. He would make it his most important mission to make her flush as often as he possibly could.

"I want to understand . . ." She stopped herself, as if she'd thought better of what she'd planned to say.

"What is it you wish to understand?"

"How it's possible for you to feel the way you do about me when there are so many far more suitable women you could've chosen to marry."

Where did he begin? "First of all, despite how it might

seem after I spent several Seasons in London, I was in absolutely no rush to get married. My mother was the one pushing me to find a wife while I was still young enough to father children."

"You're hardly in your dotage."

"Try telling her that. When I reached thirty, she turned up the pressure, probably because my two brothers are destined to be bachelors for life and as such the family name is in jeopardy if I don't produce a son."

"I see."

As he watched her sip the champagne and take delicate bites from her plate, he thought she looked every bit the society matron taking luncheon with her husband. The dress she'd donned for their wedding and the way she wore it spoke of breeding far above a housekeeper's station. It would be possible to pass her off as a member of upper-crust society if it were not for her delightful Irish accent.

Aubrey topped off both their glasses. "Second of all, I was holding out for something more than a traditional society marriage."

"What do you mean by 'more'?"

"It wasn't enough for me that my potential wife had the proper pedigree. I also wanted someone I could converse with, who had some experiences that would make her appreciate the simple things in life."

"What do you consider the simple things?"

"A picnic at the shore on a beautiful spring day. The bloom of the daffodils in the garden. Magnificent sunsets, the sound of the waves hitting the rocks and the smell of the sea air. Despite the extravagance of this house, I am, at the end of the day, a rather simple sort of fellow."

Maeve listened attentively, seeming to mull over what he'd said. "I find that quality almost as attractive as your kind eyes."

He took hold of the hand she'd placed on the table. "Do I have kind eyes?"

"You do. I have put all of my faith in the fact that your eyes are kind and thus the rest of you must be as well."

"Maeve . . ."

"Yes?"

"I would like to spend some time alone with my new wife." He swallowed the lump that formed in his throat. "Upstairs."

Before she could reply to his audacious statement, Mr. Plumber appeared at the door to the dining room. "Pardon the interruption, but Mr. Jarvis is here to see you, sir. He's waiting in the parlor."

Under his breath, Aubrey cursed Mutt's poor timing. Rising, he placed a kiss on the back of Maeve's hand. "We shall continue this conversation later."

"Is Mr. Jarvis here about me?"

"Yes."

"May I join you?"

He could say no, and she would yield to his wishes. But he didn't wish to deny her anything. "Of course. Please do join us." Extending his arm to her, Aubrey escorted her from the dining room to the formal parlor where his mother often greeted guests when she was in residence.

Matthew stood at the window and turned when he heard them coming, his mouth falling open at the sight of Aubrey with a woman on his arm.

"Matthew Jarvis, allow me to introduce you to my wife, Maeve. Maeve, this is my friend Matthew from Yale."

For a long moment, Matthew stood frozen in place. "Your *wife*? Didn't I just see you a couple of days ago when you didn't have a wife?"

"Indeed, you did," Aubrey said, amused by Matthew's reaction. "Things moved somewhat rapidly."

"I should say so." Matthew came over to properly greet them with a handshake for Aubrey and a kiss to the back of Maeve's hand. "Congratulations."

"It's a pleasure to meet you," Maeve said.

Upon hearing her distinctly Irish accent, Matthew stood up straighter and eyed Aubrey with thinly veiled curiosity.

"Have a seat, and we will explain."

Matthew took one of the high-backed chairs while Aubrey and Maeve sat together on a love seat. This room was done in shades of light green with splashes of vivid color provided by pillows and jewel-toned vases awaiting daily blooms once the Season began in earnest.

Aubrey walked his friend through the events of the day while Matthew listened with rapt attention. When Aubrey was finished, Matthew's gaze shifted to her.

"You really killed a man?"

"I did." She diverted her gaze. "Although it's not something I'm proud of."

"If she hadn't killed him, there's a good chance he would've killed her." Aubrey needed his friend to understand the stakes.

"What can I do for you?"

"Tornquist is staying at the Marlborough Inn while he's in town. I would like to hire you and your father to represent Maeve and find a way to make this go away for her."

"It may not be that simple," Matthew said. "A man is dead. His family most likely will not accept that his death was an act of self-defense."

"I'm prepared to make a sizeable financial offer if they are willing to drop any charges against her. They should also understand that if it comes to a trial, Maeve is prepared to testify to the abuse he inflicted upon her."

"I'll mention that. How much are you offering?"

"One hundred thousand dollars."

Maeve gasped, and Matthew stared at him, agog.

"That's far too much," she said, sputtering. "I can't allow you to spend that kind of money on my behalf."

"I'd pay five times that to free you from this situation."

"I certainly won't tell them that," Matthew said.

"But you will take the offer to Tornquist?"

"After I discuss it with my father, I'll present the offer to Mr. Tornquist. It's apt to take some time as he'll have to consult with his clients by overseas wire."

"We understand and appreciate whatever you can do."

Matthew stood to leave. "It was a pleasure meeting you, Mrs. Nelson."

"Likewise, Mr. Jarvis. I appreciate your help and your discretion."

"Let me walk you out," Aubrey said.

When the two men were out of earshot of the parlor, Matthew took Aubrey by the arm. "What've you done?"

"Pardon me?"

"You *married* the Irish housekeeper? What were you thinking, man?"

"The woman I'd come to care for needed my help. I didn't think. I acted."

"It's not done, Aubrey. I know you're still new to the rules that govern the upper echelons of polite society—"

"I don't give the first fuck about polite society. I wasn't raised in it and have no compunction whatsoever about telling them all to stuff their rules up their fat asses."

"You know as well as I do that it doesn't work that way. You'll be *shunned*."

"No, I won't."

"And how can you be so certain?"

"Because polite society, as you call it, wouldn't dare turn their backs on the Duke and Duchess of Westwood, and where they go, I go. And where I go, my wife goes."

"You'd subject her to being ignored and belittled? Because that's what they'll do. You know it as well as I do."

"They wouldn't dare ignore her. If they do, the duchess will ignore them."

"And you know this how?"

"I know *her*, and she disdains polite society almost as passionately as I do. When I present her with my concerns, she will become Maeve's fiercest ally."

He wished he could contact them ahead of their arrival, but they were still at sea on their way to New York and would be traveling upon their arrival. Though he would have no chance to give them fair warning, he had full faith in how they would react to learning that Aubrey had married the Irish housekeeper. They would see that he was delighted by her and would take up her cause. He'd stake his life on it.

"I hope you know what you're doing, Aubrey, because if you're wrong, this is going to be a very long summer for you and your new wife."

Maeve could hear the two men whispering, and while she couldn't make out what they were saying, she sensed they were arguing.

Probably about her, a thought that made her stomach ache.

She couldn't believe Mr. Nelson had offered a hundred thousand dollars to get her out of the charges looming in Ireland. What could he be thinking offering a king's ransom on her behalf?

She couldn't allow him to do such a thing.

But when she considered the alternative . . .

It didn't bear considering.

He returned a few minutes later and took the seat next to her. "Matthew will do what he can to help us."

"To help me."

"*Us*. We're in this together now."

"You can't give them a hundred thousand dollars."

"I can and I will if it'll lead to them dropping the charges against you."

"It's an obscene amount of money."

"It's worth every penny if it ensures your safety and security."

She shook her head, her dismay obvious.

"What is it?"

"I never imagined what would transpire when I allowed Mr. Farthington to court me. He was sweet and charming and persuasive. My father urged me to marry him because his family owns a fleet of ships and are considered quite prosperous in our area. My father desperately wanted to land the Farthingtons' account for the bank. 'You won't ever do better than him,' my father said. He was much older than me but seemed quite sincere in his affections at first. But everything about him was false, and I realized it almost immediately after we were married. The night of our wedding . . ." She swallowed hard, wiped away a tear. "When he tried to consummate our marriage, his . . . phallus . . . would not . . ."

"Harden?"

Nodding and mortified, she wiped away more tears. "He said it was my fault because I wasn't attractive enough to make him want me. That was the first time he beat me."

"It wasn't your fault."

"How do you know that?"

"Because any man with a pulse would want you. Something was wrong with him. Not you. It happens to some men."

"It does? Really?"

"Yes." He brushed away her tears. "Really."

"I have never heard of such a thing."

"It's not something men speak of as it's a very embarrassing and frustrating situation. But I promise you that it had nothing whatsoever to do with you."

"How can you know that for sure? Perhaps there is something wrong with me."

He took her hand and placed it over the hard ridge of flesh between his legs. "Do you feel that?"

Maeve's face burned with embarrassment as she tried to pull back her hand. "Mr. Nelson!"

He tightened his grip to keep her hand in place. "My name is *Aubrey*, and *this* has been a problem for me from the first instant I laid eyes on you wielding the largest feather duster I've ever seen. It didn't matter to me that you were the housekeeper or that you're Irish. All I saw was one of the most exquisitely beautiful women I've ever met, and I wanted you fiercely." After a pause, he said, "Look at me, Maeve."

She forced her gaze to meet his while knowing her mortification would be apparent in the rosy hue of her burning cheeks.

"*He* was the problem. Not you. There is absolutely nothing wrong with you." Leaning in ever so slightly, he kissed her and then released her hand to put his arms around her. "Do you believe me?"

"The evidence you presented was rather convincing."

He laughed as he caressed her face. "May I ask you . . ."

"What?" she said, feeling breathless.

"Was he ever able to . . ."

"No, and each time he tried and failed, he was more violent toward me."

"So that means you're a virgin?"

Her inclination was to tell him it was none of his business, but as he was her husband now, it was his business. "I am."

Aubrey expelled a deep breath that sounded like equal parts relief and desire.

"D-does that please you?"

"It pleases me greatly. I would like to be the one to teach you about the act of love, to introduce you to the pleasure we can find together."

"I would like to learn." The words were out of her mouth before she could stop them, and the heat in her face intensified when he directed a hungry look her way.

He shifted his body, drawing her attention to the bulge between his legs.

As she stared at the thick ridge of flesh, she licked her lips, fascinated by the way his body responded to their conversation.

"I believe we should retire to our chamber for the remainder of the day."

"But there is work to be done!"

"Not by us."

"We have so little time and much more to accomplish."

"Tomorrow, we'll return to work. Today, we shall celebrate our marriage."

She rolled her bottom lip between her teeth as she thought about what he'd said and the implications of taking the rest of the day to be alone together. "The army will need supervision. They should be finishing your sisters' rooms."

"I'll ask Mr. Plumber to supervise them for the remainder of the day. Where do you want them to go next?"

"The guest rooms assigned to the duke and duchess

as well as the others in their party. I had them tend to the family rooms first since they will be here at the end of the week."

"I'll pass along your instructions and ask Mrs. Allston to serve dinner in our chamber tonight."

At the thought of Mrs. Allston serving them dinner in their bedroom, Maeve wanted to die from the mortification.

"Go on upstairs. I'll meet you in our suite in a few minutes."

He got up and adjusted his coat to cover the obvious protuberance and made for the door with all due haste.

Maeve watched him go, wishing she had someone to talk to about what was going to happen. Her mother had fumbled her way through the explanation of marital relations, but Maeve still had many unanswered questions that filled her with nerves as she went upstairs to prepare for her husband.

Chapter Ten

The first thing she did was draw the heavy drapes to reduce the light in the room. It was unseemly to think of embarking on such activities in the bright light of day. Her mother had told her that marital relations happened in the dark under the bedcovers, and that was most definitely her preference. Did he expect her to be clothed or unclothed? She didn't know, but quickly struggled her way out of her one good dress as well as the corset and into an unadorned muslin nightgown so she would be covered when he appeared.

Thinking back to the night he'd brought the cake to her room, she recalled his reaction to seeing her hair down around her shoulders and reached up to release the pins holding it in place. The heavy lengths cascaded down, and Maeve rubbed her head, which was always sore from bearing the weight of her thick hair for so many hours.

She stood before the mirror, running a brush through her hair when the door opened and then clicked shut. In the mirror, his gaze connected with hers, and as he slid the door lock into place, her heart began to beat so fast she feared she might do something embarrassing such as faint.

He went to the windows and opened the heavy brocade

curtains, letting in the bright sunshine. Then came up behind her and reached for the hairbrush. "Allow me?"

Maeve gave a quick nod and relinquished her hold on the brush handle to him. The rub of his skin against hers sent a shiver through her body, making her feel more alive than she ever had before.

Mr. Nelson—Aubrey—ran the brush through her hair gently, reverently, making her scalp and other parts of her tingle. Her nipples tightened and an odd sensation between her legs had her closing her thighs in an effort to contain it.

"What do you know about what transpires between a man and woman in the marriage bed?" His soft tone was in keeping with the easy strokes of the brush.

"I—I know that the man has a phallus that goes inside the woman, and that's how they create babies."

"That's right." He sounded gruffer now. "What else do you know?"

"It's done in the dark, under the covers."

"That's not exactly true." Now he sounded amused.

"You find me humorous, Mr. Nelson?"

"I find you delightful, Mrs. Nelson."

"What did I say that amused you so?"

"That the act of love is done in the dark and under the covers. I aim to show you otherwise."

"You aim to embarrass me terribly."

"To the contrary, my dear. I aim to please you greatly." Reaching around her, he put down the brush, and with his hands on her shoulders, he turned her to face him. "You're extraordinarily beautiful, my sweet Maeve." He placed a hot, openmouthed kiss on her neck that sent goose bumps skittering down her arms and made her backbone tingle with awareness of him. "This elegant, graceful neck was the first thing I noticed that day when I came upon you in the drawing room. I wanted to kiss it and taste it and lick it." He did all of those things now, and only the arm he wrapped around her waist kept Maeve standing. "I've never been so fascinated by a neck or the person attached to it."

"I'm not that fascinating."

"That's not true. You may be the most fascinating person I've ever met."

"You have met dukes and duchesses."

"They have nothing on you."

She wanted so badly to believe him, but how could that be true? Before she ran from her former home, she'd never been more than fifty miles outside Dingle, had never seen or done anything of any interest to anyone.

"It's true that I have met dukes and duchesses, earls and countesses, and once, I met the king, while at court with my friend the duke. I have attended university with some of the brightest minds of our time and traveled the world, but I have never once been entranced by the curve of a woman's neck the way I am by yours. I have never wanted to get to know someone, every part of someone, the way I do you. And I've never actually married anyone until I married you."

Moved nearly to tears by his kind words, she found herself believing him. If she was wrong about him . . .

"Come to bed with me, sweet Maeve. Let me show you how it should be." He took her hand and led her as he walked backward to the four-poster bed with the lace canopy. A warm, soft breeze came in through the open window, ruffling her hair and his. Standing next to the bed, he untied his tie and unbuttoned his vest and starched white shirt, letting the fabric fall to the floor behind him.

"You don't wear a combination?" she asked of the all-in-one male undergarment that had become popular with upper-crust men.

"I hate them. Old-fashioned drawers work fine for me."

Maeve let her greedy gaze take in her first look at his chest and abdomen. Unlike Mr. Farthington, who'd been thick through the middle, Mr. Nelson had a lean, muscular build that made her want to touch him, to explore the ridges and valleys of the muscles that covered his midsection.

"Touch me, sweetheart. Touch me anytime you'd like, anywhere you'd like. I'm your faithful servant." He took her hand and placed it flat against his chest where she could feel the rapid beat of his heart.

Using only her fingertips, she explored his chest, the soft hair that covered it and the ropey muscles of his abdomen.

He let out a hiss that startled her. "Don't stop. Your touch feels better than anything ever has."

Maeve made note of the fact that the hiss was a good sound. When she reached the lower portion of his abdomen, she noticed that the tip of his hard phallus had breached the waistband of his trousers. "You . . . Your . . ."

"Cock."

She shook her head.

"Say it."

"I couldn't."

"Oh, but you can," he said, laughing softly. "My cock is hard for you and only you, sweet Maeve." He nuzzled her neck and combed his fingers through her hair. "Say it."

"Your . . . your cock is hard. For me."

"Yes," he said, triumphant. "You must never be embarrassed or ashamed of the way we express our affection for each other or the words we use in private. They're the words of love and desire."

The desire she understood, because she too had felt it for him from nearly the beginning of their association. But his use of the word "love" left her feeling hollow and empty. He had done her an enormous favor by marrying her and making his considerable resources available to extricate her from a thorny dilemma. But she didn't believe he would ever love her.

He began to unbutton his pants, moving with haste now to free himself, and when his hard . . . cock . . . sprang free, he wrapped her hand around it, letting his head fall back in apparent surrender to the sensations. "Yes, Maeve. *Yes*." Tightening his hold on her hand, he stroked himself, making shameless use of her hand.

She hadn't expected the skin there to be so soft and was fascinated when he grew harder, longer, thicker in her hand, sparking a beat of distress. How would *that* fit inside her?

He placed his free hand on her back and began to gather the fabric of her gown until it was traveling up her legs.

Maeve knew a moment of panic at the thought of being completely nude before him in the bright light of day.

"Easy, love," he whispered as the fabric slid over her backside and moved up her back.

Her first impulse was to cover herself, but she couldn't seem to move, even when the gown cleared her head and was tossed aside by her eager husband.

While she tried not to die of mortification, he took a long look at what he'd uncovered.

"You're so exquisitely beautiful, as I knew you would be." He eased her back onto the bed and came down on top of her, arranging her so her legs were splayed open and her feet propped at the edge of the mattress.

"Please, Mr. Nelson, this is indecent."

"It's Aubrey, and there's nothing indecent about it. You're my wife, and this is entirely appropriate behavior between a husband and wife."

"Surely it's not appropriate to be completely naked in broad daylight."

His low chuckle rumbled through him. "It's very appropriate. Be still, and I'll show you."

Be still? How was she to be still when he was doing . . . *that*? Oh dear God, were those his lips on her breast? And his tongue . . . She wouldn't survive this.

"Mr. Nelson . . ."

"*Aubrey*. Let me hear you say it."

"Aubrey."

"Yes, love?"

Oh, she liked when he called her that. She liked it too much. "You don't need to—" The words died on her lips and her mind went completely blank when he sucked her nipple into the wet heat of his mouth.

"I do need to." He licked and sucked her nipple, setting off a wave of need in her so strong she nearly levitated off the bed.

He kept it up until she was certain she would go mad if he didn't either stop or do something to relieve the relentless ache between her legs. Rather than stop, however, he switched to the other side, moving back and forth until she was delirious from the sensations cascading through her. She'd had no idea, no idea at all, that her body was capable of feeling this way.

Maeve realized he had moved down, that his lips were skimming over her belly and below. Surely he didn't mean to . . . "*Aubrey!*" She tried to cover herself, but he pushed her arms aside.

"Leave them there."

"You can't . . . Not there . . . Dear *God*."

His tongue and fingers destroyed what was left of her composure while his shoulders forced her legs even farther apart. How could he be licking her *there*? Certainly, civilized people didn't do *that*. Her legs trembled violently, and she felt herself climbing toward something that remained just out of reach until he curled his fingers inside her and sucked on the tight bundle of nerves at the apex of her most private place.

Maeve screamed from the feelings that converged on her all at once—pleasure, pain, need, embarrassment and fear. If he could do that to her, she was giving him far too much power over her, power she'd never intended to surrender to him.

Pressure between her legs brought her down from the incredible high to realize he was pushing his phallus into her body and her body was resisting him with everything it had.

"Relax, sweetheart." His lips moved over her neck and ear. "Relax and let me in." He rocked against her, giving her a little more each time.

Maeve took a tremulous breath, trying to give him what he wanted but also keep something for herself for when this interlude with him was but a distant memory. She refused to give him everything. He could have her body, but he would never touch her heart.

"Nice and easy. That's it." He moved slowly and carefully, as if he were afraid to hurt her.

Right when she was becoming accustomed to the motion, a tearing pain had her crying out from the agony that gripped her.

He held himself up on his hands so he could see her face, and his dark hair slid down over his damp brow. "That was your maidenhead giving way. It shouldn't hurt anymore."

While that might be true, Maeve remained tense and fearful of the pain.

"Move with me, love." He slid his hands under her

bottom and squeezed her cheeks, guiding her. As he slid deeper inside her, he tugged her upward to meet his thrust. "God, yes. Like that. Just like that."

His eyes closed, his lips parted and his cheeks flushed with heat.

Her heart contracted at the sight of him in the throes of passion. If she'd found him attractive before, now he was magnificent.

"Maeve." He gathered her into his tight embrace. "Wrap your legs around my hips."

She did as he asked, gasping when she realized the position sent him even deeper into her.

"Yes, like that. Does it feel good?"

"It feels . . ."

Because she was so close to him, she felt him hold his breath in anticipation of her response.

"Incredible."

"Yes, it does." He released his tight hold on her and reached down to where they were joined to touch the place she had only just discovered. Like before, her body seized with contractions that made him groan as he picked up the pace until he was hammering into her, the fingers on his other hand digging into her shoulder.

All at once, he pulled out of her to spend on her belly. When he was finished, he left her to grab a towel to wipe her clean. "I don't think we're ready for offspring."

"N-no." She felt boneless, like a lump of clay. If someone said the house was on fire, she feared she wouldn't be able to react.

Then he wiped up the dampness between her legs, and Maeve noticed blood on the towel.

"Is that . . ."

"It's perfectly normal the first time. It won't happen

again." His brow furrowed with concern. "Are you quite all right? I wasn't as gentle with you as I should have been."

"I'm rather well except for the fact that I can't seem to move."

His laughter lit up his face and only added to his appeal. "Come, let me make you more comfortable." He helped her up and pulled down the sheet and quilt and settled her on a plump feather pillow.

"Is that better?"

"It is. Thank you."

"Why can't you bring yourself to look at me?"

She kept her gaze fixed on the sheet. "Because I'm embarrassed."

"By what we did?"

She nodded tightly.

"There is nothing to be embarrassed about."

"Oh, but there is. I didn't know that men did . . . those things . . . to women."

"What things?"

She felt the dreaded flush creep back up her neck to her face. "Don't make me say it!"

"I won't make you say it, but you can't deny you enjoyed it." As he spoke, he dragged a light fingertip from her neck to her chest to her breasts where he teased both nipples before continuing down to the cleft between her legs.

Maeve gasped from the light touch to her sensitive flesh.

"Tell me you enjoyed it."

"I did."

"Then don't be embarrassed. Before long, what we do here will seem normal."

She laughed from the preposterousness of his statement. "I'm not sure *that* will ever seem normal to me."

"I promise you that it will. We'll do it so frequently that you'll no longer be embarrassed."

"I'll have to take your word for that."

Smiling, he kissed the end of her nose and then her lips. "I'll be right back."

Maeve watched him walk into the adjoining bathroom, taking note of broad shoulders, a narrow waist and tight buttocks. It would take months to comprehend the events of this day that had led to Mr. Nelson—Aubrey—becoming her husband. Her stomach ached when she thought of the man who had come looking for her and the money Aubrey had offered to make him go away.

What if he rejected the offer and insisted on taking her into custody? The thought of having to go back to Ireland, to face Mr. Farthington's family, not to mention the possibility of a hangman's noose, had her paralyzed with fear.

"Whatever is the matter?" Aubrey returned with a fresh towel, got on the bed and eased her legs apart.

Before she could form a protest, he had placed the delightfully warm towel against the sore area between her legs.

"You were relaxed and now you're tense again."

"I'm wondering if your friend Mr. Jarvis found the man who's looking for me."

"I have no doubt that Matthew will succeed in his mission."

"How can you be so certain?"

"When Mr. Tornquist came earlier, I noticed a few things about him."

"Such as?"

"He was missing several buttons on his jacket, his shirt was dingy and his shoes were in need of a shine."

"What does any of that have to do with me?"

"I believe Mr. Tornquist is down on his luck and will leap at the offer of one hundred thousand dollars to tell the people who hired him that he was unable to locate you."

He tapped on the bottom lip she had drawn partially

between her teeth. "Rather than worrying that delicious lip, tell me what you're thinking. Let me ease your concerns."

"I would like, at some point, to be able to go home again, to see my family. I'll never be able to do that as long as Mr. Farthington's family is accusing me of murder."

"That is a very real concern and one we will address in due time."

"How will we address it?"

Aubrey appeared to give that significant thought. "I'll write a letter to the authorities in Ireland, detailing the events as you relayed them to me." He took hold of her right hand and placed a kiss on the soft pink skin that had finally replaced raw blisters. "I'll attest to the fact that your hand showed signs of recent healing from a burn."

"You noticed that?"

"I noticed it the day of the picnic and suddenly understood why you always wear gloves while you work."

"I was desperately afraid of infection. A doctor in New York provided me with a salve that aided in the healing, but he warned me about the threat of infection until the wound healed."

Aubrey continued to press soft kisses to the new skin. "And then you came here and faced calamity with a hand that was still healing. In case I forget to tell you, I think you're a very impressive young woman."

"I'm not impressive. I was desperate for a job and willing to do whatever I had to in order to survive."

"You *are* impressive, and I'm so very happy that your desperation led you here to me."

"I fear that you will not be so happy once your family learns of our marriage."

"You must hear me when I tell you that there is nothing they can say or do that can come between us unless we allow it. I, for one, will not allow it." With his finger on her chin, he turned her face toward him, forcing her to meet his gaze. "I don't want you to worry about anything."

"That is much more easily said than done."

"You're no longer alone with your worries, lovely Maeve. You have me now, and I won't let any harm come to you." He brought his lips down on hers and wrapped his arms around her.

With his warm body pressed against hers and his tongue teasing its way into her mouth, she found it hard to think about anything other than the way she felt when he touched her. But in the dark recesses of her mind, the fears refused to be silenced.

Chapter Eleven

Matthew waited for more than an hour in the parlor of the Marlborough Inn, with only a tepid cup of tea for refreshment. If Mr. Tornquist didn't return soon, he would head out to find more robust spirits and try again tomorrow to find Tornquist.

While he waited, he thought about Aubrey and his new wife and the scandal their marriage would set off when word got out that the youngest of the Nelson children had married the Irish housekeeper. In New York, where there was so much else to entertain the upper crust, Aubrey might've been able to pull it off by giving his wife a pedigree and spinning a yarn about how she came to America when her aristocratic husband died, or some such thing—until she opened her mouth to speak in the tongue of Ireland. In Newport, where there was little to entertain the privileged beyond their mindless trips to Bailey's Beach, the Casino and the afternoon promenade on Bellevue Avenue, the scandal would be the talk of the Season.

Like so many who flocked to Newport for the Season, the Nelsons were "new" money, having found their fortune in the railroad. As the daughter of a British earl, Mrs. Nelson enjoyed lording her aristocratic heritage over the other women in Newport, who tolerated her at best.

Matthew looked forward to the Season each year because it was the only time there was much of anything interesting to do in a town that was sleepy and rather boring the other ten months of the year. Speaking of boring, he'd had about enough of cooling his heels in the frilly parlor. He got up to leave and nearly collided with a man coming in the door.

"Are you Tornquist?"

"Who wants to know?"

"Matthew Jarvis, Esquire, on behalf of Mr. Aubrey Nelson."

"I'm Tornquist."

Matthew gestured toward the parlor. "Might I have a word in private?"

Tornquist nodded and led the way.

Matthew closed the door, hoping they wouldn't be overheard.

"What can I do for you?" Tornquist asked.

"The woman you seek . . ."

"Maeve Sullivan. Here is a photograph."

Matthew took the sepia-toned photograph from him and pretended to study it. A passing glance had confirmed this was the same woman that Aubrey had married. "A lovely young woman."

"Perhaps so, but she is wanted for murder in Ireland."

"Are you familiar with the facts of the case?"

"I know that she murdered her husband, a man named Josiah Farthington, with a cast-iron pan to the head."

"And this was done with no provocation?"

"None that we know of."

"'We' being you and his family?"

"That is correct. Why do you ask?"

"Mr. Nelson has asked me to convey to you that there is indeed another side to the story, one in which

Mr. Farthington severely beat his wife, who defended herself by striking him."

"Mr. Nelson told me he did not know Mrs. Farthington."

Matthew gave Tornquist a scathing look. "He was not about to admit to knowing her when he had no idea why you were looking for her."

"He is harboring a murderer."

"It's not considered murder if she was defending herself."

"And how does she intend to prove that?"

"She doesn't. Mr. Nelson is prepared to offer one hundred thousand dollars in exchange for you informing Mr. Farthington's family that you were unable to locate her in America."

Tornquist's eyes lit up with barely restrained glee—and greed. Aubrey's hunch had been spot-on.

"If he pays me off, others will come looking for her. It was incredibly easy to follow her from New York to Newport."

"I'll be sure to mention that to Mr. Nelson. Do we have a deal?"

"When would I receive the money?"

"As soon as three days from now. Mr. Nelson will need to have it wired from his bank in New York. Again, I ask you—do we have a deal?"

Tornquist leaned forward in his seat. "Your Mr. Nelson should know that Farthington isn't the only man to come to a bad end at Miss Sullivan's hand."

"What're you talking about?"

"There was another man who showed an interest in Miss Sullivan, courted her for some time, only to be found dead of possible poisoning. As far as anyone knows, she was the last one to be seen with him before he died."

"Was she charged with a crime?"

"From what I'm told, the inquest was inconclusive, but

the young man's family believed she was involved. She married Mr. Farthington several months later, and we know how that turned out."

In Matthew's opinion, Mr. Tornquist had missed his calling as the author of cheap novels. "In that case, I see no need to make mention of it. If there's no proof she was involved, why would you bring that up?"

"I thought your client might wish to know what kind of woman he's protecting. But if he doesn't care, why should I?"

Becoming annoyed, Matthew stood to leave.

"Where are you going?"

"Anywhere but here."

"I'll take your deal, but I won't tell Farthington's family that I was unable to locate her. I'll let them believe I'm still looking."

Matthew gave him a disgusted look. "Wait here for further word." He walked away, wishing he could take a bath to wash off the slime of his brief association with Tornquist. The man had presented him with a rather thorny dilemma, however. Did he tell Aubrey about the second man who'd turned up dead or keep that to himself?

He puzzled it over as he got into his buggy and directed his horse up the hill toward the Casino in search of some badly needed spirits.

On the one hand, Aubrey seemed extraordinarily pleased to have married the woman. In fact, Matthew had never seen his old friend looking more elated than he had earlier. But on the other hand, if something were to happen to his friend, Matthew would hate to live with the guilt of having kept vital information from him.

He was truly torn about what was best for Aubrey in this situation. After several glasses of the Casino's best scotch, he came to the conclusion that he must tell his friend what he'd uncovered. But not right away. He'd give the man a week or so to enjoy his new wife before he dropped the anvil.

Paradis, the French word for paradise, described the first days of Aubrey's married life. He had never known such happiness. He and Maeve worked from sunup to sundown, alongside the growing group of locals who were being shaped into maids, footmen and kitchen workers by the capable Mr. Plumber and Mrs. Allston.

They had been fitted for uniforms and livery and had worked so hard, they were actually slightly ahead of schedule. As such, Aubrey talked Maeve into taking an afternoon off on the third day since their wedding. He had the buggy brought around and loaded her and the picnic basket Mrs. Allston had provided into the vehicle for the ride to Bailey's Beach, one of the prime social locations during the Season.

With more than a week to go until the Season began in earnest, they had the beach largely to themselves that late June day.

Aubrey spread a plaid blanket on one of the few sandy spots and held Maeve's hand until she was seated.

"This is very decadent, Mr. Nelson. Stealing away in the middle of a workday."

"We are on track to have everything ready before Mother arrives, and that is due in large part to your efforts. The least I can do is take you away from it all for a few hours for some rest and relaxation."

She gave him a side-eyed look. "Rest has been in short order the last few days."

"Indeed, it has. My wife is insatiable in the bedchamber."

She sputtered with outrage. "*I* am not the insatiable one!"

Aubrey collapsed into laughter. He laughed so hard he held his sides. And when he finally got himself together, he found his adorable wife trying not to laugh herself. He could not recall the last time he'd laughed like that. Before Annabelle died, to be certain. His face actually hurt from all the smiling he'd done in the last few days, but like Maeve, he was exhausted from being up most of every night gorging on his new wife's considerable charms.

He couldn't get enough of her, and despite her claims to the contrary, she was equally enthusiastic.

"Are you still sore, my love?" he asked as he poured each of them a glass of the champagne Mrs. Allston had chilled at his request.

"I am. I fear you've quite broken me."

"I'm sorry for your discomfort but not for how it transpired."

"It's proof that four times in one night is not healthy."

"Once you're more accustomed, you will see how very healthy it can be."

"I fear I'll not survive the first month of my marriage if we are any more 'healthy.'"

Aubrey grinned as he leaned in for a kiss. "Personally, I have never felt better in my life, although I'm sorry that you're hurting. I promise to thoroughly kiss it better later."

Predictably, her face flushed with heat that left her cheeks rosy and glowing. "You mustn't say such things out loud."

"Whyever not?"

"Because!"

"Because why?"

"Because your wife said so."

"As much as I adore my wife, she is going to have to give me a better reason than *because*."

"You know I despise how my face flushes when I'm

embarrassed, so I have asked you not to say things that embarrass me."

"And I have told you how much I delight in your rosy cheeks, and as such, I'm required to regularly embarrass you to ensure they remain rosy."

"That logic is maddening. *You* are maddening."

"And you're stuck with me and all my maddening comments."

"I was deceived by your charm."

"You were deceived by your desire for me. It's all right. You can go ahead and admit it."

She gave him a gentle shove.

He grabbed her hand and pulled her down with him, so she was partially reclined on top of him.

"Release me at once!"

"Not until you kiss me."

"Mr. Nelson!"

"Aubrey." He rubbed his lips against hers. "You were doing so well. Why are we back to Mr. Nelson?"

"Because you're being scandalous."

"I'm kissing my wife. There is nothing scandalous about that."

"There is when you're carrying on in a public place where anyone might see you."

"Kiss me, and I'll let you go."

She gave him a quick peck on the lips.

He tightened his hold on her. "You can do much better than that."

"Not here, I can't."

"Yes, you can." He raised his brow and pursed his lips, hoping she would rise to the challenge. Did she ever!

She touched her lips to his in the softest, sweetest, gentlest kiss he'd ever received. "Now let me go, or that's the last kiss you'll get today."

He let her go, but he did not want to. Flopping onto his back, he groaned as he stared up at the sun. "It's not fair for you to rile me that way and then tell me I have to let you go."

"It's not fair for you to force me into embarrassing situations in public."

Aubrey propped his head on an upturned hand so he could look at her, which had become one of his favorite things to do. He was well aware that they were living on borrowed time, inside a bubble of happiness where no one could touch them. Once his family arrived, their bubble would burst, and he wasn't looking forward to that.

Matthew had dispatched Tornquist and was keeping an ear out for anyone else who might be looking for her. While the immediate threat was gone, they still had to deal with the fact that she was wanted for murder in Ireland. He hadn't the first clue how to approach that dilemma, and was hoping Derek might be able to help him figure out a solution.

They had one more day until his mother would arrive with Aubrey's sisters and their children in tow. He fully expected a row of epic proportions to erupt when his mother found out he'd married the Irish housekeeper. The very thought of it had him wishing he could take his wife and run away. But that wasn't an option with Derek and the others arriving next week. He would have to stay and face his mother while hoping his new marriage was strong enough to weather the coming storm.

Maeve had wrought a miracle. Aubrey could think of no other word to describe what she had managed to accomplish. The house fairly sparkled and smelled fresh as a field of lilies. Between Maeve, Aubrey, Mr. Plumber and

Mrs. Allston, they had whipped their ragtag army and the family members and friends the army had recruited into a passable staff, outfitting them with uniforms they wore with unmistakable pride.

Were they the professional, flawless staff that would be found in the other fine Newport homes? Not even close, but Aubrey would take them, their sincerity and work ethic over the more polished group from last year that had left the windows open to the elements for the winter.

On the eve of his family's arrival, Aubrey walked from room to room, on a final inspection. In the massive ballroom, there was nary a spiderweb to be seen or a speck of dust to be found. His mother's room had been redecorated with a striped coverlet and floral pillow coverings that were nicer than what had been there before, in Aubrey's opinion anyway. What his mother would think was anyone's guess. If one didn't know of the disaster that had occurred here, it certainly wouldn't be apparent now.

"Ah, there you are," Maeve said when she joined him, wearing one of the smart new dresses the local dressmakers had provided. This one was white silk with thin red stripes that reminded him of peppermint candy.

Aubrey loved to suck on peppermint candy. The thought gave him ideas pertaining to his delectable wife.

Her brows furrowed. "What is it?"

"Your lovely dress is giving me interesting ideas."

"What sort of ideas?"

"The kind that would have me sucking on peppermint candy. Among other things."

Predictably, the comment set her cheeks to flame in a matter of seconds. "Stop it."

He put his arm around her waist and leaned in close enough that his lips brushed against her ear. "I'll not stop it."

"You must learn to control yourself. As of tomorrow, we will no longer have the house to ourselves."

"As you well know, I can't control myself when you're around, and we'll just have to become more creative about finding time alone once the house is full of family and friends."

"You're going to embarrass me, aren't you?"

"As much and as often as I possibly can."

"That's not very nice."

"It'll be very, very nice. I promise." He patted her on the backside to direct her toward their bedchamber.

"Where are we going?"

"We are retiring early so we will be well rested for tomorrow's invasion."

"Excellent. I could use a full night of sleep."

"I didn't promise a full night of sleep when I said we'd be retiring early."

Her delicate laughter had become one of his favorite things, along with the many expressions that crossed her flawless face in the course of a day and the way her hair looked down around her naked shoulders. He adored how the tips of her succulent breasts would peek out from under her hair, the way her face flushed at the slightest provocation, and he could listen to her speak about the most mundane of things in that lyrical accent for hours at a time and never grow tired of the sound. In fact, it was becoming quite clear to him that he loved absolutely everything about her.

He loved his wife and had no idea whatsoever if she returned the sentiment. Yes, she was an enthusiastic bed partner, and he had no doubt she enjoyed that part of their relationship. They talked freely on a wide range of topics, had worked closely together to get the house into tip-top shape and had developed an easy, comfortable rapport with each other. But did she have feelings for him? He didn't know and was afraid to ask out of fear of what she might say.

She valued the protection he had provided for her and had thanked him repeatedly for paying off Tornquist. He knew she appreciated that he was continuing to look into what could be done to fight the charges pending against her in Ireland. Gratitude, however, was last on the list of things he wanted from her. Aubrey wanted her heart and her soul. He wanted her every thought, wish, dream. He wanted everything with and from her, and while their physical connection seemed to become more intense with every passing day, the rest didn't seem to be keeping pace.

Inside their bedchamber, he released the buttons down the back of her dress while dropping kisses along the neck that had held him in its thrall from the first. He would never tire of that elegant stretch of soft skin or the bewitching scent that drove him to drink in the middle of the day so he wouldn't be tempted to waylay her and have his wicked way with her every hour on the hour.

Aubrey found himself counting down the hours until they could be alone, locked away from the rest of the world until sunup, when another long day would begin. After the Season, he would take her for a long honeymoon so they could spend every day together, in bed if they so wished. The thought of spending full days alone with her made him giddy.

"As soon as my guests depart, we shall take a wedding trip." He slid the two sides of the peppermint dress down her arms and then over her narrow hips, holding her hand so she could step out of it. The dressmaker had provided undergarments made of the finest silk, and he found her impossibly alluring in them. Releasing the pins that held her hair up during the day, he watched it fall in a fiery river. He was absolutely mad for her hair.

"A wedding trip is not necessary, Mr. Nelson."

Raising her shift up and over her head, he took in the creamy length of her back. "Aubrey, and a wedding trip is very necessary."

"A wedding trip is not necessary, Aubrey."

"I need time alone with my wife."

"You have time alone with me every night."

"It's not enough."

She laughed, and oh how he loved the sound of her laughter. "And you say *I'm* insatiable." When she would've turned to face him, he stopped her.

"Wait." Dropping to his knees behind her, he cupped her bottom through the filmy drawers and squeezed.

Her legs began to quiver, so she reached for the back of one of the Louis XIV chairs that populated every room in the house. "Aubrey . . . Whatever are you doing?"

"Shh." He pulled the drawers down and licked his lips at the sight of soft, supple flesh.

"Aub . . . Aubrey."

"Hold on to the chair."

She did as he directed, casting a wary look at him over her shoulder.

He grasped her cheeks, separated them and dove in, licking a long line from top to bottom and everywhere in between.

"Oh . . . Oh no. *Aubrey*." Her legs trembled so hard he feared she would fall, so he stood, wrapped an arm around her waist and lifted her.

She released the chair, uttering an inelegant squeak as he transported her to the bed, bending her over so the top half of her body was supported by the mattress and her feet were on the floor. Over her shoulder, she looked at him with big, wild eyes. "This isn't decent."

"I assure you it is." He dropped to his knees behind her

and went back to what he'd been doing, loving the sounds she made as he devoured her. Still from behind, he slid two fingers inside her, curling them forward toward the spot that had her gasping and clutching the quilt.

"Oh lord. Oh please . . . *Please.*"

He withdrew his fingers and sucked the hard nub of nerves into his mouth until she seized with contractions and her entire body turned a fetching shade of light pink. God, he *loved* that.

As she panted in the aftermath, he tore off his own clothes, freeing his cock and pressing into her from behind. They hadn't done this yet, and judging from the way she tensed, she wasn't sure this was decent either.

"Easy, love." He flattened his hand on her back to keep her in the position he wanted.

"You want to do it this way?"

"I do. You'll love it. I promise."

"Are you sure?"

"I'm so sure." Aubrey could tell she wasn't entirely convinced, as her muscles remained rigid and tense, so he reached under her to cup her breasts and tweak her nipples. The distraction helped to ease the way for him as he fully entered her. "How does it feel?"

"Different but good."

"Does it hurt?"

"No."

"Tell me if it does. It's supposed to feel good."

"It does."

He gave her a few minutes to adjust to the new position before bringing his hands to her hips to hold her still for his fierce possession. And when he reached around to caress the tender bud between her legs, she screamed as her internal muscles tightened around his cock and had him biting his lip to hold back a scream of his own as he found his release.

Coming down from the incredible high, he rested his head on her back, both of them breathing hard. Aubrey nearly stopped breathing when he realized he'd gotten so carried away that he'd spent inside her, which he hadn't intended to do.

Damn it.

He no sooner had that thought than he imagined Maeve round with their baby, and his heart lurched with the emotion that hit him when he thought of having children with her, a life with her, everything with her.

She squirmed under him, and he lifted himself up, planted a kiss in the center of her back and withdrew to help her up and into bed. "Be right back."

Aubrey went into the bathroom to clean up, returned with a towel for her and got into bed to help her clean up. "Um, Maeve?"

"Yes?"

"I . . . at the end there, I . . . I was still inside you."

Her eyes widened with understanding. "*Oh*."

"I'm sorry. I got carried away and forgot to be careful."

She rolled her bottom lip between her teeth.

"Say something."

"Would you . . . welcome . . . a child?"

Aubrey stared at her, drunk on the sight of her, the taste of her, everything about her. "I would welcome our child with every fiber of my being."

"I had always dreamed of being a mother, but had all but given up on the notion."

"Because of what happened with Farthington?"

She nodded. "Since I fled Ireland, I pictured myself working to survive, not marrying or having a family."

Twisting a strand of her hair around his finger, he gazed at her. "The picture has changed now. You're free to dream those dreams again."

"I'm still adjusting to the changes that have transpired."

"Are you happy, Maeve?"

"Yes, I'm happy—and relieved. You saved me from certain death."

"But are you happy with me?" Aubrey wanted to curse at how needy he sounded, but he had to know.

"Of course I am."

"You are? Really?"

"Yes," she said, smiling. "I'm happy, but I'm also nervous about what tomorrow will bring."

Linking his fingers with hers, he brought their joined hands to his chest. "No matter what tomorrow brings, no matter what they say or think or do, you're my wife and you shall be treated with the respect you deserve."

"You can't make them respect me, Aubrey."

"Watch me."

Her deep sigh conveyed her true feelings on the matter.

"I don't want you to worry. Whatever happens, I'll handle it. You're safe with me, always, against any foe, even my family."

As he said the words and saw the apprehension in her eyes, he vowed to protect her with everything he was, everything he'd ever be. For she had become the most precious thing in the world to him, and there was nothing he wouldn't do for her. Nothing at all.

Chapter Twelve

With Aubrey's family due to arrive within the hour, Maeve took a last stroll through the house, checking every room with an eye toward the fine details. Vases filled with freshly picked blooms positioned in the center of a table, a fold removed from the tieback of a drapery, a chair moved slightly to the left to better align with its companion, a framed landscape nudged ever so slightly to make it perfectly straight.

It was probably just as well that Mr. Tornquist had shown up and terrified her to the point that she'd jumped at the chance to marry Aubrey and be protected by him, for it probably would've taken Mrs. Nelson mere minutes to realize that Maeve was patently unqualified to run a house the size and scope of Paradis Trouvé.

Mrs. Nelson had been described to her as a "dragon lady," and thoughts of how she might react to her youngest child's marriage to the Irish housekeeper had kept Maeve awake long after Aubrey had fallen asleep the night before. He'd tried to reassure her that everything would be fine, but the hollowed-out feeling in her stomach couldn't be ignored.

They'd been fooling themselves these last few days, living as if they were the lord and lady of the manor when they weren't. His parents were, and soon they would arrive to the news that Aubrey had done much more than prepare the house for their arrival. If the rumors about Mrs. Nelson's famous temper were to be believed—and after seeing the wreckage brought about by the former staff, Maeve believed the rumors—this peaceful, sunny day was about to turn dark and stormy.

In the ballroom, she glanced up at the sparkling chandelier where there was nary a single cobweb to mar the glory of the gleaming crystals. Thinking of the day Aubrey had startled her and then caught her when she fell off the ladder made her smile. He was such a sweet man, even if misguided at times. He'd tried to rescue her when she didn't need rescuing, but then she had needed it, and he'd been quick to offer her his name and protection.

Her feelings for him were a jumbled mix of gratitude and desire and concern about what might be ahead for them. Would he tell his family *why* he'd felt compelled to marry her? They'd never discussed what he planned to tell them, and before they came, she needed to find him to ask him.

If they found out she'd killed a man . . . Her stomach lurched, and she feared she might cast up her accounts into a potted palm. She was so intent on finding him that she took a corner without looking and crashed into a hard wall of chest. Only his quick thinking kept her from falling from the impact.

"Wherever are you going with such haste, my dear?" His kind eyes danced with amusement as they so often did when he looked at her. They laughed a lot, so much so that she wondered if it were normal to be so entertained by one's spouse, even at the most intimate of times. She couldn't remember her parents laughing with each other and had no one else to ask if such things were normal. "Maeve? What is it?"

"I . . . I was looking for you."

"Well, you found me. What's wrong?"

"I was wondering about your family."

"What about them?"

She swallowed hard, hoping the bile in her throat wouldn't come rushing up to mortify her in front of her husband. "Are you going to tell them why you married me?"

"Why, yes, of course I will."

Her stomach dropped. "Oh."

With his hands on her face, he compelled her to look at him, which was certainly no hardship. His handsome face had become one of her favorite things to look at. "I'll tell them I married you because after knowing you for a short time, I realized I would never be complete without you. I'll tell them I married you because I quite simply couldn't live without you." He punctuated his tender words with a soft kiss that had her heart beating fast and her head swimming from the need to breathe.

"You won't tell them about Mr. Farthington?"

"Not unless I absolutely have to, and I can't imagine why I'd have to."

Relief flooded through her, leaving her almost as breathless as his kiss had. "Thank you."

"Please do not worry about anything, sweetheart. I'm going to take care of you."

To her tremendous mortification, her eyes filled with tears that she tried to blink back, but they spilled down her cheeks anyway.

Aubrey kissed them away. "No tears, my sweet. Everything is going to be all right. You have me now. You're not alone anymore."

Maeve slid her arms around his waist, under the elegant gray coat he wore, and held on tight to him and his assurances.

They were still there when the sound of a throat clearing startled them apart.

"Pardon the interruption, Mr. Nelson, Mrs. Nelson." Plumber glanced toward the foyer. "But the family is arriving."

"Thank you, Mr. Plumber. We'll be right there." After the butler had walked away, Aubrey looked down at her, smiling. "Are you ready?"

"As ready as I'll ever be. Stay close."

"Nowhere else I'd rather be than close to you."

When he said such things and looked at her with tenderness, her insides felt like they were full of butterflies in flight.

He tucked her hand into the crook of his arm and led her to the foyer.

Mr. Plumber opened the big door for them, and they went outside to await the four carriages as they came through the ornate black wrought-iron gate. The family had traveled on a steamship from the Fall River Line that conveyed passengers between New York and Boston, with stops each way at Newport's Long Wharf. There they'd been met by hired carriages for the journey up the hill to Bellevue Avenue. Since Newport was located on the southernmost portion of Aquidneck Island, it was more convenient to take the steamship than the railroad that served the mainland.

Aubrey had explained the logistics to her the night before, while warning her that the travelers were apt to be weary after the overnight trip. Maeve had taken the train from New York to Providence and a smaller ferry to Newport, which had been more economical than the deluxe accommodations the Nelson family had probably secured on the overnight boat.

Maeve marveled at how he'd settled her nerves and calmed her fears. Today, she'd worn the dress she'd been married in, hoping it would bring her the same luck it had on her wedding day. Watching the Nelsons pour out of the carriages, she had a feeling she would need all the luck she could get.

Watching his mother alight from the carriage, Aubrey was filled with dread. He'd promised Maeve he would protect her, but the sight of his mother's face reminded him of whom he was dealing with. It would take all his considerable fortitude to manage this situation and ensure that no harm would come to his fragile union at the hands of his mother.

Next came his father, and Aubrey gasped at his obvious decline in the last few weeks. Aubrey's mother shouted orders to anyone who would listen, instructing them to tend to her husband. Wiggie and Kaiser appeared, each of them offering an arm to Mr. Nelson to help him up the stairs.

Aubrey's mother, Eliza, did a double take at the sight of the men. Even dressed in red livery, their rough edges were still readily apparent in their awkward, unpracticed movements.

"Mother." Aubrey kissed both her cheeks in the European way she preferred. Once upon a time, Eliza Nelson had been beautiful. Now she would be considered attractive for her age with her blond hair gone brassy and deep lines around her mouth giving her the look of a perpetual frown. Aubrey shook his father's hand while Wiggie and Kaiser stood by in case they were needed. "Father, it's good to see you. Meet our new footmen, Wiggie and Kaiser. Gentlemen, these are my parents, Mr. and Mrs. Nelson."

"Pleasure to meet you, sir, ma'am." The men recited the line Maeve had instructed them to use when they met their employers.

"What happened to George and Tim from last summer?" Eliza breezed past Plumber and Maeve and into the house. His father followed behind her, moving much more slowly.

Aubrey offered his arm to Maeve as he followed his parents inside. "They left."

As she removed her hat, his mother turned to him, her gaze zeroing in on Maeve's hand tucked into the crook of his elbow. "They *left*?"

"The entire staff left at the end of last Season."

"That is not true. Corrigan continued to pay their wages."

"You would have to consult with Mr. Corrigan about that." The family's man of business took care of paying the household bills in New York and Newport. "But I can assure you the staff departed en masse at the end of last summer. I have taken the liberty of hiring a new staff, including Mr. Plumber, our new butler."

Plumber bowed in greeting. "It's a pleasure to meet you both. I'm honored to be working at such a fine home."

"And this is Maeve—"

"Ah yes," Eliza said, "the housekeeper. The agency in New York informed us of your hiring."

Aubrey and Maeve spoke at the same time.

"Pleasure to meet you, ma'am."

"She's no longer the housekeeper."

Eliza eyed her youngest son. "I beg your pardon."

"Maeve is no longer the housekeeper." He put his arm around her. "As of a few days ago, she is my wife."

Eliza stared at him for the longest time, during which Aubrey refused to blink.

His mother began to laugh. "You can't be serious. You aren't *married* to the Irish housekeeper."

"I'm married to Maeve Sullivan Nelson, formerly of Dingle, Ireland."

"Is this some sort of joke, Aubrey? Because I assure you, it's not funny." The laughter of a moment ago had been replaced by a fierce scowl.

"It's no joke, Mother, and I would advise you to think carefully about what you say or do next. Maeve is my wife, and I care for her very much. You will show her the respect she deserves or else."

Eliza's eyes narrowed. "Or else what?"

"I'll take my wife and my friends, the duke and duchess, and we will spend our summer—as well as the rest of our lives—elsewhere."

"Don't make idle threats. The duke and duchess aren't going to want to summer anywhere but here."

"They will summer wherever I am, Mother, and whether or not I'm here will depend entirely on you."

Before his mother could form a response, his father spoke up. "I'd like to lie down if that's all right."

"Of course, Father." Aubrey signaled to the footmen, who again came to his father's aid. Aubrey would've helped his father himself, but he didn't want to leave Maeve alone with his mother.

As the footmen helped his father up the stairs, Aubrey's sisters and their children arrived in a noisy, happy gaggle of words and laughter that seemed to die when they realized they were walking into something.

Aubrey ventured a glance at Maeve, and noted her face was pale and her lips set with displeasure. He hated that she'd had to witness such ugliness. Hopefully, his mother had heard what he'd said and would take him seriously. Aubrey had no doubt that Derek, Catherine and the others would take their lead from him, and if he said they needed to relocate, they would.

They couldn't care less about hobnobbing with society. They were coming to see him, and Aubrey was thankful for that. His mother was looking forward to enjoying the stature that would come with hosting the duke and duchess and wouldn't want to have to explain to the other hostesses why her illustrious guests were no longer planning to come to Newport. The humiliation would be greater than her mortification over her new Irish daughter-in-law—or so he hoped.

Aubrey was putting great faith in his friendship with Derek and Catherine. Their pending visit gave him cachet within his own family, and with the social doyennes who could make or break the Season. If the duke and duchess were to snub the Nelson family, that would be a disaster for his mother and sisters—and his mother knew it.

He took hold of Maeve's hand, which was freezing, and gave it a squeeze. "Maeve, I'd like you to meet my sisters— Adele, Audrey, Alora and Aurora. Alora and Aurora are twins, as you can probably tell. And these are my nieces and nephews—Margaret, Augusta, Jane, Samuel, James and Sally." The children ranged from the oldest at eleven to the youngest at three, and living as they did in close proximity in New York, were nearly constant companions. They too looked forward to the summers in Newport when they lived under the same roof for a couple of months. "This is my wife, Maeve."

"You got *married*, Uncle Aubrey?" Augusta asked. At nine, she had strawberry-blond hair and big blue eyes.

"I did. Come say hello to your new aunt Maeve."

Augusta led the other children over to greet Maeve. "You're very pretty."

"Thank you." Maeve hugged each of the children in turn. "You are as well."

"You talk funny," James said.

"James," Aubrey said sternly. "That's not polite. Maeve is from Ireland, and that's why she speaks differently than you and I do."

"I'm sorry," James said.

Maeve patted James on the top of his dark-haired head. "No apology needed. I do talk funny compared to you."

James, who was seven, giggled.

"James has no right to say anyone talks funny," Margaret said. "He says a lot of words wrong."

Aubrey embraced his eleven-year-old niece. "Spoken like an older sister."

"It's true," Margaret said.

James made a spitting noise at his sister.

"That's enough, children." A team of governesses materialized to usher the children upstairs to unpack.

"Can we play croquet on the lawn, Uncle Aubrey?" Samuel asked on the way up the stairs.

"Absolutely. We'll set up the game after lunch."

"They're delightful," Maeve said.

"They're a handful, but we love them." At times, he wondered how many children he would've had by now had Annabelle lived. His children would've grown up among the others. Now he had another chance for a family of his own, and he couldn't be more excited by the prospect of children with Maeve.

"Aubrey, may I have a word in private, please?" Eliza asked.

"Of course, Mother." He released Maeve's hand. "I'll find you shortly?"

"We'll take care of Maeve." Audrey hooked her arm through Maeve's. "Don't worry, Aubrey."

"Be nice, or else," he said under his breath to his sister.

She rolled her eyes at him and escorted Maeve toward the back veranda with their other three sisters in tow. Over her shoulder, Maeve glanced at him, looking uncertain. As Aubrey followed his mother into the parlor, he hoped his sisters would be kind to his wife.

The door closed with a loud thud.

"What is the meaning of this, Aubrey?"

"Of what, Mother?"

"You *marrying* the Irish housekeeper."

"I love her." He loved her and would do anything it took to make their marriage succeed.

His mother's brown eyes flashed with rage. "You *love* her? You barely know her!"

"I know her better than I have ever known anyone, including Annabelle."

"How is that possible when you only met her two weeks ago?"

"I can't explain the how of it. All I can tell you is it's the truth. She is the woman I have been hoping to find ever since I lost Annabelle, and I won't stand for anyone, even you, making her feel less simply because she was born in Ireland."

"She won't be received here or in New York."

"Yes, she will. The same people who would shun her will wish to entertain my friends, the duke and duchess. We come as a group. All or nothing."

"You show astonishing hubris in pretending you speak for the duke and duchess."

"The duke and duchess are my dear friends, and I have no doubt whatsoever that they will embrace my wife and will follow my lead when it comes to contending with Newport society."

"How could you do this to me, Aubrey? I'll be mocked from one end of Bellevue Avenue to the other."

"I haven't done anything to you, Mother, except marry the woman I love, the first woman to truly catch my attention in the ten years since I lost Annabelle. I would think you'd be happy for me."

"You would think wrong. I'm appalled, and if your father was in his right mind, he would be, too. People of our class don't *marry* the help, for God's sake." Her harsh words were spoken in the crisp British accent that indicated her aristocratic upbringing.

"People of our class also don't mistreat their help."

"What is that supposed to mean?"

"When Maeve arrived here, she found a complete disaster. Last year's staff left the windows open all winter to invite in the seagulls, rodents and other feral guests. In your room, we believe they left food to ensure maximum wreckage. Everything in your room and Father's had to be burned. She has worked her fingers to the bone for weeks, at first completely alone, to ensure the house was ready for your arrival. If not for her extraordinary efforts, you would've been arriving to a mess that defied description. In all my years, I've never seen anything like it."

"They should be prosecuted," she said, sputtering with outrage.

"*You* should be prosecuted for treating them so badly that they would do such a thing. Henceforth, you shall have no authority over the household staff in this house. They will answer to me and only me."

Her face turned an alarming shade of red. "Who do you think you are?"

"I'm your son, and I'm *appalled* by your behavior." He let that sit for a long moment before he continued. "In light of Father's precarious health, I see no need to tell him about what transpired at the end of last Season, unless, of course, you continue to be abusive to the hardworking men and women who depend upon us for their living. In that case, I would have no compunction whatsoever about telling him what happened and why."

Rage rippled from her in waves that Aubrey could feel as much as see.

"You will treat my wife and our staff with courtesy and respect, or I'll make sure you're the social pariah of the Season."

"You would do such a thing to your own mother?"

"Try me, and you'll find out the lengths I'll go to in order to ensure my wife is embraced by my family and that the people whose life's work is to serve us are well treated."

"You have disappointed me greatly, Aubrey."

"Likewise, Mother. You should know that I couldn't care less what you or anyone else thinks of me, my choice of a wife or anything else I do. I have nothing at all to lose here, whereas you care so greatly what others think and have everything to lose. I truly hope that you will hear me when I tell you to tread carefully."

Feeling as if he'd made his point, Aubrey walked away, eager to find his wife and make sure his sisters weren't peppering her with questions that she wouldn't want to answer.

Chapter Thirteen

"You have to understand." Adele said along with expressive hand gestures. "Aubrey hasn't shown the slightest interest in *any* woman since he lost poor Annabelle, so it's a shock to us to arrive and hear that he has gotten *married*."

Aubrey listened in for a minute before he made his presence known.

"I'm sure it's very startling," Maeve replied.

"You must tell us everything!" Alora declared.

"No, she mustn't," Aubrey said as he came through the door to join them. "Mind your own business, you annoying harpies."

"When have you ever known us to do that?" Aurora asked.

Aubrey laughed. "Very true."

"Well, one of you needs to tell us how this happened," Adele said. "We have a right to know."

"You do not have a right to know," Aubrey said, "but all I'll say is that the moment I met Maeve, I wanted to know her. I wanted to know everything about her, and when I was lucky enough to convince her to become my wife, I was smart enough to get it done before you ladies could arrive and talk her out of it." He put his arm around Maeve and glanced her way to make sure she was all right.

She smiled, and he felt something inside him settle. She'd met his mother, father and sisters and was still smiling at him. He recorded each of those things as victories. "I require a moment alone with my wife."

"Honestly, Aubrey," Aurora said. "In the middle of the day?"

"I wish to *speak* to her."

"Of course you do," Audrey said as the others cackled with laughter. "We've been newlyweds, too."

Aubrey pulled a disgusted face. "Don't put those thoughts into my mind." Before the girls could pursue that line of conversation, he led Maeve inside and up the backstairs, hoping to get to their bedroom before they encountered family members. He was relieved to see the hallway clear of relatives and followed her into the room, closing the door behind him. Leaning against the door, he released a long breath full of relief. "All things considered, I think that went rather well, don't you?"

"Your mother was very displeased."

"She often is displeased, but I made it clear to her that I'm quite delighted with my choice of a wife, and I'll tolerate no detractors, even my own mother." He pushed himself off the door and went to her, putting his arms around her waist and kissing her.

"Did you tell her about the house?"

"I did, and she suggested the former staff ought to be prosecuted. I suggested *she* ought to be."

"You didn't!"

"I did, and I meant it. I put her on notice that the staff no longer reports to her and that unless she wishes to be shunned by polite society, she will be kind to my wife as well as the men and women who work for us."

"She must be so angry."

"I care not if she is. I have always been a good and faithful son who respected his mother and father, but as I grow older, I have learned that respect must be earned, not bestowed."

Maeve placed her hand over his heart. "I find this protective, fiercely loyal side of you very . . . attractive."

The statement became his favorite thing anyone had ever said to him. "Do you?"

"Mmm-hmm." Going up on her tiptoes, Maeve kissed him while Aubrey stood perfectly still, stunned and aroused to nearly the point of madness by her taking the initiative for the first time.

He forced himself to stay still, to see what she would do, and she didn't disappoint.

With soft, almost delicate brushes of her lips over his, she had him clinging to the edge of sanity, and when she added light dabs of her tongue, he snapped, wrapped his arms around her, hauled her as close to him as he could get her and devoured her.

She met every stroke of his tongue with one of hers, buried her hand in his hair and tugged on it to get him even closer.

Aubrey lost track of time and space and anything that didn't include her and having more of her right now. It didn't matter to him that they were in a house full of family members or that they'd given his sisters plenty to talk about by disappearing this way in the middle of the day. As he continued to kiss her, he eased them onto the floor, making sure he was under her to soften the landing.

She broke the kiss and stared at him, seeming as stunned as he felt. "What're you doing?"

He grasped handfuls of her skirts and eased them up and

over her fine backside. "This." As he spoke, he turned them so he was on top of her.

"Aubrey, we can't. Not now. We're expected for luncheon with your family."

"We can. We're newlyweds. They'll understand if we miss luncheon." He focused his attention on her neck, nuzzling her with kisses and light dabs of his tongue as he pressed his rigid erection against her core. "You can't leave me in such a state. They'll surely notice and be relentless in the grief they'll give me. You wouldn't do that to me, would you?"

The withering look she gave him was one that wives everywhere would recognize.

Freeing himself from his trousers with one hand, Aubrey kissed his way back to her lips, which were swollen from their earlier kisses. "We'll be quick and only a few minutes late to lunch."

"You're never quick."

He snorted with laughter. "I'll be this time. I promise. You've got me so worked up, I won't last but a minute."

"Why am I always the one who is blamed for these situations?"

"Because it's your fault that you're so beautiful and alluring and soft and sweet and . . . ah, God, so ready for me." The flood of moisture between her legs was nearly his undoing.

"That is *your* doing."

"Ah, love, that is *our* doing." He slid into her and bit his lip—hard—to keep from spending as soon as her tight, wet heat surrounded his cock. In all his life, nothing had ever felt better than being inside his lovely wife. "You feel so sinfully good."

"As do you." She combed her fingers through his hair

in a gesture so loving and tender it made his heart skip a beat and the breath get caught in his throat.

He'd promised to be quick, but he hated to rush something that felt so damned good. Sliding a hand under her, he grasped her bottom and held her tight against him as he began to move faster.

She looked up at him, his gaze connecting with hers in a moment of perfect harmony that made him shiver and falter.

"Are you all right?"

He shook his head. "I'm quite undone by you."

"And that is a bad thing?"

"On the contrary. It's the best thing to ever happen to me." He captured her lips in another torrid kiss as he continued to move inside her, the crisis growing and multiplying until it could no longer be contained or denied. "Maeve . . ."

"Yes, Aubrey. Don't stop."

He would never stop wanting her, loving her, needing her. The realizations came over him like a tidal wave, one after the other. In her he had found his perfect match, like Derek with Catherine and Simon with Madeleine. He understood now why they had risked anything and everything to have the women they loved, because he would do the same to protect Maeve and their fragile bond.

He would do whatever it took to feel this way for the rest of his life.

She raised her hips to meet a deep stroke of his cock, and that's all it took to break him.

Aubrey reached the summit with a shout that came from the deepest part of him, his fingers digging into her hip and shoulder to hold her still as she experienced her climax right along with him.

"Shhh, they'll hear us."

"I don't bloody care."

Breathing hard, he collapsed onto her, every muscle in his body lax in repose. He couldn't have moved if he'd had to.

Her arms encircled him as her fingers continued to comb through his hair, filling him with a profound feeling of well-being and contentment.

"That was *not* quick."

His low chuckle rumbled through his chest. "I found myself exceptionally inspired by the magnificence of my wife and couldn't rush perfection."

She laughed, and as always, the sound of her laughter delighted him. "You've made a terrible mess of me. I'm going to need to change my wrinkled dress."

"I love to make a mess of you." He cupped her cheek and gazed down at her. "I love every minute I spend with you."

"I quite enjoy our time together as well."

"It makes me very happy to hear you say that."

"I hope you didn't wonder."

"No, not really." Aubrey still wondered if she were with him for the protection he could provide or because she genuinely cared for him. He didn't know, and that uncertainty was the only thing keeping him from telling her the truth of how much he cared for her. Taking a deep breath, he let it out slowly as he realized he'd once again been careless about preventing conception. If she ended up pregnant, that would keep her with him, or so he hoped.

The uncertainty detracted from the happiness she had brought to his life and left him with a grinding fear of what would become of him if it turned out that she was only with him so she wouldn't be taken home to Ireland to face murder charges.

* * *

Over the next week, Maeve found herself waiting. For what, she didn't know, but she fully expected something to happen, something unpleasant that would destroy the bubble of happiness she had found with Aubrey.

His sisters had been friendly if reserved in their welcome of her. The children had been lovely, but they were unaware that they shouldn't be too warm toward their uncle's new wife due to her lowly heritage.

In America, the Irish were treated as second-class citizens, which she had known before she came, but with few options available to her, she'd come knowing she would most likely be able to find work there. She hadn't expected to meet a man of society who had taken an immediate and overwhelming interest in her, nor had she ever expected to find herself married to such a man.

When he'd told her Mr. Tornquist had come looking for her, at the behest of Farthington's family, she'd experienced panic so deep and pervasive it had stolen the breath from her lungs. Aubrey had been right there, offering her protection and affection and a solution to her most pressing problem.

Desperation had driven her to accept his outlandish proposal, and his obvious desire for her had added to the appeal of his offer. And in the days since then, he'd introduced her to pleasure beyond anything she could've imagined before she had known him. Maeve found herself anticipating time alone with him with a nearly sinful enthusiasm for what would transpire when they were behind closed doors.

He continued to surprise and delight and yes, embarrass her with the things he convinced her to do, but the end result was always the same—dizzying pleasure.

Since her arrival, his mother had kept her distance from both of them, but her disapproval of Aubrey's choice of a wife was apparent in everything she said and did. She had completely ignored Maeve, apparently deciding that if she pretended her youngest son hadn't married the Irish housekeeper, then maybe it would be like it hadn't happened.

For a woman known for her volcanic rages, her silence spoke volumes.

Aubrey hadn't noticed the way his mother completely ignored her, but Maeve had, and wondering about Eliza's strategy kept Maeve in a constant state of disquiet, her stomach upset and her nerves stretched thin. Silence, in this case, wasn't golden. If her intent was to keep Maeve in a perpetual state of dread, she had succeeded brilliantly. Not for one moment did Maeve believe that Eliza was going to accept her son's marriage to the former housekeeper.

By the time a week had passed, the house was on full alert for the imminent arrival of the duke and duchess and the rest of their party, and no one was more excited to greet them than Eliza. Perhaps their pending visit was the only thing keeping Eliza from finding a way to banish Maeve from Aubrey's life.

At the moment, she seemingly cared more about the social boost she would receive from the arrival of the duke and duchess than she did about the woman her son had married. But Maeve knew her day of reckoning was coming. Dread had her nerves stretched so thin it was all she could think about as she moved through her days pretending to be part of the Nelson family while knowing these halcyon days would soon be relegated to memories she would cherish forever.

Aubrey was attentive, sweet, loving and tender with her, seemingly delighted to be spending time with her and his extended family at his favorite place in the world. He appeared to be a man without concern as he kept his pledge to oversee the staff, including a new housekeeper named

Sarah who had arrived three days prior. Aubrey spent time every morning in the office with his father, catching up on business reports from his brothers in New York.

Maeve used the time he spent tending to work to walk the grounds of the estate and the nearby shore so as not to chance an encounter with Eliza while Aubrey was otherwise occupied. She had come to rely on his steady presence to keep her calm when she felt the grip of fear over what would become of her when his mother prevailed in convincing him to turn his back on her.

It would happen. Maeve had no doubt whatsoever about that. But not knowing when or how it would happen had her clinging to the edge of sanity while everyone around her indulged in summertime frivolity.

The day the duke and duchess were due to arrive, Maeve walked farther than she had before, traversing the path that wound along the shoreline. With warm sunshine beating down on her and a soft, early summer breeze coming from the ocean, she could almost convince herself she was back home in Dingle, except that the ocean faced the other direction here, something she had found remarkable when she first realized it. Naturally, that made perfect sense, but until someone had been on both sides of the vast ocean, the difference didn't register.

When she'd walked to the end of the long path, she turned back, every step toward "home" making her more anxious. She was more than halfway back when she noted a familiar man coming toward her. After weeks as his lover, she recognized the shape of his body and the unique way in which he moved. A shiver of anticipation rippled down her back when she realized he had been looking for her.

In the seconds it took for him to reach her, she realized she'd made the critical, devastating error of allowing herself to fall in love with the remarkable man she had married, even knowing that at any moment, the dream they had created for themselves would turn into a nightmare. A woman like his mother would settle for nothing less than complete and utter destruction.

"There you are." His face lit up with pleasure at the sight of her, as it always did.

Had anyone ever looked at her the way he did? No, never. She would miss him so much when she was forced to leave him. "Here I am." She made an effort to match his cheerful tone so he wouldn't know how tortured she was. Had he known, he would've reassured her, told her there was nothing anyone could do or say to make him not want her. He would say all the right things, but there were things that could tear them apart, and when—not if—his mother learned of how Maeve's first marriage had ended, she would do everything within her considerable power to drive them apart.

Aubrey extended his arm to her. "Why do you seem troubled, my dear?"

Maeve tucked her hand into the crook of his elbow, realizing as she did it, that holding on to him had become as natural to her as breathing. How had she allowed that to happen? "I'm hoping your friends are having an uneventful journey and that they will find the accommodations to their liking."

"I'm sure they will be delighted with everything you did to prepare for their arrival. I know I am."

His approval meant the world to her. Pleasing him had become her most important daily task, because when she pleased him, he directed that warm, loving smile her way. That smile calmed and soothed her the way almost nothing else could. It gave her hope and faith that maybe they would survive whatever his mother cooked up to ruin them. But then she thought of the condition the house had been in and the lengths the previous staff had gone to exact their revenge on the woman who had tormented them, and the feelings of hope deserted her.

"Tell me about them," she said, desperate to find something to talk to him about so she wouldn't be tempted to unload her fears on him. "You've talked of them so often, but I still don't know how you met the duke or much about the others in his party."

"Derek and I met a couple of years ago when my mother strong-armed me into spending the Season in London in the hopes that I would land an aristocratic wife."

"How devastated she must be now." The words were out before she could consider whether she should say them.

"Her feelings have no bearing on mine. I was always very clear with her that I would only marry if I met someone I couldn't live without, and that's exactly what I did."

His words went straight to her heart, making it flutter with delight. He really was the sweetest man she'd ever known. "How did you come to be acquainted with the duke?"

"You know the saying misery loves company?"

"I do."

"Well, neither Derek nor I, nor his cousin Simon or dear friend Justin Enderly, wished to be anywhere near the ballrooms of London or the desperate mothers looking to make an aristocratic match for their feather-headed daughters."

She glanced up at him, raising a brow. "Feather-headed?"

"That's really the only way to describe the way they flit about, preening and posing and hoping against hope to land a duke or an earl or, if all else fails, a man whose family has struck it rich in the railroad in America. Although, compared to Derek, the rest of us may as well have been two-day-old haddock. He was the big prize—a wealthy, titled duke under the age of fifty who still had all his teeth and a face so handsome as to make the mamas weep. I quickly realized that having him for a friend meant that we would be surrounded at all times by diamonds of the highest caliber."

The thought of Aubrey being surrounded by beautiful women made Maeve seethe with jealousy. "It must've been a terrible hardship to be so in demand."

He stopped walking and turned to her, flashing that irrepressible grin. "Is my lovely wife jealous?"

"Of course not. You chose me over all those diamonds you could've had. What reason do I have to be jealous?"

"No reason whatsoever." His expression became more serious. "It's apparent to me now that I was waiting for the most flawless of all diamonds to cross my path." He caressed her face and turned her chin up to receive his kiss. "The diamond I married has no peer on this or any continent."

Maeve sighed with pleasure and delight at how efficiently he dispatched her unsettling thoughts. "You're quite accomplished at flattery, Mr. Nelson."

"I speak only the truth, Mrs. Nelson."

"You mentioned Derek's cousin, Simon, and his friend Justin. Are they also your friends?"

They began to walk again, taking their time returning to the house full of people that was about to get even more crowded with the arrival of the duke, duchess and their party.

"Indeed they are. The three are—or I guess I should say were—constant companions before Derek and Simon married the McCabe sisters."

"And how did cousins end up marrying sisters? You told me some of it, but not the whole story."

"Well, Derek had decided he'd had enough of the social

Season in London, and even though he was under pressure to marry by his thirtieth birthday—"

"How come?"

"A ridiculous and legally questionable provision in his family's primogeniture, inserted by the first Duke of Westwood, that compels all future dukes to marry by age thirty. While none of the previous dukes had come close to missing the deadline, Derek hadn't wanted to question the legality of the provision with his scurrilous uncle waiting in the wings, panting for the power Derek possesses. The last thing he wanted was to cede to Anthony, but he couldn't bear the Season for even one more day. He took his leave and headed home to Essex on his beloved horse, Hercules, and was nearly home when he found a woman digging on his property. At first, he thought it was a man, but it turned out to be Catherine McCabe, who had run away from an arranged marriage with a nasty viscount. I don't know all the details, but upon learning of her disdain for the aristocracy, apparently Derek convinced her he was the estate manager, Jack Bancroft—"

"Jack Bancroft? That was the name you used the day we met!"

"It was," Aubrey said with a sheepish grin. "It was the first name that popped into my head after I realized you thought I was the new butler."

"I see that deception is a trait you and your friend have in common."

"We have both learned from our mistakes. I assure you of that. Derek and Catherine fell madly in love, and when the viscount came looking for her, Derek spirited her away in the night to Gretna Green where they were married."

"Did he tell her then that he was really the duke?"

Aubrey winced. "Unfortunately, he did not. He decided to give them both a week of happiness that included his formerly dreaded thirtieth birthday, before he broke the news to her."

"He must've been relieved to have met the deadline."

"Indeed. That was a huge relief to him. His parents were killed in a carriage accident when he was just a boy, so he had always endeavored to make them proud. He felt that his failure to meet the deadline would've devastated them, especially seeing everything go to the brother his father had despised, who it turns out, was the one who orchestrated the deaths of Derek's parents."

"Oh, my lord. And that man is Simon's father?"

"Yes, but fortunately, Simon is nothing at all like the man who fathered him. A more affable chap you'd be hard-pressed to find."

"How did he end up married to Catherine's sister?"

"Derek sent him to London to find out what was being said about Catherine and to determine if her fiancé, the viscount, was looking for her. While he was there, he met Madeleine, and I was there that night. He was instantly smitten by her, to the point that Justin and I couldn't believe what we were witnessing. Simon had been somewhat of a rake, and to see him dazzled by a woman was startling, to say the least. And that the woman he'd fallen for was also considered the belle of the Season . . . We found it highly entertaining. There's much more to the story but I'll let Catherine and Madeleine tell you about it."

"Do you think they will like me?"

"They will adore you."

"How can you be so certain?"

"Because I know them, and they're delightful women. Did I tell you they were raised in a small village where their father was the local blacksmith?"

"No, you didn't mention that."

"Their father was a second son, and when his older

brother and nephew succumbed to fever, he became the earl. Catherine and Madeleine were already in their twenties when this happened, so they weren't raised as aristocrats. I guess it was quite a shock to them to be suddenly thrust into society and all its many rules."

Maeve shuddered. "I understand somewhat of how they felt. It's a shock to one's system to suddenly be considered *more* simply because someone dies or marries."

"Life can change so suddenly. That's what happened to Derek and Simon and then to me when I walked into the ballroom and saw you there, looking so appealing as you wielded that massive feather duster."

"I still say there is something wrong with your vision."

He laughed. "There is nothing at all wrong with my vision. It was your delectable neck that sealed your fate, my love."

"I've never heard of a man being attracted to a woman's neck."

"Until you met me, that is."

"Yes, until I met you. It's an odd fixation you have developed for my neck."

"I find myself fixated on your neck and every other part of you. I have never been more thankful that my thoughts are private than I have since my family invaded our idyllic existence. For if they had any idea of the indecent thoughts I have about my wife while surrounded by sisters and nieces and nephews, I'd be drummed right out of the family."

Heat flooded her face, which of course he noticed with a bark of laughter. "I love that sweet flush more than anything else in this life."

"You're completely daft."

"I'm daft about you."

She wanted so badly to ask him if he still would be once

his mother played her hand and tried to destroy them. Would he still feel the same way about her as he did now when his mother forced him to choose between his wife and his family? Because she would. Of that Maeve had no doubt whatsoever. It would come down to a choice. And how could Maeve expect him to choose her over those he had loved all his life?

He wouldn't choose her, and she needed to prepare herself for that inevitability and make plans for what she would do when this beautiful moment with him came to an end. In the meantime, she would do her very best to enjoy every minute she got to spend with him and to record the memories upon her heart and soul to sustain her during the empty, lonely years she would spend without him.

Chapter Fourteen

Derek, Catherine, Simon, Madeleine and Justin arrived late that afternoon in a flurry of carriages that included ladies' maids, valets and a governess for baby Grace, a cherubic six-month-old with golden ringlets and big blue eyes who instantly captivated Aubrey.

"She's beautiful," he told her parents. "Well done, you two."

"It was all Catherine," Derek said with a wide grin for his wife. "She did all the hard work. My part was exceedingly pleasurable."

"Hush, Derek," his wife admonished. "Don't speak of your pleasure in front of the baby."

While the others laughed, Derek made a comical face at his wife.

Aubrey was delighted to see that the two couples were happier than ever, and clearly still besotted. It gave him hope that he and Maeve might fare similarly in the years to come. "Dear friends, I have someone very special I would like you to meet." With his arm around Maeve, he drew her into their group. "This is my wife, Maeve. Maeve, meet Derek, the Duke of Westwood, his wife, Catherine, the Duchess of Westwood, their daughter, Lady Grace,

Derek's cousin, Simon, and his wife, Madeleine, and our dear friend Justin Enderly."

"You have been keeping secrets from us, Aubrey!" Catherine handed the baby to Derek so she could hug Maeve. "Welcome to the family, Maeve. I'm so happy to meet you."

Aubrey could tell that Maeve was taken aback by Catherine's effusive greeting. "Thank you, Your Grace."

If his friends were startled by Maeve's Irish brogue, they gave nothing away. God bless them. He'd never been more thankful for their friendship than he was in that moment.

"Please call me Catherine. We're going to be great friends. There's no need for formality."

"Thank you," Maeve said.

Madeleine hugged her next. "It's so nice to have another woman in our midst. Catherine and I are woefully out-numbered in this group."

"You think it's easy being me," said Justin, "known as the fifth wheel, stuck in the midst of all these lovebirds? I'm devastated to hear you've joined their ranks, Aubrey. You were my only hope for this summer."

"So sorry to disappoint, dear friend, but I'm happily shackled."

Simon hugged Maeve. "Welcome and congratulations. I can't wait to hear how you brought Aubrey up to scratch."

"Oh, um, I didn't really do that."

The flush that overtook her cheeks had the same effect on him it always did, and he had to remind himself he wasn't allowed to ravish her in front of their guests. "That's exactly what you did, my sweet, and I've never been happier."

"This is quite a development, old friend," Derek said. "We're going to want to hear the full story."

"We'll be happy to tell you, but first I have to introduce

you to my mother and sisters, who are waiting not-so-patiently to meet you." Aubrey led them to the back veranda where he'd asked his family to wait so their guests wouldn't be overwhelmed the second they arrived. His mother had been none too pleased with the request, but had ceded to his wishes about that, the same way she had about everything else since her arrival.

He felt confident that he'd succeeded in making his stand with her by outlining the consequences that would accompany bad behavior on her part. As he was fully prepared to make good on his threats by taking his illustrious friends and departing, he expected her to toe the line and show his wife the respect she deserved.

So far, she had left them alone and had allowed Aubrey to oversee the staff.

Even his sisters had commented on their mother's unusually docile behavior. Perhaps it was their father's worsening health that had her preoccupied. They were all preoccupied with concern for their father, who seemed to be withering away before their eyes. He was making a valiant effort to participate in family activities, but he tired easily and was often in bed for the night before dinner.

"Mother, I'm delighted to introduce you to my dear friends." Aubrey went through the introductions again, cringing when his mother curtsied before the duke and duchess, knowing they wouldn't expect such a gesture. "And these hellions are my sisters." He introduced them and then signaled to Mrs. Allston, who'd been hovering nearby, to go ahead and serve the refreshments he'd requested.

"I hope you'll make yourselves entirely at home," Eliza said, beaming with excitement.

Derek and Eliza launched into a "who's your mother, who's your father" conversation that further delighted

Aubrey's mother. She loved nothing more than discussing her aristocratic lineage with anyone who would listen.

To his credit, Derek paid rapt attention and asked all the right questions, which endeared him to Eliza for life. She could talk endlessly about her upbringing in England, the people she'd known, the balls she'd attended and the other trappings of a pampered, privileged life.

"How did you end up marrying Mr. Nelson?" Catherine asked.

Eliza's displeasure with the question wouldn't be apparent to their guests, but Aubrey saw it and resented it. His father may not have been the world's most exciting man, but he'd been a wonderful husband and father, and his wife owed him more than her disdain. "My father, the earl, met Mr. Nelson at White's and they became friends due to their mutual love of horse racing. My father introduced me to Mr. Nelson and suggested I allow him to court me, and here we are forty-five years later." She added a fake smile to the end of the statement that only her children would recognize as disingenuous.

Aubrey had been in his late twenties when he learned, quite by accident, that the man she had desperately wanted to marry, the Duke of Ellington, had led her to believe a betrothal was imminent before eloping with one of Eliza's closest friends, setting off a scandal that had rocked the *ton* to its core. She'd never recovered from the deception— or the scandal—and carried the bitterness of the duke's betrayal with her to this day. The offer of marriage from his father was the only one she received, and her father demanded she accept or end up a spinster sitting on a dusty shelf.

Hosting the Duke and Duchess of Westwood, the current toast of the *ton*, would give her something to crow about to the people at home in England who still talked about her humiliation in hushed whispers. Meanwhile Ellington and his wife went on to have ten children who were now adults and among the cream of society themselves. Aubrey had actually met a few of them during his first Season in London, not knowing at the time of their father's former connection to his mother.

The group passed an entertaining and relaxing afternoon on the veranda, enjoying the warm summer air and the company of friends. Grace snoozed through most of it on her mother's shoulder. When the governess appeared in the doorway to take the child upstairs, Catherine waved her off, preferring to tend to her daughter herself.

"I'm not sure why we brought Miss Ames with us, my dear," Derek said with a tender smile for his wife.

"She is here so we can attend events. Otherwise, I wish to care for Grace myself, as you well know."

"I do know and wouldn't have it any other way."

Aubrey noticed that Maeve paid close attention to the conversation but didn't contribute to it at all, as if she didn't think she ought to. He looked forward to being alone with her to encourage her to fully participate. She had every right to as his wife, and he would remind her of that the first chance he got.

"Shall we adjourn to dress for dinner?" he asked.

The others agreed and were shown to their rooms with two hours to rest and prepare for dinner.

When they were inside their bedroom with the door closed to prying eyes, Aubrey wrapped his arms around her and held her tight against him. "I have needed this for hours."

"You showed remarkable restraint."

"I did, didn't I?" He drew back so he could see her face. "Did you enjoy yourself?"

"Very much so. Your friends are delightful, just as you said they would be."

"You were very quiet. I hope you know you're welcome to fully participate."

"That is kind of you to say, but I didn't want to intrude in any way. I know how much you've looked forward to seeing them."

"You wouldn't be intruding. They will want to get to know you, and you should feel free to speak up."

"I'll try."

He studied her face more closely. "Is there something else troubling you?"

She schooled her features and shook her head. "No."

"You would tell me if there was something, wouldn't you?"

"Yes, of course. Everything is fine."

She said what he wanted to hear, but he wasn't sure he believed her.

"I would hope you know that there is nothing you could say to me that would be wrong. If you're upset about something, I want to know."

"Thank you."

"I don't want your gratitude." The words came out harsher than he intended, so he softened his tone. "I want you to share your concerns with me so that we may resolve them together."

"I wonder about Mr. Tornquist and whether there may be others looking for me."

"If there are, we will dispatch them the same way we did him."

"You can't pay off everyone who comes looking for me."

"Who says?"

"I say. That's not the way to handle it. Eventually we are going to have to contend with the fact that I'm wanted on serious charges in Ireland."

"I'm going to speak to Derek about that. He will know what we should do, and if he speaks up for you, that will matter."

She recoiled. "You can't ask him to do such a thing for someone he doesn't even know."

"He would do it for me, Maeve. Because I ask him to."

"I wouldn't feel right about asking him."

"If he could help to free you from the weight of your concerns, you wouldn't want to at least try?"

"I would like nothing more than to be free of those concerns but asking your friend to intervene on my behalf is too much."

"I do not agree. He is a powerful man with powerful connections. We would be foolish not to at least ask for any assistance he can provide."

As she thought about what he'd said, she rolled her bottom lip between her teeth.

Aubrey tapped on her chin with his fingertip. "Don't hurt that lip. It's one of my favorite lips in the entire world."

Maeve released the lip from between her teeth.

He framed her face with his hands and kissed her gently. "I don't want you to worry about anything. There is nothing that could happen, nothing at all that would change how I feel about you or how much I want to make our marriage work. You have become the most important person in the world to me, and you must believe me when I say I'll do whatever it takes to keep you safe and happy."

"You're very kind."

"I'm not being kind. I'm being a selfish bastard, because if you're happy, I'm happy. It's that simple."

"What do you think your friends really think about you marrying the Irish housekeeper?"

"I'm sure they can plainly see how very pleased I am to be married to you, and that will be enough for them."

"After spending the afternoon with them, I begin to see why you care so much for them. They are just like regular people. If you did not know of their titles, you'd never suspect they held them."

"I'm glad that you were able to discern that. They are very humble people, who are not at all impressed with themselves, unlike many of the people you will meet this summer who are *extremely* impressed with themselves." As he spoke, he began the task of unbuttoning her yellow shirtwaist, enjoying each inch of creamy skin he uncovered. "It's going to be a late night. Shall we take a rest?"

Her brow arched. "Will this rest involve sleeping?"

"How suspicious you are, wife."

"I have come to know you quite well, husband."

Her teasing words hit him like a punch to the gut. He had a *wife*. He was her *husband*. And she was absolutely perfect for him in every way.

"What is the matter?" she asked after he had stared at her for a full minute.

"I'm continuously amazed that you agreed to marry me and that I get to spend my life with such an extraordinary woman."

"You flatter me, Mr. Nelson."

"I adore you, Mrs. Nelson." He kissed the back of her neck, pulled the pins from her hair and watched her glorious hair cascade down her back. Then he began to quickly remove his own clothes and followed her into their bed where she welcomed him into her outstretched arms.

Every time they were together this way, Aubrey felt as if he'd come home from a long journey to the place he was always meant to be. He could look at her exquisite face for hours on end and never grow tired of the view or of the way he felt when she gazed back at him, seeming equally enamored. He wanted to ask her if she felt the way he did, but something continued to hold him back from posing the question. Perhaps it was the fear he sensed in her. He had reassured her every way he knew how, but still he could see her wrestling with concerns she kept from him.

It was a lot to expect of his new wife that she take on his mother, sisters, illustrious friends and Newport society all at once, but the woman who had defended herself against a violent man and escaped to a whole new country wasn't one who would be easily cowed. He was counting on her inner strength to help propel her through the summer of social obligations.

Anxious to quiet the thoughts that swirled through his mind, he placed his hand on her face and kissed her, intending to actually allow her to get some rest. But one kiss became two and her eager response had him forgetting all about sleep to indulge in pleasure so profound he often felt as if he'd consumed half a bottle of scotch after being with her this way.

His head spun and his heart beat faster than was probably healthy. He could barely breathe from wanting her so desperately. "Tell me you feel it, too." He uttered the words between urgent kisses and then remembered he hadn't planned to push her to reveal her feelings.

"Feel what?"

"*Everything*. Every single thing there is to feel when we're together this way."

As he watched her contemplate what he'd said, he felt as if his entire life was on the line along with any chance he had to be happy. For without her, he wouldn't be happy. He already knew that much for certain. "I feel it, too."

Relief flooded him, along with gratitude and love. So much love. "Maeve, I—"

She drew him into a kiss that smothered the words he'd planned to say. Had she known what he would say and didn't want to hear it?

For the longest time, they only kissed, arms wrapped tight around each other, his leg between hers as their kisses became ever more desperate. Until Aubrey broke the kiss to stare at her once again. "I've never wanted anyone the way I want you." The statement surprised her as much as it did him because it was acknowledgment that as much as he'd loved Annabelle, it hadn't been like this with her.

He was a heel for even having such a thought, but he couldn't deny the truth of it. As much as he'd loved Annabelle—and he'd truly loved her—what he'd felt for her paled in comparison to his feelings for Maeve.

"I still can't believe that this has happened," she said.

"Believe it. It's the very best thing to ever happen to me."

"Me as well. I have been so afraid of what would become of me, especially if Mr. Farthington's family tried to find me, and then there you were to fix everything that was wrong."

"I'll always fix what is wrong, sweet Maeve. You only have to tell me what you need and I'll see that you get it. Whatever you want you shall have."

"I want to be safe. That's the only thing I need."

"You're safe with me. I would kill to protect you."

"Please don't say such things!"

"It's true."

"Aubrey, please don't say that. I can't bear the thought of such a thing."

"Shhh. I'm sorry. I wasn't thinking about what happened with Mr. Farthington. This is Newport. Things like that don't happen here. You've nothing to worry about."

As he said the words, he could only hope they were true, but he meant what he'd said. If it came to it, he would kill to keep her safe.

Chapter Fifteen

Much later that night, after a delightful dinner full of laughter and stories, Aubrey entered the billiard room with Derek, Simon and Justin. Since Catherine and Madeleine had retired, Maeve said good night and went to bed rather than spending time alone with his mother and sisters. He noticed she went out of her way to avoid being with them if he wasn't there, too. Aubrey hoped that in time she'd become more comfortable with his family.

However, if that never happened, so be it. After the summer, they wouldn't have to spend time in close proximity to his family unless they chose to. He had his own home in New York where they could hibernate together and venture out only when they both wished to. They just had to get through the summer.

"All right, Aubrey," Derek said when each of the men had glasses of scotch and the finest cigars money could buy. "Start talking."

Startled, Aubrey wasn't sure how to reply. "Pardon?"

"Don't play coy, old chap," Simon said. "We're dying to know how you ended up married to Maeve."

Justin took a long drag on his cigar and blew out the smoke. "We stood by your side through several tedious Seasons during which the cream of London society was paraded before you, and you barely took notice. Imagine our surprise when we arrived to find you *married*."

"Ah, I see. Well, I was rather surprised myself to arrive to a complete disaster when my mother sent me ahead to get the house ready for guests."

"A disaster?" Derek asked. "How so?"

How to tell them without speaking out of turn? If there was one thing his mother did not tolerate, it was the airing of the family's dirty laundry in public. But his friends weren't "public," and he trusted them. "Between us?"

"Of course," Derek said as the others nodded in agreement.

"My mother can be a bit of an ogre at times, and the former staff quit en masse at the end of last Season, leaving the windows open to the elements."

"*Good lord*," Justin said.

"The house was a total wreck, and when I arrived, Miss Brown—Maeve—was trying to make it right almost entirely on her own. We began to work together, and one thing led to another . . ."

Derek sat back, eyeing him with friendly suspicion. "And that was all there was to it? Please don't be offended, Aubrey. Your Maeve is lovely, but this must've happened very quickly and marriage is a big step."

"Yes, it is, and the circumstances were somewhat similar to those under which you and Catherine were married."

"Ahh," Derek said. "So she was in some sort of danger?"

"Yes." Aubrey hadn't planned to tell them any of this yet, but now that the door had been opened, he decided to take the plunge. "First, I must beg for your discretion. My family knows none of this."

"Of course you have it," Simon said, answering for all of them.

"Thank you. Maeve was married in Ireland, to a man who

mistreated her. He was unable to perform—sexually—and took out his frustrations on her, beating her repeatedly. The last time she was convinced he was going to kill her. She grabbed a pan off the stove, threw hot soup at him and when he charged her, she hit him with the pan itself, killing him."

"Dear God," Justin muttered.

"She burned her hand rather severely on the handle of the pan, and the skin on her palm was still healing when we met."

"How did she end up here?" Derek asked.

"She took money from her husband's boot and booked a passage to America, fearing she would be hung if she stayed in Ireland. In New York, she made contact with an employment agency that offered her the position here, not mentioning that it was open because no one else wanted it. She found that out when she got here."

"I can't imagine what she must've encountered after a winter with the windows open," Simon said.

"Your imagination isn't vivid enough to conjure the filth. They left food in my mother's room to ensure maximum carnage. There are no words to describe the nightmare we encountered."

"Dear God," Derek said in a whisper.

"Poor Maeve was trying to address it all by herself, with an injured hand, no less. I was immediately and irrevocably attracted to her. We struck up a friendship of sorts as we worked to restore the house. And then a man came looking for her, sent by her dead husband's family. That's when she told me what had happened in Ireland. I offered her the protection of my name and resources."

"I'm sure she was very relieved," Justin said.

"She was actually reluctant to involve me in her problems."

"I'll admit to being relieved to hear that," Derek said. "Otherwise I might've been concerned about her motives."

"I assure you they are pure. I had to plead with her to let me help her. In addition to marrying her, I paid off the man looking for her with the provision that he report to his clients that he was unable to locate her in Newport."

"But they are still looking for her?" Derek asked.

"I assume so. I was going to ask if you have any suggestions of how we might reach out to the authorities in Ireland to convey her side of the events."

"I would be happy to reach out to my contacts in Ireland to see what might be done."

"Thank you, Derek. I was hoping you might say that."

"Whatever I can do to help. What was her husband's name?"

"Farthington."

Derek glanced at Simon. "Why do I know that name?"

"I was thinking the same," his cousin replied. "Something about it is familiar, but I can't say how I know of him."

"Maeve said his family is in shipping in Ireland."

"We must think about it," Derek said, rubbing his chin before returning his attention to Aubrey. "I ask this with the utmost respect for you and your wife, but have you prepared her for what it will be like for her in not-so-polite society?"

"We have already spoken extensively about that, and while we are nervous about how she might be received, I believe that my affiliation with the visiting duke and duchess will help to smooth the way for her."

"How so?" Justin asked.

"Allow me," Derek said, amusement etched into his expression. "Aubrey is well aware that the local hostesses will be panting over the thought of entertaining a duke and duchess, and he intends to make his lovely wife part of the package. Am I close?"

"You're spot-on. Please accept my apologies for shamelessly using you to my own benefit."

Derek barked out a laugh. "Use me to your heart's content. If I can help to make things easier for you and Maeve, I'm all for it, and I know Catherine would say the same."

"I told Maeve that you would probably say that."

"As you well know, I have no patience for bullies, especially those dressed in the finest silk who think they should be allowed to determine who passes muster. By the end of this summer, we will see to it that your wife is the toast of Newport society."

"Wouldn't that be something?" Aubrey gave silent thanks for the blessing of good friends. He'd had many friends in his lifetime, but these three men were the best of the best, which is why he'd always be thankful his mother had insisted he partake in the London Season. He may not have come home with the wife she'd dreamed of for him, but he'd made lifelong friends.

"It's not outside the realm of possibility," Justin said. "Things are changing. It's a new century, and people need to get over their fear of anything foreign. If it weren't for her Irish brogue, you could pass her off as a member of any high-brow family."

"I have had that very thought myself."

"It's the twentieth century," Derek declared. "I have no patience for this type of nonsense."

"Which type of nonsense are you referring to, cousin?" Simon's eyes glittered with amusement. "He has a well-known lack of patience for many kinds of nonsense."

Derek rolled his eyes at his cousin. "I'm referring to the kind of nonsense that would have an innocent young woman like Maeve shunned simply because she was born in the wrong country. It's outrageous and high time we stopped judging people for things they have no control over."

"Amen," Justin said.

"Couldn't agree more," Aubrey added. "Thank you for taking such a stance. I assured Maeve that you would be inclined to help make her entrée into Newport society smoother than it would've been without your assistance."

"Most of the time, my title is more of a hindrance than an asset," Derek said.

"Especially when he was on the marriage mart," Simon added, snorting with laughter.

"Especially then."

"The desperation," Justin said, "the mothers, the beautiful debutantes. It was all so *arduous*."

"Enough out of you," Derek said with a playful scowl for his friend. "It was extremely arduous. Thank God I found Catherine digging on my land. She saved me from a lifetime of monotony with—"

"The braying donkey?"

Justin's comment set off a wave of hilarity among the men.

"Wait," Simon said. "What'd I miss?"

"Hours upon hours in more ballrooms than we can count," Aubrey said, "in which we entertained ourselves by listing the reasons certain debutantes were unsuitable for His Grace."

Never one to stand on formality, Derek frowned at the words "His Grace."

"He was particularly concerned about becoming shackled to the one who sounded like a braying donkey when she laughed," Justin said.

"Ah," Simon said, smiling. "I see."

"*You*, on the other hand," Derek said to his cousin, "managed to land the belle of the Season after attending exactly *one* ball. That's hardly fair to those of us who tolerated multiple Seasons and came home empty handed—for the most part, anyway."

"And thank God for that." Justin poured himself another drink before topping off the others.

"I did get extraordinarily lucky to find my Madeleine in a sea of people at the Crenshaw affair."

"You got extraordinarily lucky when I sent you to London to find out if anyone was looking for Catherine."

"That too," Simon said, grinning at his cousin.

"I still can't believe the three of you have abandoned me to marriage and left me to my own devices," Justin said glumly. "Just over a year ago, we were all free as birds, and look at you now."

"Happier than pigs in shit," Simon said.

"Hear, hear," Derek said, holding up his glass.

Aubrey touched his glass to Derek's and then Simon's. "I'll drink to that."

"Maybe we can find our boy Justin a nice American girl this summer," Derek said.

"Shut your filthy mouth," Justin retorted. "Justin is *just fine*, thank you very much."

The others laughed at his quick comeback.

Derek yawned dramatically. "I for one need to hit the hay. Lady Grace will be up before the chickens."

"Lady Grace has a perfectly capable governess to get up with her," Justin said. "Why don't you just admit that you want to get naked with your wife?"

"I want to get naked with my wife," Derek said, deadpan.

The other three howled with laughter.

Simon downed the last of his drink, snuffed out his cigar and pointed to his cousin. "What he said."

Aubrey rose. "I'm off to bed as well. Will you be all right on your own, Justin?"

Justin waved him off. "I've been traveling with the lovebirds for weeks. I've become adept at entertaining myself."

"Very well then. We shall see you in the morning."

"Good night."

For a moment, Aubrey felt bad about leaving Justin alone, but when he thought of Maeve asleep in their bed, he headed up the stairs, eager to be with her—even if she was asleep. He let himself into the dark room and made quick work of removing his clothing before stepping into the adjoining bathroom to brush his teeth.

When he slid between the cool sheets and reached for her, he found the other side of the bed empty. A beat of panic had him scrambling for the pull cord on the bedside light. He looked around frantically until he found her, asleep on the window seat. Aubrey got up and went to her, noting the odd angle of her head and neck. She would feel that in the morning if he didn't make her more comfortable. Moving carefully, he slid his arms under her and lifted her to carry her to bed.

She roused when he set her down on the mattress, looking up at him with sleepy, confused eyes.

"Sorry to wake you, but you would've had a terrible knot in your neck if you slept like that all night." He kissed her forehead and pulled the covers up and over her.

"I was looking out at the moon and stars and must've fallen asleep."

"Close your eyes and go back to sleep." He went around the bed to get in the other side, sliding an arm around her and breathing in the scent that drove him to distraction.

"All is well with your guests?"

"All is well."

"You had a nice time with the men?"

"I did. They're some of my favorite men, and as I predicted, Derek is very eager to assist with your situation."

"Oh. You told him then?"

"I did. I hope that's all right. We had discussed requesting his assistance."

"It's all right. Do you think . . ."

"What, love?"

"That he will mention it in front of your mother and sisters?"

"I'm all but certain he never would, but tomorrow I'll ask him and the others again for their discretion."

"That would be for the best."

"Try not to worry. Everything will be fine. I'll see to it."

"What if you can't see to it? What if you're not with me and they find me? What if—"

"Maeve, sweetheart, please don't think like that. I'll spend every waking minute by your side if that's what it takes to ensure your safety and peace of mind. There's nowhere I'd rather be than by your side anyway, so it wouldn't be a hardship of any kind."

"It's sweet of you to make such an offer, but it's not realistic. Just this evening, you were off with your friends—"

"I didn't have to do that. I could've stayed with you."

"They have come all this way to spend time with you. Of course you should be with them. I was merely pointing out the futility of such a plan."

"It hurts me to know you're unsettled. I want you to be happy and at peace."

"I don't want you to be hurt by my concerns."

"I can't help it. If you hurt, I hurt."

"I ask myself . . ."

"What?" He felt breathless waiting to hear what she would say.

"What I did to get so lucky to find such a devoted, wonderful husband."

"All you had to do was come here where I was lucky enough to find you wielding that massive feather duster."

"You'll never forget that feather duster, will you?"

"How could I? It played a role in the most important moment of my life."

"You honestly feel it was the most important moment of your life?"

"I absolutely do."

"That is very sweet of you to say."

He cupped her cheek and stroked her soft skin with his thumb. "I wish there was something I could say to ease your worries."

"It helps that you're here and that you're trying to help. I don't know what I'd do if I had to face this on my own."

"You already faced the worst of it on your own. I have every confidence that you could handle any challenge that comes your way. Your resilience is admirable."

"I like the way I look to you."

"I would hope that someday you would see yourself as I do—strong, endlessly capable, resilient, determined, lovely, sweet." He punctuated his words with a soft kiss. After a long, contented silence, he said, "Tell me more about your life in Ireland, before your marriage. I want to know everything."

"I told you I have three younger sisters."

"Bridget, Aoife and Niamh."

"Your memory is quite good."

"I remember everything you've ever said to me. Tell me more."

"We had a lovely upbringing in Dingle, close to our extended family that included both sets of grandparents, aunts, uncles and lots of cousins who were close in age."

"That must've been fun."

"It was. We were together all the time."

"Did you like school?"

"I loved it. I did very well in all my subjects."

"I have no doubt. What was your favorite?"

"I liked mathematics."

Aubrey groaned. "I knew there had to be something about you that wasn't perfect."

"I take it you did not like maths?"

"It was my nemesis all the way through university. I just was terrible at it. But I did very well with Latin and history and I was told I was an excellent writer on more than one occasion."

"My best subject was religion. For a time, I thought about entering into the holy order."

"Is it all right to say I'm extremely thankful that you didn't?"

She offered a small smile. "Sometimes I think I would've been better off. The fact that I'm responsible for taking another's life weighs heavily on my soul."

"I'm sure it does, but you should take comfort in knowing that you did what you had to in order to protect yourself from someone who would've thought nothing of taking your life."

"That brings small comfort. I fear that I'll be damned in the afterlife for breaking one of the Ten Commandments. Thou shalt not kill."

"Maeve, sweetheart, I have to believe that God would forgive you for defending yourself. You did what anyone would do when faced with certain death."

"I guess I'll find out when I reach the afterlife."

"Which will be many, many, *many* years from now, during which you will absolve yourself of your sin over and over again by performing acts of kindness. By the time you reach your day of judgment, there will be no doubt whatsoever about where you belong."

"I hope you're right."

"I'm almost always right. The longer we are married, the more you will realize that."

She laughed—hard, which delighted him. Making her laugh had become one of his primary reasons for being. "I had no idea you had such a large opinion of yourself, Mr. Nelson."

"Sure you did, and don't call me Mr. Nelson. That's my father."

"How is he feeling? I've hardly seen him since the family arrived."

"He is declining by the day. My brothers and I fear he won't last the summer."

"And the doctors can't do anything?"

"Unfortunately, they believe that by the time he began showing symptoms, his illness was too far advanced to be treated. I spoke at length with my brother Anderson about it two days ago, and he and Alfie have taken on nearly all of my father's duties within the company. They are looking forward to my return after the Season. Had I not invited friends to join me here, I'd be on my way back to New York now."

"I'm sorry to hear he's declining so rapidly."

"As am I, but I'm glad he could be here with us for the summer. Perhaps the sea air will prove restorative to him."

"I'll pray for him."

"Thank you." He caressed her back in small smoothing circles. "Tomorrow the Season begins in earnest. I've hired Mrs. Allston's niece, Kathleen, to be your maid. She has extensive experience working in other Newport households during the Season and will make sure you're properly prepared for every event."

"It would be fine with me, you know, to not participate

in the Season. I could stay here while you accompany your friends."

"It might be fine with you, but I'd like to show off my beautiful new wife and introduce her to friends."

"They will never accept me."

"We don't need them to accept you. I accept you. That is the only thing that matters."

"We both know that is not true."

"Maeve, sweetheart, it's the absolute truth. I do not care about society. I do not care what anyone thinks of me or my choice of a wife. We will go through the motions during the summer. We will enjoy our time with Derek and Catherine and the others, and we will spend as much time alone together as we possibly can. If or when it gets to be too much for you, all you have to do is look to me. I'll be your port in the storm."

"You make it sound so simple."

"It can be simple. No one can touch us unless we let them, and I, for one, will not let them."

"The women will be vicious. That is how they are."

Aubrey sighed, knowing it was true. "Stay close to Catherine and Madeleine. They will not allow anyone to disparage you."

"That is an awful lot to ask of two women who have only just met me."

"They like you, but they would do it for me. That is what friends are for. When Derek fell terribly ill with influenza, Justin and I were there for Catherine."

"I didn't know he was ill."

"It was dreadful. We were so certain we were going to lose him."

"Oh my goodness."

"The night he became ill, we carried him to an icy bath that helped to lower his fever. There is nothing I wouldn't do for any of them, and I know they return the sentiment. When I tell you they will care for you, I'm sure of it. Remember, too, that Catherine has no patience for the nonsense that perpetrates so-called polite society, and she will not allow anyone to be unkind to you. She and Madeleine were not raised in the aristocracy. Catherine wears her new title somewhat uncomfortably, going through the motions because it's expected of her, not because she necessarily enjoys it. When you get to know her better, you will discover that most of the time she'd much rather be curled up with her husband and daughter or a good book and a cup of tea than hobnobbing with snobs."

"Thank you for trying to make me feel better. No one has ever been as concerned about my well-being as you are."

"I'll always be concerned about your well-being, my sweet. It's my job as your husband to make sure you're happy. That is my most important job of all." He kissed her lips, the tip of her nose and both eyelids. "Now close your eyes and get some rest." He kissed her button nose every chance he got now that he was allowed to.

With his arms around her and her head cushioned by his chest, Aubrey was relieved to feel her relax into sleep sometime later. He would give everything he had to protect her from ever being hurt again. So many of the Season's events kept the men and women separate, which meant he couldn't be there any time she needed him. While he was confident that Catherine and Madeleine would be good friends to her, he couldn't help but fear that others wouldn't be so kind.

Chapter Sixteen

Maeve slept fitfully and woke to whispered voices. Aubrey stood fully dressed by the doorway, conferring with someone. She sat up, ran her fingers through her hair and tried to prepare herself to face this day. In all her life, she'd never imagined a scenario in which she'd be participating in the Newport Season as a member of society rather than as a member of the working class.

Despite Aubrey's thoughtful assurances the night before, Maeve had few illusions about how she would be received. People would be polite until she spoke and revealed her nationality. Her stomach turned with dread. While things had greatly improved for Irish immigrants coming to America since the Civil War, in which many Irish enthusiastically fought on behalf of the Union, they were still seen in many circles as "less than." This was especially true of Catholics like herself. Though many second- and third-generation Irish Americans had begun to gain political offices and other positions of prominence, the hundreds of thousands of Irish living in poverty and working in service helped to perpetuate the stereotypes.

Maeve had little doubt of how she would be received by the Knickerbocker set she had heard so much about from her benefactor in New York, who'd had nothing but disdain for the women who lorded over society.

Aubrey closed the bedroom door and came to the bed, sitting on the edge of the mattress. "Sorry if we woke you. Kathleen is here to help you prepare for the day, but first I've asked to have breakfast sent up."

"You didn't have to do that. I can go down."

"No need." He kissed her forehead. "You must allow me to pamper you."

"That doesn't come naturally to me. I'm used to working and contributing to the household. We were expected to help out at home."

"I understand this is a big adjustment for you, but over time, you will become accustomed to it."

"If you say so."

A smile lit up his lovely, kind eyes. "I say so."

A soft knock on the door had him getting up to receive her breakfast tray, which he brought to her, resting it on her lap.

"Have you already eaten?"

He expertly poured her tea. "Some time ago."

"I didn't hear you get up."

"You slept fitfully."

"I hope I didn't disturb you."

"I like being disturbed by you." When he was satisfied her tea had properly steeped, he stirred in the cream and spot of honey she preferred.

"You're exceptionally good at preparing tea."

"Two Seasons in London served me well."

He stayed with her while she ate the scrambled eggs, sausage, oatmeal and kidneys.

She glanced up at him. "This is an awful lot of food for one person. Won't you have a little?"

Aubrey shook his head. "You need sustenance to prepare you for a busy day."

The reminder of the day ahead had her stomach turning with nerves. "I think I've had all I can manage."

"If you're sure."

"I am, thank you."

"I'll take your tray down and tell Kathleen you're ready to get dressed."

"When will I see you?"

"At the luncheon on the Astors' steam yacht in the harbor. Derek, Simon, Justin and I'll meet you and the other women there."

Though Maeve had paid very little attention to the who's who of society, even she recognized the name Astor from the information her benefactor had shared in New York. The Astors were among the cream of New York society and presumably held the same stature in Newport.

Her breakfast wanted to come back up at the thought of having to socialize with people of that caliber. Of course, they would all know by now that Mr. Nelson had married the housekeeper and she could only imagine the things that were being said about her—and him.

She took a deep breath and released it slowly, determined to make an effort for his sake, but having no illusions about what this day might entail.

Kathleen came bustling in a short time later, a ball of energy and speaking in the accent of Maeve's home, as she got busy choosing attire from the wardrobes that had been packed with Worth gowns, gloves, hats and other items she would need for the multiple changes of clothing that would transpire each day. Kathleen told her a new outfit for every occasion would be required, along with matching hat and parasol, and as many as five pairs of gloves would be needed each day.

Maeve tried not to react with horror, as she didn't want to offend the young woman, who had expertise in the attire required for the Season. She knew she ought to be grateful, but all she felt was deep, pervasive dread over the entire production.

Her maid had dark hair contained in a neat bun, dark brown eyes and a keen fashion sense that would serve Maeve well. If she was going to be labeled an outsider, at least she would be wearing the latest fashions when she was ignored. To her credit, Kathleen never said a word about the elephant in the room—that an Irishwoman had married a man like Aubrey.

By a quarter to nine, Maeve was decked out in a yellow day dress for the morning drive on Bellevue Avenue that would take place, as Kathleen informed her, in a phaeton, preferred for the lower sides that allowed for the best view of everyone's outfits.

"The first time you pass a carriage, nod to any acquaintances," Kathleen said. "The second time you smile, and the third time, you look away. This is a very important tradition, and you must never allow your carriage to overtake a social superior, although with the duchess and her sister riding with you, everyone else is inferior."

Maeve listened to everything Kathleen told her, committing the rules to memory and hoping she wouldn't commit a faux pas that would be discussed for years to come. Although she'd already committed the greatest of faux pas by marrying Aubrey in the first place.

After the morning parade, the ladies would be conveyed to the Casino where they would watch the tennis matches and exchange gossip. After that, they would be taken to Bailey's Beach for ladies' swimming before luncheon onboard a steamship in the harbor, followed by a stop at the polo grounds to watch the matches and an afternoon promenade on Bellevue Avenue. The evenings would consist of five-course dinners, parties, weekly Casino dances, debutante balls, theatrical performances and midnight suppers.

Maeve was exhausted, and she hadn't even left the house for the first day of the two-month ordeal.

When Kathleen declared her ready, she steeled her nerves and headed downstairs. Naturally, the first person she encountered was her mother-in-law, who gave her a withering look that made her want to shrivel into a ball and hide in a corner. But then she remembered the things Aubrey had said to her, his sweet sincerity and desire to make their marriage successful. His affection gave her the courage to keep her chin up and meet Eliza's steely glare head on.

"Good morning, Mrs. Nelson." Maeve clasped her hands behind her back so the woman wouldn't see the way they trembled.

Eliza was about to say something when she apparently thought better of it, turned, and walked away.

"That was rather chilly," a voice behind Maeve said.

She turned to find Madeleine. "Oh hello. I mean good morning." The other woman's delicate beauty was on full display this morning with her light blue day dress perfectly complementing her dark blue eyes.

"Good morning to you, too."

"I'm sorry you had to see that." Maeve glanced in the direction Eliza had headed. "She is unhappy with her son's choice of a wife."

"Simon told me last night that Aubrey is positively smitten over you, and since we adore him, we adore you. Try not to worry. You're not without friends here."

"Thank you," Maeve said, genuinely moved by Madeleine's kind words, not to mention hearing that her husband was smitten over her. "I rather adore him, too."

Mr. Plumber gestured for them to head for the front door.

As she walked by, her arm linked with Madeleine's, the butler offered a wink and smile that further bolstered

Maeve's confidence. To know he was pulling for her helped to settle her nerves somewhat.

Catherine was already in one phaeton while Aubrey's sisters occupied another.

Wiggie and Kaiser were there to help them into the vehicles.

"You look mighty fine, Mrs. Nelson," Wiggie said.

"Mighty fine indeed," Kaiser said.

"Thank you both," she said, taking a seat across from Catherine and Madeleine.

When they were ready, the driver—a man Maeve didn't recognize—took the reins and directed the matched pair of horses down the driveway toward the avenue.

"I did a lot of research about Newport prior to our visit," Catherine said.

"She reads *everything*," her sister added in a teasing tone.

Catherine raised a brow in her sister's direction. "How else would we know what to expect?"

"How else indeed." Madeleine gestured for Catherine to continue. "Educate us."

"It's all about the women in Newport. The men are mostly absent during the week and take the Fall River boat up from New York on weekends and often leave before dessert is served on Sundays to return to the city for another workweek. In addition, since there is nothing else of import occurring during the summer in Newport, society is all there is. No business is conducted or stock market or any of the other distractions that are part of life in New York. Here it's all about socializing and the women are in charge. Three in particular—Mrs. Astor, Mrs. Mills and Mrs. Goelet. They decide who is *in* and who is *out*, and from what I read it can take five years for someone to work their way into proper Newport society, and even after putting in all that time, there is still no guarantee of success."

"Why would anyone care to bother?" Madeleine asked, her lips pursed with distaste.

"You know why," her sister said. "It's all about prestige."

"Eh." Madeleine waved her hand disdainfully. "Who cares?"

"These people care greatly," Catherine declared as women in every carriage they encountered waved to them, hoping to gain the duchess's attention.

"How do they know it's you?" Maeve asked, fascinated.

Catherine returned every wave she received. "I presume they know everyone else, so they have identified me through the process of elimination."

Maeve chuckled softly. "I'll never understand how all of this works."

"Don't worry, dear." Madeleine patted Maeve's knee. "We don't understand either."

The three of them shared a laugh that further settled Maeve's uneasiness. To have two such wonderful allies and friends as they headed into "battle" was truly a blessing to behold.

"May I speak to you about a matter of somewhat grave concern?" Maeve asked the question hesitantly, but Aubrey had assured her she could trust these women, and she was about to take his word for that.

"Of course. Madeleine and I hope the three of us will be the best of friends."

"You have no idea how much I appreciate that."

"We have a small idea," Catherine said. "Two years ago, we were living in a tiny village with our mother and father, who was the village blacksmith. Today, I'm married to a duke and Madeleine is married to his cousin. We understand what it's like to be thrust into something for which you're woefully unprepared."

"I suppose you do understand."

"What is troubling you?" Madeleine asked, her kind eyes portraying nothing but sincere concern.

"Mrs. Nelson."

Catherine's delicate brows furrowed with confusion. "Aubrey's mother? She seems like a nice enough lady."

"How can I say this tactfully?"

"Is she putting on a show for Aubrey's illustrious guests?" Madeleine asked.

"*Yes*." Maeve liked Madeleine more with every minute she spent in her presence. "You must never let on that I told you this, but the previous Newport staff disliked her so intensely, they left the windows open for the entire winter. They put food in her room to ensure total destruction."

"Good lord," Catherine whispered.

Maeve spoke in a low tone. "By all accounts, the woman is a monster."

"She'd have to be for her staff to react that way," Madeleine said.

"Needless to say, she was apoplectic when she heard that Aubrey had married the Irish housekeeper. But since then, she's been . . . quiet. Which has me worried—"

"About what she is planning," Catherine said, nodding. "I would be concerned, too."

"This is not something I can discuss with Aubrey. While he is well aware of his mother's shortcomings, she is still his mother."

"That is true," Madeleine said. "It's indeed a predicament."

Their support gave Maeve the courage to air out her greatest fear. "Not for one second do I think she is going to peacefully accept his choice of a wife and carry on as if nothing untoward has occurred."

"I believe you're right to be concerned," Catherine said.

"I expect whatever she does to be cataclysmic, something

so grave as to drive a permanent wedge between Aubrey and me."

"He won't let that happen!" Madeleine's outburst took the other two by surprise. "I told you what Simon said. He is positively smitten with you."

"Derek said the same. He said the last thing he expected when he came to Newport was to find Aubrey married, but he couldn't deny that his friend seems deeply pleased with his choice of a wife."

"It's nice to hear that from people who know him so well. I find myself equally surprised most of the time by everything that has happened. From the day we met, there was something different about him and how I felt when he was around."

"I know that feeling," Catherine said with a small, intimate smile. "I met Derek when I was delirious with fever and was instantly attracted."

"The same with my Simon, although I didn't have a fever. However, being around him made me feel quite feverish in an altogether different way."

The three women giggled like schoolgirls.

"Aubrey told me I would adore you two, and he was absolutely right."

"We adore you right back," Catherine said. "In my new life, I have found it difficult to find genuine people who are unaffected by the trappings of wealth and society. It's indeed refreshing to find a true friend in you, Maeve, and I mean that sincerely."

"I feel the same way. I'm thankful for both of you. I couldn't face this day or this Season without your support."

"We'll be right there with you through it all," Catherine assured her.

"What exactly is the point of this outing we are on?" Madeleine asked as they pulled up to the Casino.

"I believe the goal is to see and be seen," Maeve said. "And everyone who is anyone wants to see the two of you."

"Oh joy," Catherine said as her companions laughed.

With the two of them by her side, this day was looking far less daunting to Maeve.

Chapter Seventeen

Aubrey spent the morning reviewing the cables he'd received from his brothers in New York, providing business updates that he was to pass on to his father, all the while fretting about how Maeve was faring with the sharks.

Worrying about people being unkind to her had him on the verge of doing something stupid, such as venturing to the Casino to check on her during the period of the day that was reserved for the women.

He couldn't bear the thought of people shunning her, simply because she was born in Ireland and had been their family's housekeeper. Although, he knew it was foolish to expect her to get a rousing welcome. Hopefully, Catherine and Madeleine would provide a suitable buffer, but still he worried.

Perhaps he shouldn't have encouraged her to fully participate in the Season. He should've kept her at home with him where he could protect her from the vipers. Except, the biggest viper of all was living in this house, and her unusual reticence had him on edge. He knew better than to expect that his mother would passively cede to his choice of a wife and allow them to live happily ever after, and her silence on the matter had him on edge.

He'd told Maeve they would stand up against any obstacles

together, and he'd meant it, but that didn't mean he wasn't worried about what those obstacles would be.

Taking the cables from his brothers, he went upstairs to his father's room and knocked softly on the door, hoping he wasn't waking him.

His father's devoted valet, Harrison, answered the door. "Good morning, Mr. Nelson."

"Good morning, Harrison. Is my father up for a visit?"

"He is. Please come in. While you're with him, I shall venture downstairs to fetch him some herbal tea."

"Very good."

"If you could stay until I return, that would be appreciated."

"I will." Realizing that Harrison didn't want his father left alone only added to Aubrey's already considerable anxiety. Had it come to that? Was his father so bad off that he couldn't be alone? Aubrey closed the door behind Harrison and went to his father's bedside.

Anderson Nelson Senior had his eyes closed and his hands crossed at his lap. Seeing him propped against the pillows, Aubrey noted the sallow tone of his father's complexion and that he'd lost more weight he couldn't afford to lose. Not wanting to disturb him, Aubrey took a seat next to his father and read through the cables from his brothers Anderson and Alfie again:

> NEW ORDER FOR A DOZEN REFRIGERATION CARS
> FROM HORMEL, WILL NEED TO ADD ANOTHER SHIFT
> TO THE PRODUCTION LINE. PLEASE ASK FATHER TO
> AUTHORIZE ADDITIONAL COST.
>
> MEETING WITH MEMBERS OF VANDERBILT FAMILY
> THIS WEEK ABOUT NEW TRAVEL CARS. ALFIE
> TRAVELING TO SAN FRANCISCO NEXT WEEK TO TAKE

MEETING WITH UNION PACIFIC, WHICH NEEDS NEW
PROVIDER OF COUPLINGS AND COMPONENTS. IF HE
LANDS THAT ACCOUNT, WE WILL NEED TO QUICKLY
MOVE FORWARD WITH CONSTRUCTION OF SECOND
PLANT TO MEET INCREASED PRODUCTION DEMANDS.

HEARD YOU GOT MARRIED. WHAT THE HELL,
AUBREY? REQUIRE DETAILS IMMEDIATELY. HOW
IS FATHER?

The business was clearly booming, which was one thing
to be thankful for, Aubrey thought, amused by his brothers'
request for information about his marriage. He wasn't surprised they had gotten the news. They stayed in close touch
while the rest of the family was in Newport. In fact, he
fully expected his brothers to make a rare appearance in
Newport to meet his new wife.

Aubrey was a decade younger than his older brothers,
but the three had become closer after working together in
the family business. Anderson and Alfie had come to rely
on Aubrey's business acumen, not to mention the contacts
he'd developed as someone who participated in society,
which they actively shunned. Perhaps they had the right
idea. After this summer, Aubrey and Maeve would be stepping away from society to focus on more important things,
such as starting a family.

His father came to, clearing his throat and opening his
eyes. "Morning, son."

"Morning, Papa." He hardly ever called him the name
they'd all used as children, deferring to "Father" most of
the time. But seeing as they were alone, Aubrey went
with the more personal title, pleased when his father's lips
curled into a small smile.

"Been a while since any of you called me that." He

grimaced as he tried to find a more comfortable position. "I've missed it."

"I have, too."

Nodding to the papers Aubrey had brought with him, Anderson said, "What've you got there?"

"Cables from New York." Aubrey read them to his father.

"That's some excellent news about Union Pacific and Hormel."

"Indeed, it is. The business is growing faster than expected."

"The railroad is opening up the country to the kind of commerce and travel that was all but impossible before. It's an exciting time, to be certain. I wish I was going to be here to see what becomes of it all."

"Don't say that. You were well enough to make the trip to Newport. Surely that's a good sign."

"I made the trip because I wanted to be with you all when I draw my last breath."

"Papa—"

"Aubrey, listen to me. I don't have much time left, and there are things we must discuss."

Aubrey didn't want to hear that. He couldn't imagine life without his father, but he also couldn't deny the obvious evidence that his father was far more ill than he'd previously let on. "What things?"

"Your wife, for one thing."

That was the last thing he'd expected his father to say. He'd anticipated something about the business. "What about her?"

"Your mother is very angry that you married the Irish housekeeper."

"I'm sure she is, but that doesn't mean—"

"Aubrey, listen to me!"

Taken aback by his father's forceful statement, Aubrey sat back in his chair and crossed his arms. "I'm listening."

"She's not going to take this lying down. You must be vigilant and pay close attention to everything she says and does. She is determined to rid you of this woman, no matter what she has to do."

Shock reverberated through Aubrey. He'd known she would be unhappy, but never for a minute did he imagine anything like what his father was telling him. Although, in light of the nightmare he'd found when he arrived in Newport, he probably should've considered that possibility. His stomach began to ache like a bastard. "What is she going to do?"

"I don't know, but you must be vigilant. The first day we were here, I saw how you looked at your wife, and I can tell you're happy."

"I'm happy. I love her, Papa."

"Then you must protect her. Get her out of this house, away from your mother."

"That's not possible. I have guests who've come for the summer."

"Take them with you and go, Aubrey. Go before it's too late."

"Papa, please don't overly excite yourself."

"I fear you're not taking me seriously, son."

"I'm taking you very seriously. I just don't know what to do. Derek, Catherine and the others have traveled so far to be with us this summer."

"From what you have said of Derek, he is a man who protects the ones he loves. I would think he'd be keen to help you do the same."

Aubrey was reeling from the things his father had said. "You honestly think she would hurt me that way, Papa?"

"I honestly think she would do anything to preserve her

social standing, even at the expense of her own son." Anderson sagged into the pillows, seeming to have spent his small reserve of energy. His eyes closed and within seconds he was asleep again, his chest rattling with the dreadful sound that had become so familiar to them in recent months.

Aubrey was still contending with shock and confusion—and dread—when Harrison returned.

"Ah, good. He is resting." The older man sounded relieved. "He's been extremely agitated, which is new. I fear he hasn't much time left. I've read about the agitation increasing when the end is near."

"When you say agitated, how do you mean?"

"He's extremely concerned about things that aren't going to happen, such as the house burning down the way the first Breakers did. He's concerned about the company going bankrupt and his children falling on hard times—all things that aren't going to happen. I've tried to reassure him that all is well, but he's become increasingly paranoid."

Aubrey was actually relieved to hear that, since it would explain the things his father had said about his mother. Although painfully aware of her many faults, Aubrey couldn't imagine her deliberately hurting him. "I'm going to leave him to rest. Please let me know if either of you need anything."

"I will, sir, thank you."

"No, thank you, Harrison, for your dedication to Father. We all appreciate it."

"He's a great man, and it's my honor to serve him."

Aubrey shook the man's hand and then left the room, feeling unsettled by the conversation as much as his father's declining health. He'd held out hope that his father would rebound after the latest treatments, but it was now clear that they hadn't had the desired effect. There could be no denying the inevitable now, and Aubrey needed to notify his brothers, so they could come to Rhode Island to say good-bye to their father.

After yet another morning promenade, Maeve begged off on the daily trip to Bailey's Beach. The smell of the seaweed turned her stomach, which had gotten touchy lately. While wondering where Aubrey had gotten off to, she wandered down to the kitchen to visit Mrs. Allston and was pleased to find the older woman alone.

"This is a nice surprise," the cook said, her face alight with pleasure.

Hearing the sound of home in the other woman's voice had been a comfort to Maeve from her first days in Newport. "I don't mean to disturb your work."

"It's no bother. I've been hoping to see you." The older woman dried her hands on a dish towel and took an assessing look at Maeve. "Marriage seems to be agreeing with you."

Maeve's face flushed with predictable heat. "I quite like being married to Mr. Nelson."

"He does seem like a sweet sort and keeps his word, too." Mrs. Allston lowered her voice. "Haven't seen hide nor hair of the missus since she arrived, thank goodness."

"Oh, that's very good news indeed."

"Is she treating you all right?"

Maeve glanced over her shoulder to make sure they were still alone. "She mostly ignores me, but I don't delude myself into thinking that'll last forever. It's only because of the duke and duchess that she's tolerating me at the moment."

"Perhaps she also sees that her son has tender feelings for you."

"I highly doubt she cares about such pedestrian things as feelings."

Mrs. Allston cut a piece of chocolate cake and slid it across the counter to Maeve. "This'll make what ails you better."

"You know me too well, Mrs. Allston."

The older woman smiled and served up tea for both of them.

"How's the new housekeeper working out?" Maeve asked between bites.

"She's no Maeve Brown, but she'll do."

Maeve took pleasure in the compliment. "I so appreciate your many kindnesses to me, Mrs. Allston. I'm sure you've been shocked at times . . ."

Mrs. Allston reached across the counter to cover Maeve's hand with her work-roughened hand. "I can see that you and Mr. Nelson are happy, and it makes me happy to see good people get what they deserve."

"Thank you," Maeve said softly.

She would never know what she'd done to deserve Aubrey Nelson, but she would be thankful for him for the rest of her days, no matter what became of them.

After another week of morning carriage rides, trips to the Casino and Bailey's Beach, regular stops at the Worth boutique to see what had arrived from New York, luncheons aboard steamships in the harbor, polo matches, afternoon teas and long, leisurely dinners filled with laughter and teasing, Maeve had begun to relax somewhat. As Aubrey had predicted, the society doyennes were polite to her because everywhere she went, Catherine and Madeleine were with her—and they and the men from England were the toast of the summer Season.

Everyone wanted an audience with the duke and duchess, and if they had to go through a lowly Irish housekeeper who'd "married up," then so be it. To her amazement, she'd found herself actually enjoying the social interactions and meeting new and interesting people. She'd expected the Knickerbocker set to be nothing but snobs, and there were plenty of those, but among them were also people who had amazing stories to tell of travel and adventure and discovery.

Sir Walter Green, a dear friend of the duke's, had come for dinner two nights ago and had entertained them with stories of his archaeological dig in Africa that had yielded priceless artifacts from an ancient civilization. Derek had partially funded the expedition and had shared in Green's glory upon his victorious return from the Dark Continent. Both men were also friends and supporters of the Wright brothers, from Dayton, Ohio, who many believed were on the verge of accomplishing manned flight.

The dizzying speed of advancement, invention and commerce made for interesting and lively conversation around the dinner table. Maeve enjoyed listening to the various points of view and the opinions about President Roosevelt and his recent twenty-five-state tour that took him out west on the *Elysian*, a seventy-foot railway car from which he made speeches along the way.

"He's still making a case for last year's Reclamation Act," Aubrey said, noting the benefits to ranchers and farmers in the West who would share in the cost of building the irrigation systems called for in the act. "I think it's brilliant the way he's convinced those who will benefit most from bringing in the water to invest in the process."

"And in turn, we will all benefit by an improved food supply," Aurora said.

"Not to mention, Nelson Industrial will benefit from

increased demand for our refrigeration cars," Alfie noted. He and Anderson had arrived two days earlier to spend time with their ailing father.

"However," Anderson Junior said, "he is increasing scrutiny of big business." The family called him Junior, but only when his father was present. He and Alfie were dark-haired and handsome like Aubrey, but in Maeve's opinion, her husband was the most handsome of the three brothers. She could look at him all day and never get tired of the sight of him.

"Only in how it affects regular citizens," Aubrey said. "I don't believe he's looking to limit commerce, but more to make business responsible to their communities, which is a fair ask."

"He is so much bluster," Eliza said in her haughty British accent. "So uncouth and uncultured."

"People like him because he's real, Mother," Aubrey said.

"The British find him to be an interesting character," Derek said. "A man of the people."

"They say he has charisma and is reshaping the presidency for the modern times," Alfie said.

Eliza dismissed their comments with a roll of her eyes. "He's everything America and Americans are known for—boorish, uncivilized, vulgar."

"You're aware, Mother, that your husband and seven children are Americans, aren't you?" Anderson asked.

"I'm *painfully* aware of that," Eliza said.

"America has been very good to our family," Alfie said. "We should be counting our blessings."

"Hear, hear," Aubrey said, earning a glare from his mother. Under the table he reached for Maeve's hand and linked their fingers, giving a gentle squeeze that set off flutters inside her. How he did that so effortlessly was a source of continuing fascination for her as no other man had ever had such an effect on her.

She sent him a warm smile that he returned and the connection between them crackled like a radio seeking reception. When he looked away to reply to his sister, Maeve caught Eliza staring at her with abject hatred. Maeve's entire body went cold in the second her gaze was trapped in her mother-in-law's evil net.

She actually shivered.

"Are you all right, my dear?" Aubrey asked.

"I'm feeling a little off, actually. I think I'll retire early if you don't mind."

"Of course I don't mind." He kissed the back of her hand. "I'll be up to check on you shortly."

"Good night, everyone." Maeve made a hasty retreat and then hated herself for being so easily cowed by Eliza. She should've stayed and pretended to be unbothered by the other woman's hatefulness. Had Aubrey or anyone else seen the way she'd looked at Maeve? Probably not, because Eliza was nothing but careful in how she went about keeping her displeasure toward Maeve hidden from the others.

But Maeve saw it on a daily basis, and it was becoming ever more difficult to pretend that it didn't bother her. She kept telling herself she only had to survive the latter half of July and August. After that, she and Aubrey would go to New York where they would live alone in his town house without his extended family underfoot.

But with six more weeks in Newport to get through, she had cause to wonder how she would endure the other woman's hatefulness. If only she too had been born into an aristocratic family rather than the middle class, maybe Eliza could swallow her revulsion and tolerate her new daughter-in-law.

That, however, was a pipe dream. The woman would

never accept her and was probably biding her time until she found a way to convince Aubrey that he'd be better off without Maeve. She ached at the thought of him rejecting her, of him choosing his mother over her, which of course he would do. She was his *mother*. She wanted the best for him, and Maeve didn't come close to meeting Eliza's exacting expectations.

After changing into one of the silk nightgowns and matching robes Aubrey had bought for her, Maeve curled up in the window seat, which had become one of her favorite spots in the enormous house. The cozy corner reminded Maeve of her bedroom at home in Ireland, which had also included a window seat. Here she could look out over the vast ocean, lit by moonbeams, and wonder about her family back home in Dingle. Had Aoife and her husband Thomas succeeded in conceiving the child they wanted so badly? Had Bridget delivered her third baby, and had her husband's mother recovered from her recent surgery? Niamh would have graduated from school last month and would be looking for a job. How, Maeve wondered, was her father's gout and the arthritis in her mother's knee that pained her so?

Tears ran down her face as she stared out into the darkness. The ones she loved were on the other side of that vast ocean, but they might've been a million miles away. She missed them all terribly, as well as her familiar routine of helping to care for the neighbor's children, checking in on several elderly relatives and working as needed at the bank her father owned. It had been a small but satisfying life that had changed forever the day her father informed her that he'd given Mr. Farthington permission to court her.

She cringed at that memory, the first time her beloved father had ever asked her to consider the suit of a man. Prior to that, she had been courted by several of the boys she'd grown up with, but never by anyone she didn't know personally. For a while, she had thought she would marry her dear friend Padraig. But then he had taken his own life after realizing he was attracted to men, not women. His death had shaken her to her core, especially when people had briefly suspected her of having something to do with it. Only when one of his sisters had publicly speculated on the possible reason for his death did the gossip surrounding Maeve come to an end.

From the first time she'd met Farthington, shortly after Padraig's death, she'd been dazzled by the handsome, charismatic older man. Underneath his shiny veneer, however, she'd sensed a dark side that he kept well hidden. She'd tried to tell her father that, but he'd been so excited by the prospect of landing the Farthington family business for the bank that he'd been deaf to her concerns.

What he must think of her now. A sob escaped from her tightly clenched lips, and then Aubrey was there, kneeling beside her and drawing her into his warm embrace.

"My darling, whatever is the matter?"

"I'm feeling terribly homesick."

"Oh, my poor sweet." He rubbed her back soothingly. "I'm sure your homesickness is made more difficult being surrounded by Nelsons."

"Maybe a little. I do enjoy your family though."

"They enjoy you, too."

"They do?"

"Of course they do. My sisters think you're delightful."

That was news to her. While the Nelson sisters were never rude or dismissive the way their mother was, they weren't overly friendly either. They were, at best, polite and cordial. Without Catherine and Madeleine in her daily life, Maeve would feel truly lost in a sea of strangers with varying agendas. "They said as much?"

"Adele said she quite enjoys your company, and Alora noted how wonderful you are with the children."

"I adore them."

He wiped away her tears. "They adore you right back. James asked me earlier when you would play croquet with them again."

"They are far too good for me. I don't stand a chance."

"I think they enjoyed finally finding an adult they could beat."

Maeve laughed, which she wouldn't have thought possible a few minutes ago. Leave it to Aubrey to make her feel better. She caressed his face, running her fingers over the rough late-day whiskers on his jaw while he gazed at her with the wild hunger she'd come to expect from him. "You're very good at making me feel better."

"I never want you to be sad. You should've come to find me."

"It came on all of a sudden, and I knew you were enjoying time with your friends."

"Nothing is more important to me than my beautiful wife." He slid his arms under her, picked her up and carried her to bed. After helping her out of her robe and gown, he shed his own clothes and climbed in with her.

"You're taking an early night this evening." He often sat up with Derek, Simon and Justin until long after midnight.

"I came up to tell you some very big news. After dinner, we were playing billiards when Justin suddenly remembered where he had heard Farthington's name before."

Chapter Eighteen

Maeve gasped as shock rippled through her. Hearing the man's name was enough to make her blood run cold. "Justin knew of him?"

"Yes, he, Derek and Simon all felt the name was familiar the first time they heard it, but they couldn't place it. Justin was lining up his cue when he stood upright and said 'I've got it. I remember where I've heard of Farthington before.' It seems he was arrested in London several years ago for beating up a prostitute and leaving her nearly dead."

Maeve gasped.

"He was brought up on charges but managed to escape from custody before he could be tried. Once Justin mentioned this, Simon recalled hearing that the man is wanted in England and his company's ships were banned from British ports of entry."

"I can't believe this!"

"It's a pattern, Maeve. When he couldn't perform, he took his frustrations out on the woman. It wasn't just you."

She broke down into sobs that came from her very soul, the relief so profound it left her drained in the aftermath of the emotional outburst.

"There, there," he said softly. "Get it all out. You've been so strong and courageous. I'm so proud of how strong you've been."

"I haven't been strong. I'm terrified all the time that they are going to find me and take me home to hang."

He pushed the hair back from her face and kissed away her tears. "That's not going to happen."

"How can you be so certain?"

"Because we have the truth on our side—and a very well-regarded duke who has made quiet inquiries on your behalf."

"He has?"

"Yes, and he's got contacts in the highest corners of the Irish government. They've promised to do anything they can to assist his friend, the former Mrs. Farthington."

"I can't believe it, Aubrey. That he would do such a thing for me."

"My sisters aren't the only ones who find you delightful. My friends do as well, and Derek has no patience for bullies or men who would beat up a woman to make up for their own failings. Catherine was attacked by the man she was supposed to marry, and she too ran away to avoid her fate. The two of you have much more in common than you might think."

"I had no idea that she too had endured an attack."

"She would tell you that the attack led her to flee, which led her to Derek. I would say that Farthington's attack led you to flee, which led you to me. Happy endings in both cases."

"Well, in one case anyway. We don't know yet what will happen to me."

"We do know. You were attacked and defended yourself."

"It would be my word against his, and since he is not here to offer his input, I'll be seen as a heartless killer."

"I would be right there by your side to attest to the

injuries you still had when I met you." He kissed the palm of her hand where the new pink skin was still tender. "I don't want you to worry about anything. Whatever transpires, we will face it together."

"You make me believe that anything is possible. How do you do that?"

"The same way you make me believe in fairy tales and happily ever after."

"I do that?"

"Mmm-hmm." His lips brushed against hers, persuasive and seductive, and like every time he kissed her, she felt the impact of him from her scalp to the soles of her feet and everywhere in between. How did he do that with one soft kiss? "Close your eyes. Relax. Let me love you."

His use of the word "love" made her heart skip a beat. But before she could spend too much time thinking about whether he might actually love her, he was cupping her sensitive breasts, running his thumbs back and forth over the tips.

"So very lovely and all mine," he whispered as he drew her left nipple into his mouth while pinching the right one in a light squeeze.

The combination had her hips lifting off the mattress, seeking him. After weeks in his bed, she'd become accustomed to many of the things they did together, but she still flushed from head to toe when he kissed his way down her body, put her legs on his shoulders and opened her to his tongue. She would never get used to the nearly obscene way he used his lips, tongue and fingers to drive her mad.

He sucked on the tight nub of nerves that set her off every time he touched her there, making her cry out from the shocking pleasure that overtook her.

Maeve came down from the incredible high to find him watching her in that intense way of his.

When he smiled at her his entire face lit up. "Hello there."

"You seem rather pleased with yourself, Mr. Nelson."

He nuzzled her neck, taking a nibbling bite of her skin. "I'm incredibly pleased with myself—and yourself, Mrs. Nelson."

When he shifted to enter her, she stopped him with a hand to his chest. "Could I do to you what you did to me?"

He froze, his expression unusually blank.

Did he think her brazen for suggesting such a thing? "Never mind," she said, looking away. "I didn't mean to shock you."

"You didn't shock me. You aroused me so completely that all the blood in my body seems to be located in one place, leaving nothing to power my brain."

She glanced down to find his cock harder and larger than it had ever been, and how was that possible? How could it get *bigger*?

Aubrey released a tortured-sounding groan that alarmed her. "Please," he said softly but urgently. "Please do to me whatever you wish." He ran his fingers through her hair. "Nothing you do would ever be wrong."

Emboldened by his words and the tender way he touched her, Maeve gave his chest a gentle push to encourage him to lie on his back. He eyed her warily as he settled into the position, his hands grasping handfuls of sheet, as if he needed to hold on to something.

She sat up to study his chest and abdomen, trying to decide where she wanted to kiss first. His hard cock stretched nearly to his navel, and she watched with fascination as fluid appeared at the tip, pooling onto his stomach.

"Maeve," he said through gritted teeth, "are you going to just look, or do you plan to put me out of my misery?"

"Tell me what you like. I'll do whatever you want."

His sharp intake of breath had her glancing at his face, which was tight with tension. "I'm about to spend from merely thinking about your lips on my—"

She bent over him, wrapped her hand around the thick base the way he'd taught her to do, and took the tip into her mouth, sucking gently but insistently.

His fingers tangled into her hair, his hips came off the bed and he made sounds she'd never heard him make before. Emboldened, she took more of him into her mouth and lashed the tip with her tongue.

He moaned, and his fingers tightened in her hair nearly to the point of pain.

Maeve released him slowly, the tip leaving her mouth with a loud pop.

"Don't stop," he said, sounding desperate.

"I've no plans to stop." She moved so she was between his spread legs and bent over him again, this time cupping the soft pouch under his scrotum as she took his shaft into her mouth once again.

"Dear God," he muttered, his legs trembling violently as she sucked and licked with wild enthusiasm. "Maeve. Sweetheart, *stop*. That's enough." He tugged on her hair, trying to get her attention.

But she wouldn't be deterred from giving him the same pleasure he'd given her.

"*Fuck.*"

She'd never heard that word from him before, and knowing she'd driven him to vulgarity fueled her desire to give him everything. She squeezed, sucked and licked the soft skin until he exploded down her throat in a hot, scalding blast that she swallowed frantically.

"Holy Christ," he said as his body continued to seize

and tremble until he finally sagged into the mattress, seeming completely spent.

Maeve released his cock slowly, continuing to stroke him through the aftershocks that followed his release. When she finally looked up at him, she found him watching her with a nearly feral look in his eyes. "Did I do it correctly?"

He grunted out a laugh. "If you did it any more correctly, you might've stopped my heart." Reaching for her, he encouraged her to lie on top of him, and brushed the hair back from her face. "You're magnificent, and I want nothing more than to kiss your cock-swollen lips."

The things he said! Predictably, she felt the flush creep into her face as he kissed her senseless.

"How can you blush like that after sucking my cock until I exploded?"

"Do you have to be so vulgar?"

"It's not vulgar to speak to one's own wife about the things that transpire in the marriage bed. Now answer my question. How can you still be embarrassed after all the things we have done?"

"I'm not embarrassed, so much as shocked at my own behavior."

"Your behavior is quite shocking."

She poked him in the belly, making him startle and then laugh.

"But I wouldn't have you any other way. You're absolutely perfect."

"I'm glad you think so."

He held her close to him, running his hands over her back and down to cup her bottom. Between them, his cock hardened and throbbed against her belly.

"You have recovered rather quickly."

"That's all your fault. You're so soft and sweet, and I want you all the time." He gave her bottom a squeeze. "Sit up."

Aubrey helped her up, until she sat on top of him, her legs positioned on either side of his hips. She wasn't so far gone that she didn't immediately note the impropriety of the position. She would've moved to bring her legs together, but he stopped her. "Like this."

"Aubrey . . . You can't possibly think . . ."

"Shhhh. Trust me. Lift up a little."

"No . . . What . . . *Oh my goodness.*"

With his hands on her hips, he brought her down on his hard cock, pushing so far into her she could feel him in her belly. "That's it," he said tightly. "Just like that."

"This isn't decent."

"It's *so* decent." He raised his hips and surged deeper into her body, the base of his cock stroking the tender nub at the top of her sex, making her tremble.

"Aubrey . . ."

"Yes, love?"

"We can't . . ."

"We can." He held her hips and surged into her again. "We are. Ride me like a horse."

"*What?*"

"You heard me. Move your hips the same way you would on a horse."

"I *can't.*" The thought of it mortified her.

"You *can.*" With his hands on her hips, he guided her and helped her find a rhythm that felt shockingly good.

"I can't believe I'm doing this."

"Believe it, sweetheart." He encouraged her to move faster still and then reached between them to coax her to an orgasm that ripped through her like wildfire.

Her head fell back in complete surrender to him and the way he made her feel.

"You're perfection." His fingers dug into her hips to keep her from moving as he surged into her, finding his own release and then bringing her down to rest on his chest.

"You have made a complete doxy out of me."

His low laughter made his chest rumble under her ear. "I quite adore my wife, the doxy."

Maeve smiled at his predictable comment. "I didn't even know such a thing was possible."

"Wait until you see what else is possible."

"There's *more*?"

Aubrey ran his fingers through her hair. "So much more, and the good news is we have the rest of our lives to do it all."

One day at a time, one night at a time, one tender word at a time, one explosive encounter at a time, he was making her believe that they might just get that lifetime to spend together after all.

Eliza waited until everyone had retired for the evening to execute her plan. She crept down the stairs and into the kitchen, leaving the house through the servants' entrance and walking down the long driveway to the appointed meeting spot. Her lady's maid had followed her directions to the letter in arranging this late-night appointment.

The carriage awaited her outside the gate, the driver standing next to the open door. He nodded to her, held out a hand and helped her inside. When she was settled, he closed the door and a moment later the carriage began rolling toward town.

Her skin tingled with excitement and anticipation. It

had taken two full weeks to arrange this meeting, during which she'd had no choice but to bide her time and *tolerate* the former housekeeper her son had married. An Irish-woman, no less. Eliza shuddered. Everyone knew the Irish were good for cooking, cleaning and caring for newborns. One did not *marry* the Irish.

She would never forgive Aubrey for putting her in the position of having to defend his choice of a wife to New-port society. Everywhere she went this Season, people asked her about it, and every time she had to answer those questions, she became more enraged than she'd been before. How *dare* he do this to her? She seethed with outrage so all-consuming she could think of almost noth-ing else.

He had been given everything, including two Seasons in London during which he could've chosen an aristocratic wife, but to her great regret, he'd come home empty-handed both times. He had, however, made influential friends, and having the duke and duchess in residence was the only thing keeping her from total ruin this summer.

Without their illustrious guests, Eliza and her family would've been shunned by society. They wouldn't have been invited to any of the best parties or balls, and people would've looked the other way when they saw the Nelson family coming. They were being *tolerated* this Season, thanks to their guests, but what would happen next year?

She wasn't about to wait around to find out. No, she had to take action, and she had to take it now.

The carriage pulled up to the Marlborough Inn and came to a stop. When the driver—she couldn't recall his name—opened the door, he leaned in. "Are you sure you wish to get out here, ma'am?"

"Yes, I'm sure." Eliza didn't like being questioned by

anyone, particularly someone in service. She allowed him to help her out of the carriage. "Wait here. I won't be long." She breezed inside and looked around, her gaze settling on the man in the black suit sitting in the parlor, a glass of amber liquid in hand. She went into the room. "Mr. Dunleavy?"

He stood to greet her. "Mrs. Nelson, I presume?"

"You presume correctly. Please tell me you've brought the information I requested." The former Pinkerton inspector had come highly recommended.

"Please tell me you've brought the payment we discussed."

She handed him a bank draft, thankful to her father for having ensured that she had retained control over her own money after her marriage to the American, as she still thought of her husband after more than forty years of marriage.

Dunleavy carefully inspected the banknote before folding it in half and tucking it into the inside pocket of his coat. "Your son is married to a murderer."

Eliza stared at him. "I beg your pardon?"

"Maeve Sullivan, née Maeve Brown, née Maeve Nelson, murdered her first husband, a man named Josiah Farthington. She is wanted for murder in Ireland."

The ground seemed to shift under Eliza. She'd known there would be *something*, but murder? That had never crossed her mind. "You can't possibly be serious."

He handed her a folder. "It's all there, every sordid detail."

Eliza sat in one of the cheap armchairs and opened the folder, scanning the three-page report that laid out the case against her son's wife.

"There's more," Dunleavy said. "The innkeeper here told

me there was a man named Tornquist here a couple of weeks ago who'd been hired by Farthington's family to find the woman in question. Apparently, your son paid him off with the understanding that Tornquist would tell the Farthington family that he'd been thus far unsuccessful in locating her. Tornquist was rather indiscrete about his new-found windfall, flashing cash around left and right and not a bit reticent about how he'd come into the money. From what I was told, he's double dipping, keeping the Farthingtons on retainer and letting them think he's still looking for her when he isn't."

Eliza cringed. It was all so sordid, but then again, she'd known it would be. A mother of seven children developed intuition about such things. "So Aubrey knows that she"— Eliza had to swallow hard to keep her dinner from coming up—"*murdered* her former husband?"

"It would seem so."

Eliza couldn't believe what she was hearing. How could he have *married* a woman who was wanted for *murder*? Had he taken leave of his senses? "You have been very helpful."

"There's one other thing."

How could there be more? "What other thing?"

"I have made some subtle inquiries and, by all accounts, your son is quite taken with the woman he married, per-haps even in love with her."

Eliza scowled at him. "He's not in love. He's in lust with an Irish whore who was convenient. I never should've sent him ahead to prepare the house. That was a mistake, but I shall rectify that mistake with all due haste."

"As you wish, Madame. Do not shoot the messenger."

"Our business is complete. I trust I can count on your full discretion?"

"Of course. I'm nothing if not discreet."

Eliza rose to depart. "Thank you and good evening."

"To you as well."

She departed the squalid inn, feeling dirty for having spent even a few minutes there, and allowed the driver to help her into the carriage for the ride up the hill to the exclusive part of town where she belonged. In all her years of coming to Newport, she'd never been anywhere near the Marlborough Inn before tonight. That was just another reason to take issue with Aubrey, whose irresponsible actions had caused her such distress.

Years ago, she'd accepted that Anderson and Alfie probably wouldn't marry. Her two older sons were painfully shy around women, to the point that they'd retreated from society before they ever officially joined it. All her hopes had been pinned on Aubrey to ensure the continuation of the family name she alone had made prominent in society, and he had failed her so completely.

She needed to act and act quickly before he impregnated the Irish whore. Under no circumstances would grandchildren of hers be half Irish. The thought of such a thing gave her vapors even as she realized she might be too late to stop that secondary disaster. Every chance they got, or so it seemed to Eliza, Aubrey and that woman were sneaking off to be alone together, even with his friends in residence.

Thank goodness for the duke and duchess. They were the only thing standing between her and total ruin this summer. She walked a fine line in finding a way to dispose of the Irish whore without falling out of favor with Aubrey's illustrious friends. They would naturally side with him in any dispute. That, in and of itself, was laughable. He was a lowly American. She was the *daughter of an earl*. In her day, members of the reigning social class had taken care of one another. In these modern times, that was no longer true. No matter what happened, she had to keep the duke and duchess in residence until the end of August.

Hopefully by next summer, Aubrey's indiscretion would be replaced by someone else's and things could go on as they had in the past with her taking her place among the most respected members of Newport society. Even though her family could be considered second tier since their fortune was relatively new, she had been given her due as the daughter of a British earl and had enjoyed the acclaim that came with her title. But that could all be erased if the triumvirate turned against her.

The thought of her daughters and grandchildren being shunned because Aubrey had done such a foolish, selfish, thoughtless thing without a single regard whatsoever as to what his actions could mean for the rest of the family made Eliza feel ill.

No, she couldn't abide this, even if he had convinced himself he was "happy" with that woman, as if he had some sort of God-given right to happiness. She knew all too well what it was like to want someone with all her heart who didn't want her and then be forced to marry a much lesser choice. Aubrey was a fool brought low by a murdering whore, which was so very disappointing, but he certainly wasn't the first man to follow his baser instincts. She'd had such high hopes for him, her youngest and most favorite child. Soon her husband would be gone, and she would become the de facto head of the family. As such, she had to take steps to protect the Nelson name, such as it was.

Disposing of the murdering Irish whore would set things

to rights, as long as it could be done without displacing the duke and duchess.

Now she just had to figure out a way to accomplish both things at the same time—and quickly, before Aubrey could impregnate that dreadful woman.

Chapter Nineteen

Aubrey had never understood the expression "drunk on love" until he, himself, had been intoxicated by the incredible Maeve Sullivan Nelson. He was, quite simply, obsessed with his beautiful wife. No matter how many times they made passionate love, he wanted more. If he wasn't with her, he was thinking about her and counting the hours until he could be alone with her again.

With his friends in residence, he was forced to go through the motions of being a proper host, of ensuring his guests were happy and well entertained. However, after looking forward to their arrival for more than a year, he couldn't be less interested in doing anything that didn't also involve Maeve.

Fortunately, Derek and Simon were equally smitten with their wives and understood Aubrey's predicament— and even teased him about his obvious desire for his wife. The three couples and Justin had spent a delightful Sunday afternoon sailing in Narragansett Bay onboard the sleek, classic sailboat that Aubrey had named *Sundowner* before he'd met Maeve. Next Season, he would change the boat's name to honor her. Earlier that morning, he had accompanied her to mass at St. Mary's Church, on Spring Street and Memorial Boulevard. Though he was Protestant, he had indulged his Catholic wife's desire to attend mass, which probably had given his mother another round of fits when she heard where they had gone. Not that he cared. Whatever Maeve wanted he wanted, too. It was that simple.

"Tell me," Aubrey said to his friends that night over billiards, "does the marital madness become less so in time?"

"It hasn't for me." Derek aligned the cue with the ruthless precision that had him leading their summer billiards league by ten games over Simon, who was in second place. Not surprisingly, Aubrey was in last place because he couldn't care less about winning the games they played any chance they got between the seemingly endless social obligations. He cared only about *finishing* the games so he could join his wife in bed as early as possible. "If anything, the madness has become more so the longer we are together."

"For me as well," Simon said. "I'm well and truly besotted with my sweet Maddie."

"What a bunch of pathetic fops you've turned out to be," Justin said with his usual disdain for the lovelorn.

"So sorry to disappoint you, dear friend," Derek said with a big smile. "And I, for one, cannot wait to throw your words back in your face when you meet the one that turns you into a fool like the rest of us."

"Don't hold your breath," Justin muttered.

"We were just like you," Simon reminded him, "until lightning struck."

Justin stood next to the table, leaning on his cue. "Why do you think I prefer to be indoors?"

Derek barked out a laugh. "If you think you can avoid this sort of lightning by remaining indoors, you're the biggest fool of all."

Simon nodded. "He's right. I got struck in a ballroom, which you know because you were there."

"Yes, I was, and it was the most pathetic display I'd ever witnessed until we arrived here and were treated to Aubrey panting after poor Maeve like a bitch in heat."

Aubrey tugged dramatically at his collar, endlessly amused by his friends. "It's rather *warm* around here this summer."

"It *sure* is," Simon said. "Something about the sea air has made my wife even more *agreeable* than usual."

"Which is saying something," Derek said dryly. "From what I've witnessed at home, Mrs. Simon Eagan is nothing if not *agreeable* toward her husband."

"She does rather love me."

"Someone's gotta," Justin said, making the others laugh.

"You'd better watch out, Justin," Derek said. "You're beginning to sound like an old curmudgeon."

"I'd rather be an old curmudgeon than a pathetic, love-sick fop like the rest of you."

"We need to find him a companion," Aubrey said. "Perhaps if he was getting a little affection, he might not be so . . ."

"Grumpy?" Derek asked.

"Frustrated?" Simon posed.

"All of the above," Aubrey said.

"Sod off," Justin said. "The last thing I need is female complications."

"But those are the very *best* kinds of complications," Aubrey said.

Justin rolled his eyes. "You would say that, Mr. I-have-a-headache every day, three times a day."

Aubrey bent in half laughing because he couldn't begin to deny what Justin had said. He had gone to enormous lengths, even bordering on rudeness to his guests, to be alone with his wife. Despite the teasing, he knew none of them thought less of him for neglecting them at times to spend more time with Maeve. They were, after all, newlyweds.

When he'd recovered from the laughing fit and returned his attention to the billiards table, he was sobered by the nagging feeling that something was amiss, even in the midst of his pervasive happiness. "It's been too easy," he said, giving voice to his concern for the first time.

Derek's brows furrowed with confusion at the sudden change in tone. "What has?"

"Marrying Maeve. It's been too easy."

Justin bent over the table, the eight ball within his sights. "How do you mean?"

"Please don't misunderstand me. I'm delighted that Maeve has been so warmly received at the various events and that my sisters and the children seem to adore her nearly as much as I do."

"So what's the problem?" Derek asked.

"My mother."

"What about her?"

"She's been too quiet."

"Could it be she's preoccupied with your father's declining health?" Justin asked.

"I wish I could believe that, but she doesn't give a hoot about him. She's barely spoken to him about anything other than social obligations in decades. Even after Nelson Industrial became fabulously successful, she acted as if he'd done her a disservice by making her part of the nouveau riche. As you well know, there is nothing more bourgeois than new money."

"Ouch," Simon said. "That's cold. How did they end up with seven children if they barely speak?"

"We were all born in the first twelve years of their marriage, which we believe was the high point, if you will."

"Ah, I see," Simon said. "It's not as if your mother can do anything. You're legally married to the woman, whether she approves or not."

"There is so much she can do to undercut our union. I fear she is biding her time to make her move, hoping to ensure maximum carnage."

Derek tipped his head. "What can she really do?"

"I don't know, and that's what has me so unsettled. I know she's got to be planning something, but the not knowing has my nerves stretched to their limit. I suspect Maeve is equally concerned but doesn't speak of it to me out of respect for the fact that the woman is my mother, after all."

"Have you thought that maybe she is willing to accept and respect your choice?" Simon asked.

"Not for one second."

"That is a dilemma to be certain," Derek said. "Catherine tells me Maeve has been well received everywhere they have been so far this Season."

"Maeve believes that is because Catherine and Madeleine have made it their mission to make sure no one is unkind to her." The thought of anyone being unkind to her, even his own mother, was enough to make Aubrey want to commit murder.

"They do make for a formidable pair of bodyguards," Simon said, drawing a laugh from his cousin.

"Indeed, they do. I wouldn't want to cross the McCabe sisters," Derek said. "That's for certain."

"I hope you know how grateful we are to all of you for the way you've embraced Maeve. It means so much to us."

"You love her," Derek said. "That's all we need to know."

"Is that so very obvious?" Aubrey asked.

"As obvious as the nose on your face, old chap," Justin muttered. "You're like a lovesick puppy when she's around."

"That is not true!"

"Ah, well, it's kind of true," Simon said with a snicker.

Aubrey was about to protest when Plumber came in the room. "Pardon the interruption, but a cable has arrived that was marked urgent."

Aubrey took it from him. "Thank you, Mr. Plumber."

"Of course, sir." The butler turned and left the room.

Anxiety had Aubrey opening the envelope with the same caution one might give a container full of dynamite. What now? He read the brief message with a sinking feeling.

"What is it, Aubrey?" Derek asked.

"My God," Aubrey said, glancing at Justin. "I'm so very sorry to have to tell you that your father and brother were killed in a riding accident yesterday."

Justin's expression went flat. "*What?*" He shook his head as if he hadn't heard Aubrey correctly.

"None of the details were provided. That's all it says."

Justin found the nearest chair and landed hard, dropping his head into his hands.

Derek and Simon sat on either side of him, their hands on his shoulders.

"I'm so sorry, Justin," Derek said.

"What can we do for you?" Simon asked.

"What kind of riding accident could've killed them both?" Justin asked, his disbelief conveyed in his every word.

"I can't imagine," Derek said.

Justin looked up all of a sudden, his eyes gone wide. "Dear Christ, this means I'm the *earl* now." He moaned.

"*This cannot be happening.*" And then his shoulders heaved as a great sob shook him.

Derek moved quickly to wrap an arm around his friend while Simon patted him on the back.

Aubrey stood by, feeling inept and uncertain as to how to help. First thing in the morning, he would arrange transportation to get Justin home to England as soon as possible. That much he could do.

"I'm sorry." Justin wiped the tears from his face. "It's just such a shock."

"Of course it is," Derek said. "And please don't be sorry. You're among friends here. I just wish there was something we could do for you."

"I'm going to need you to tell me how to be an earl with holdings so vast it'll take the rest of my life to understand it all."

"That I can do. Whatever you need, whenever you need it."

"Thank you." Justin ran a trembling hand through his hair. "I suppose I'll need to go home then."

"I'll set up transport for you in the morning," Aubrey said. "I'd get you on the train to New York, but it's actually quicker from here to take the Fall River boat. From there, we'll book passage on the first liner headed to England. Don't worry about a thing. I'll take care of everything."

"That's very good of you. Sorry to ruin the party."

"You haven't ruined anything," Aubrey assured him. "We're just so sorry this terrible tragedy has happened to you and your family."

"It's truly a disaster," Justin said. "Father and Richard had heads for business, commerce, land management and everything aristocratic that I haven't the first bit of. The family will be ruined inside a year with me at the helm."

"That is not true," Derek said. "You will have my help and that of your many friends. You will not be alone in this challenge. I promise you that."

Justin wiped new tears from his face. "You have all been very kind, but I think I'd like to retire now, if that's all right."

"Of course," Derek said. "I'm right next door if you need anything during the night."

Justin went to the sideboard, poured himself a full glass of whiskey and raised it in toast to his friends. "I'll be all right. Eventually. Good night."

"Good night, Justin." When their friend had left the room, Aubrey took the seat he had occupied between Derek and Simon. "What a kick in the teeth."

"It's terrible," Derek said bluntly. "If there's anyone more woefully unprepared to step into this role, I'd be hard-pressed to think of who it might be."

"There is no one more unprepared," Simon concurred. "Justin has made a career out of avoiding responsibility. His father and brother have been aggressive in their efforts to expand the influence of the earldom. He will be stepping into rather big shoes, the poor guy."

"Worse yet," Derek said, "he has no interest in the role."

"Can he hire someone to oversee most of it?" Aubrey asked.

"He can definitely hire help," Derek said, "but he can't disengage entirely, which is what he will want to do."

"Gosh, all that on top of losing his father and brother," Aubrey said. "Were they close?"

"In their own strange way they were," Derek said. "Justin and Richard had nothing in common, but they got on rather well just the same, and his father was a good chap, always upbeat and smiling and fun to be around. It's a shocking loss no matter how you look at it." Derek sat up a little straighter. "I'm just remembering that Richard was due to be married in the spring."

"Oh dear," Aubrey said, sighing. "Such a terrible tragedy for everyone involved."

"I want to know what happened to them," Simon said.

Derek nodded. "As do I, but I suppose we'll find out soon enough. I'm going to head up to bed, too. I'll see you both in the morning."

"I'm with you, cousin. Good night, Aubrey."

"Good night." When he was alone, Aubrey poured himself a drink and took it with him when he left the billiards room and headed for the stairs, eager to be with Maeve, even if she was asleep. After receiving the dreadful news from England, he was out of sorts and sad for his friend. What a monumental challenge he faced once he returned home to a grieving family and a vast earldom in need of management from someone woefully unprepared for such a daunting challenge.

At the first landing, he encountered his mother, wearing a dressing gown as she headed down the stairs. "You're up late, Mother."

"Your father is having a difficult night. I thought some warm milk might help."

"I can go sit with him until you return." He visited his father no less than three times per day, but most of the time his father slept through the visits.

"No need. Harrison is with him."

"We have received dreadful news from England." He filled her in on the deaths of Justin's father and brother.

"They aren't leaving, are they?" She seemed horrified by the prospect of her illustrious guests departing prematurely.

"Justin will leave in the morning, but the others have said nothing about going with him."

"Thank goodness for that."

"My friend has lost two family members in a tragic accident, Mother. I find it disappointing that you're concerned about the Season at such a time."

Her eyes narrowed into the furious expression that had made his knees knock as a boy. "Are we talking about disappointments now, Aubrey?"

Thankfully, he was no longer a boy. "Something on your mind, Mother?"

"I want to know what the hell you were thinking marrying that woman." In deference to the sleeping household, she spoke in a low tone that was nearly a hiss.

"I married her because I wanted to. Not for any other reason."

"Is that right? So the fact that she stands accused of murder in Ireland had nothing to do with it?"

For a brief second, his brain went blank with shock, but he recovered before his mother could tell she'd shocked him—or so he hoped. "Of course you've hired investigators to find a way to discredit her, but I'll say this once—and only once—stay away from me and my wife, or else."

"Or else what? Perhaps you aren't aware that your father's will was updated a year ago, and once he passes, I'll control everything—the business, the money, all of it. So you'd do well to decide what's important to you before much longer."

Aubrey wasn't surprised to hear that his mother had seen to updating his father's will at the first sign of illness. "I already know what's important to me, Mother, and I'm afraid I'm going to disappoint you once again by saying good night. My wife is waiting for me in our bed, and I'd much rather be with her than arguing with you."

He left her on the landing and continued up the stairs, shaken by the ugly encounter as his father's warning echoed through his mind. Perhaps he should heed his father's advice and get out of there before she could do something to ruin everything for him and Maeve. Except, the only way his mother could succeed in ruining them was if they allowed it, and he had no intention of allowing her to do anything that would harm his marriage.

Chapter Twenty

Unsettled, Aubrey slipped into his darkened bedroom and closed the door behind him, leaning against it for a time to take several deep sips of whiskey. Closing his eyes, he felt the liquor move through him, heating him from within.

"Aubrey?"

That voice. That one in a million voice. "I'm here, love."

"Is everything all right?"

No, he wanted to say, it's not. *My mother is a monster and she's going to try to destroy us.* "Justin received some terrible news from home." He pushed off the door and went to the bed, sitting on the edge of the mattress.

"What happened?"

"His father and brother were killed in a riding accident."

"Oh no. Poor Justin."

"In addition to his obvious grief and heartache, this also means he is the new earl. He's rather overwhelmed by that prospect, to say the least."

"I'm so sorry for him."

"I am as well. He's such a good fellow. I hate to see him suffering."

"Will he leave to go home?"

"In the morning."

"One never knows what's coming next."

"That is very true. Often the not knowing can lead to beautiful things." To make his point, he reached for her hand and linked their fingers. "But not always."

"No, not always. I'm sorry your friend is sad."

"Thank you. I'm sorry, too."

"Do you want to come to bed?"

"Very much so."

She surprised him when she sat up, pushed the covers aside and went up on her knees to unbutton his shirt.

He was extraordinarily moved by her tender care and the way she touched him as she helped him out of his shirt.

"Lie back."

Aubrey put the glass on the table and did as directed, on fire with desire to know what she would do next. He wasn't disappointed when she released his belt and unbuttoned his pants. At her command, he raised his hips and allowed her to remove his trousers and unmentionables, leaving him bare to her curious gaze.

"You're so finely put together, Mr. Nelson."

He loved how she called him that now for effect, rather than out of formality. "I'm glad you think so, Mrs. Nelson."

"Everyone thinks so. I heard Abigail Gish discussing your fine physique during the Coddingtons' croquet party. She said you have a very tight derriere and wondered, aloud, if it looked as good unclothed as it does in trousers. I assured her it does."

Aubrey's face heated with mortification. "You did not!"

"I certainly did so. I won't have her discussing my husband's derriere as if I'm not standing right there."

His heart seemed to expand in his chest as he reached for her, wrapping his arms around her and burying his fingers in the thick silk of her hair. "You have made me happier than I have ever been."

"I have?"

"You have. You mustn't ever leave me. I would be entirely bereft without you."

"I . . . You . . ."

"Love you. I, Aubrey Nelson, have fallen deeply in love with my beautiful wife, Maeve Nelson, and I can't imagine a day—hell, I can hardly bear an *hour*—without her by my side."

Her eyes filled with tears as she stared at him, seeming stunned by his proclamation.

A nagging worry about whether he'd shown his cards too soon had him kissing her rather than waiting—hoping—to hear the same sentiment from her. What if she didn't feel the same way? He would die if she didn't love him. It was that simple. Judging by the way she kissed him, she had to love him. She just had to.

Tightening his hold on her, he turned them so he was on top, breaking the kiss to gaze down at her sweet face and eyes that seemed to see through to the very heart of him. As he made love to her, she gave him her body, but he wanted her heart and soul, too. Anything less wouldn't be enough.

In the morning, Maeve got dressed early to go downstairs with Aubrey to see Justin off. He looked dreadful. His eyes were rimmed with red, and his face bore the signs of a sleepless night. Her heart went out to him as she gave him a good-bye hug. "You'll be in our prayers."

"Thank you, Maeve. I'm glad I got to meet the woman who has made Aubrey so happy."

"I'm glad I got to meet you, too." She stepped back so the others could say their good-byes.

When she thought about the words her husband had

said to her in the dark of night, her heart beat faster and her mind raced with the implications. He loved her. He couldn't bear to be parted from her for even an hour. What had begun as a way to protect her had become something so much more than she ever could have imagined.

Despite his words of love and devotion, she remained unconvinced that those who truly mattered, including his own mother, would ever accept her as his wife. Having Catherine and Madeleine by her side at every social event this summer had made it impossible for anyone to be outwardly rude to her, for they feared offending her powerful friends far more than they disliked having her in their midst.

What would happen next summer when Catherine and Madeleine weren't there to smooth the way for her? Maeve shuddered imagining facing the social demands without her friends by her side. From every morning ride to every noon dip at Bailey's Beach where everyone complained about the rocks and the smell of the seaweed, to the picnics, luncheons, afternoon teas, visits to the Casino, dinner parties and formal balls, she had managed to survive only because of them.

The McCabe sisters had been formidable allies, making sure one of them was always with her, even if that meant missing out on a chance to dance with their husbands. They never left her alone.

Maeve had never in her life had friends quite like them and would be forever grateful for the way they had protected her this summer. She dreaded the day they parted company and she was left to face the mercies of a merciless group of people on her own. Aubrey would be there, of course, but so often the men and women were separated at events.

Her stomach turned at the thought of being left alone

with those people. She flattened a hand over her queasy abdomen. With every morning beginning that way lately and no sign of her courses, she'd begun to think she might be with child. Aubrey had long since stopped being careful about spending inside her, so it was entirely possible. She only wished she could allow herself to be excited about the positive things in her life—the love of a truly good man and now, the possibility of his child.

But underneath it all was the certainty that nothing this wonderful could possibly last.

As they waved to Justin when his carriage departed, Aubrey slipped his arm around her waist. She leaned into his comforting presence, wanting to steal every moment she could get with him while she still could.

They turned to go back inside and came face to face with Eliza, who trained her cold, unyielding stare on Maeve.

Did Aubrey see the way his mother looked at her? If he did, he didn't speak of it, but the enmity coming from her mother-in-law made Maeve's blood run cold.

"Good morning, Mother," Aubrey said.

"Good morning," Eliza replied. "He is off then?"

"He is. I was able to book him passage from New York to England tomorrow."

"It's a pity he had to leave. It would've been nice to have a duke *and* an earl in residence, especially for the Russells' ball tonight."

The tightening of Aubrey's hold on Maeve's waist was the only indication of his displeasure with his mother's comment. To his credit, he said nothing in response to her. After all, what could be said?

"Come, my dear," he said to Maeve. "Let's have breakfast."

They joined Derek, Catherine, Simon and Madeleine at

breakfast and then spent time on the back veranda with Aubrey's nieces and nephews as well as Derek and Catherine's baby daughter, Grace, choosing to skip the morning drive and the other customary social obligations that day so they could spend the time needed to prepare for the ball that evening.

"I read in the morning paper that Dr. Ernst Pfenning of Chicago has become the first owner of a Ford Model A," Aubrey said. "People are speculating that before long, everyone with the means will have one."

"Won't that be something?" Derek asked.

"I imagine it'll be chaotic with everyone running into each other," Aubrey said.

The others laughed.

"Until the government intervenes to figure out a way for people to get about without catastrophe," Simon said.

Maeve listened with interest to the conversation, but for some reason, the thought of the evening's ball had her on edge all day. While Aubrey went to visit his father, Maeve retired to her bedroom for some much-needed time alone before facing the crush of society that night.

She didn't expect to sleep but woke some time later to her husband's lips on her neck. His obsession with her neck continued unabated. Keeping her eyes closed, Maeve smiled. "I hope you're my husband."

"Who else would be kissing your neck?" He kissed his way from her throat to her ear, sending goose bumps skittering down her back. "Whoever he is, I'll run him through with the sharpest sword I can find."

"Is it time to get ready?" she asked with a sinking feeling of dread.

"Not quite yet, but I have good news I couldn't wait to share with you."

Intrigued, Maeve opened her eyes and looked up to find him smiling widely. "What news?"

"Derek received a cable from his contact at Scotland Yard. At his request, the Scotland Yard inspector reached out to the authorities in Ireland to make them aware of Farthington's assault on the London prostitute. In addition, he informed them of your side of the story, including Farthington's inability to perform sexually and his ensuing outrage each time he failed in that regard. That, along with my assertion about the burn to your hand that you were still nursing when we met and Derek's character reference has led them to drop all charges against you."

For a long moment after he finished speaking, Maeve could only stare up at him as she tried to process what he'd said.

"Did you hear me, sweetheart? It's over. You're free. We can go to Ireland to see your family."

Maeve broke down into deep, wrenching sobs that took them both by surprise as he gathered her into his embrace. Until he told her it was over, she'd had no idea how truly terrified she was of what might happen to her. If Tornquist had found her so easily, what would stop someone else from tracking her down? Now she could rest easy and it was all because of Aubrey and his friends.

When her sobs finally subsided, she drew back from him. "I'll never be able to properly thank you or Derek for what you have done for me. I was fully convinced I would never be free of the charges or ever see my family again."

He brushed stray hairs back from her face and kissed away her remaining tears. "You're free. *We* are free. There's nothing more to worry about."

If only she believed that to be true. But at least there was one less thing to worry about. A thought occurred to her that she had to share with him, even if he might not like it. "You married me to protect me. Now that I no longer require that protection—"

"Do *not* finish that thought," he said, scowling. "Did you hear what I said to you last night?"

"Yes," she said as heat crept into her cheeks. "I heard it."

With his fingers on her chin, he compelled her to look at him. "I meant every word, Maeve. Marrying you was the best thing I have ever done, and I don't give a flying fig about *why* I married you. That was just a convenient excuse for me to get exactly what I wanted most, which was *you*." He kissed her softly. "I love you. I'm in your thrall. I can't get enough of you."

"I love you, too."

How could she not love this kind, generous man who had helped to make all her problems go away while giving her every part of himself?

"You do?"

"I do."

"Maeve . . ." His voice caught, and his head dropped to her shoulder.

She ran her fingers through his hair, wishing they had nowhere to be so they could spend this evening together celebrating the end of her nightmare.

But that was not to be. Her lady's maid arrived a few minutes later to begin the arduous process of preparing her for the ball.

"We will finish this discussion later," Aubrey said in a low tone that only she could hear.

She shivered with anticipation of being alone with him. "I'll look forward to that."

He kissed her again. "Being alone with you shall be all I think about until such time as it happens." Aubrey nodded to Kathleen on his way out.

She took one look at Maeve's tearstained face and took

charge. "Come, Mrs. Nelson. We must get started right away."

Maeve dragged herself up and out of bed, fighting the pervasive exhaustion that came over her around this time every day lately.

Sitting at the vanity while Kathleen began with her hair, Maeve thought about the news Aubrey had brought her and the relief she felt at knowing she was no longer facing charges at home. But would her family welcome her after everything that had happened or were they embarrassed to be associated with someone who'd been accused of murdering her husband? Had she ruined her father's business with the Farthingtons' shipping company and would he forgive her for that? Those unknowns continued to torture her.

Her routine had become familiar by now. Before she allowed Kathleen to help her into her dress, she tucked the rest of Farthington's money into her bodice, as she had before every event during the Season, so it was always with her in the event that something happened that would require her to protect herself. She'd had nightmares about being sealed off from the house by Eliza's evil machinations and unable to get to her belongings, especially the money she had kept hidden even after she married Aubrey.

Having had to run for her life once before, she felt the need to be prepared for anything, especially in light of the way she'd caught his mother looking at her almost every day since the woman arrived in Newport—as if she wanted to gut her and feed her innards to the seagulls that swarmed the nearby shore.

In light of the disaster perpetrated by last summer's staff, Maeve had reason to believe that Eliza was capable of anything, even gutting her own daughter-in-law if it suited her. Having an Irish daughter-in-law most definitely did not suit Eliza, and Maeve didn't doubt for a minute that the woman was planning to get rid of her. The waiting and wondering *how* the other woman would attack had Maeve constantly on guard—and that is why she never left the house without her money.

Kathleen curled her hair with hot tongs and created an elaborate style held together by a series of well-placed pins.

"So much hair," Kathleen said as she did every time she dressed Maeve's long, thick hair.

"Too much hair." However, her delightful Mr. Nelson quite loved her hair. Thinking of him made her smile. He loved her. He thought of her every minute that they were apart. No one had ever been kinder to her than him, and the idea that she might one day have to leave him made her as sad as she had ever been.

Kathleen tied her into a corset and then helped her into the plum-colored silk gown that they had decided to hold aside for this occasion. The Russell ball was the event of the Season each year, and Kathleen had wanted her to wear the plum gown to the ball because it complemented her coloring so beautifully, or so the maid said.

Maeve had no idea what to wear to anything, so she deferred to the more knowledgeable Kathleen, who hadn't yet given her bad advice. Through multiple daily changes of clothing, Kathleen knew just what Maeve should wear to every occasion and had a new pair of kid gloves at the ready for each event. So many dresses! So many pairs of gloves! And the hats! Maeve had a separate wardrobe just for the large hats that were all the rage. Thank goodness for Kathleen, who had ensured that she was properly turned out, even if everything else about her was wrong.

"May I ask you something that may seem odd?" Maeve said when she was dressed.

Kathleen bustled about the room, gathering discarded

clothing and straightening the vanity. "Of course. What is on your mind?"

"I wondered if you have heard anything . . ." Maeve swallowed hard. "Around town . . ."

"About?"

"Me." Much to her mortification, Maeve's face flushed, making her wish she'd never asked.

"People are intrigued about Mr. Nelson marrying the housekeeper. I won't lie to you about that. Especially one of our kind."

"Irish, you mean."

"Aye. We're the working class here, even if we come from the wealthiest families in Ireland."

"Are they being . . . unkind toward me?"

"Not that I have heard, but they know I'm your maid. They'd hardly speak poorly of you to me."

"True."

"There has been much talk about Mrs. Nelson and about how last year's staff left the windows open all winter."

"It was quite shocking."

"Indeed. The stories about the missus are the thing of legend."

"She hates me," Maeve whispered, terrified she would be overheard.

Kathleen's eyes went wide with shock. "How do you know that?"

"She looks at me like she wants me dead."

"No!"

"Yes! She's horrified that Aubrey married me, and I'm quite fearful about what she's going to do about it."

"What can she do? You're legally married."

"I don't know, but I have no doubt whatsoever that she will do something." Maeve's stomach turned, and she rested her hand on it. "My stomach is upset all the time."

"You shouldn't worry over much. I have seen the way your sweet husband stares at you like a man in love. He won't let anything happen to you."

"No, he won't, but he can't be with me every minute."

Kathleen patted her arm. "Try not to worry. Your husband is a good man. Everyone says so. You can count on him to take care of you."

Realizing the conversation was making Kathleen uncomfortable, Maeve nodded. "You're right. Thank you for listening."

"Of course." Kathleen stood back to take a critical look at Maeve's finished appearance. "You look beautiful. You will be the belle of the ball."

"I quite doubt that."

"I don't," a male voice said from the doorway.

Maeve spun around to find her husband there, gazing at her with the heated look that made her insides quiver every time he directed it her way.

"Thank you, Kathleen," Aubrey said.

"Have a lovely evening." Kathleen left the room, closing the door behind her.

Aubrey walked toward Maeve, stopping a foot from her. "You have never been more beautiful."

She looked up at him, resplendent in his black formal attire. "I could say the same about you."

"I wish I didn't have to share you with Newport society or anyone else tonight."

"I wish that as well, but we must not keep the others waiting."

He extended his arm to her.

She tucked her hand into the crook of his elbow and looked up to find him gazing down at her.

"I'm the luckiest man who ever lived to be married to you, my love."

"And I'm the luckiest woman. Thank you for everything you have done for me. You will never know how much I appreciate you."

"I have a small idea because I appreciate you just as much, if not more."

They descended the stairs arm in arm, "arguing" about who appreciated whom the most.

"Let's call it a draw, shall we?" Aubrey said when they were in the grand foyer where the others awaited them.

She smiled at him, delighted by their witty banter. Being with him was such great fun. After the misery of the months she'd spent as Mr. Farthington's punching bag, Aubrey was a breath of fresh air on a bright sunny day in comparison.

He was the sun, the moon, the stars, the entire universe. He was everything she'd ever wanted and never dared to dream for herself.

She tightened her hold on his arm, almost afraid to let go out of fear of somehow managing to lose what she had waited so long to find.

"Are you all right?" he asked, his brows furrowed.

"My stomach is upset." She spoke the truth, even if that wasn't her primary concern.

"That seems to be the case quite often these days. Is it possible . . . ?" His voice faltered, and his eyes widened. "Maeve . . ."

"It's possible," she whispered.

"How soon can we find out for certain?"

"Another week or two."

"I'll never last that long. The curiosity will kill me."

"Don't say such a thing!" The possibility of anything—or anyone—killing him was horrifying to her, so much so that tears sprang to her eyes.

While the others chatted and admired each other's

evening wear, Aubrey led her off to the side of the foyer for a private word. "Maeve, honey, whatever is the matter?"

"I . . . I don't know." Using her handkerchief, she dabbed at her eyes. "I'm so very emotional and overwrought as of late."

His tender smile warmed the places inside her that had gone cold with the fear his mother inspired in her. "I remember when my sisters were expecting. Audrey would cry if the cats fought with each other. Her husband would poke terrible fun of her histrionics."

"That makes me feel a little better. It's not just me."

"Definitely not. Do you feel unwell? Should we stay home tonight?"

"No, of course not. I'll be fine as long as you don't talk about anything killing you."

"That's what did it?"

Feeling madly vulnerable, she looked up at him and nodded.

Ignoring the others, he held her chin in place for a soft kiss. "I'm going to live so long you will beg me to finally die so you can get some peace."

She shook her head. "Never. I'll never beg you to die."

"We'll see about that. You may soon tire of my three-times-a-day demands."

"I won't."

"You say that now."

"I say that forever. I love your demands."

He wrapped his arms around her and held her as close as he could without crushing her dress. "And I love you. No more tears or worries or anything but happiness and fun, all right?"

Nodding, she said, "I'm sorry to be so silly."

"You're not silly, but I do think you might be pregnant, and that makes me so happy I'm floating on air."

"I feel the same way." She held on tight to the man who had become the center of her life. How was it possible that she'd only known him for six weeks? It seemed like so much longer.

"Come along. Let's go dance the night away."

She released her hold on him and turned toward the door, her gaze colliding with Eliza Nelson, who glared at her with unfettered hatred that made Maeve shiver in fear.

Chapter Twenty-One

Aubrey had taken a moment to smooth Maeve's skirt and missed the vile look on his mother's face, but Maeve would never forget it.

Eliza joined them as they went out to the carriage. As the others had already departed, the three of them ended up alone in a carriage together, which only added to Maeve's nervousness. She had been trying to avoid being anywhere near Eliza and was now seated across from her for the thankfully short ride to the Russells' home.

"Father seemed a little better today, don't you think?" Aubrey said, breaking an awkward silence.

"No, I didn't think so. I know you're hoping for a miracle, Aubrey, but that's not going to happen. I'm surprised he's lasted this long. The doctors in New York told us he'd be lucky to see Independence Day, let alone the end of the month."

Only because Aubrey was pressed against her from shoulder to knee did Maeve feel him sag from the way his mother's callous words dashed his hopes. Maeve reached for his hand and cradled it between both of hers while sending his mother a defiant look. How dare she do that to him when he was looking for hope anywhere he could find it?

"We will need to discuss what happens after your father passes," Eliza continued, with no sense whatsoever that she had wounded her son.

"We will discuss that only after he is gone," Aubrey said.

"You're soft like him," Eliza said with obvious disdain.

"I'd rather be soft like him than hard like you."

Oh God, Eliza had not appreciated that.

"You disappoint me, Aubrey."

"So you've said, Mother. But I find that I no longer care whether you hold me in high regard. I have been a good and dutiful son to you and to my father. After what Maeve and I encountered when we arrived in Newport, I find that I've lost respect for you. Grandfather used to say we are only as good as the way we treat others. I believe he would be appalled by the way you treat others."

As Eliza fumed, the carriage came to a stop and the door opened to the Russells' footmen, eager to help them out. Eliza extended her hand to the first footman. "I'm glad we had this conversation, Aubrey. It clarifies things for me." And with that, she was gone, swept up into the crowds entering Chateau de la Mer, or House of the Sea. It was grander by far than the Nelsons' home, with a ballroom big enough for the five hundred invited guests who filled the massive room. Scoring an invite to the Russells' ball was the goal of every Newport socialite, or so Maeve had been told.

She held on tighter to Aubrey's arm, fearful of being separated from him in the crush. Derek and Catherine were in front of them, Simon and Madeleine behind them. To her left, Maeve saw Aubrey's sister Adele and her husband, Edward, who had come up from the city for the weekend.

The massive crowd only added to Maeve's anxiety, which had spiked during the tense conversation with Eliza in the carriage. If she'd maintained a small hope that her mother-in-law was going to accept her son's choice of a wife, those illusions had been shattered in the last few minutes. The woman was up to something, and whatever it was would be ugly for Maeve.

Did Aubrey feel the same way? She wished she could ask him but had tried not to say too much to him about his mother, out of fear of offending him. As bad as she could be, Eliza was still his mother, and even though Maeve was now his wife, she had known him for such a short time. How could she possibly compete with the mother he'd known for thirty-two years?

Her stomach turned, and she felt overly warm. Waves of queasiness added to her discomfort, making her fearful that she would toss up her accounts right there in the foyer of the Russells' palatial home.

She faltered, and Aubrey turned his attention toward her.

"Sweetheart, you're so pale. Are you all right?"

Maeve shook her head because she was afraid to open her mouth to speak.

He moved quickly, dodging people and skirts and footmen to get her to the ladies' retiring room with all due haste. It had a sign on the door designating it for ladies. She went inside, hoping he hadn't followed her into a space reserved for women. Several ladies were gathered around mirrors at a long vanity table.

Maeve zipped past them and into one of two stalls that was thankfully open. She leaned over the stool and heaved up the light snack she had eaten that afternoon. Her entire body hurt from the effort to be quiet as she was sick.

". . . the Irish housekeeper."

". . . would've been a terrible scandal were it not for the duke and duchess."

". . . never leaves her side."

The scandalized whispers of the other women had Maeve's face burning with embarrassment. Of course they were talking about her every chance they got. She hadn't given them sufficient opportunity with Catherine or Madeleine always by her side, but she'd deluded herself into thinking she'd somehow managed to evade the gossip. It had probably been happening all along, just not where she could hear it.

". . . if she's pregnant, Eliza will die."

Maeve used the tissue to wipe her mouth and hoped she hadn't ruined her appearance by being sick.

"Ladies, if you'll excuse us for just a moment. I'd like to check on my wife."

Aubrey. Dear God, he couldn't be in here.

"Of course, Mr. Nelson," one of the whisperers said. "We hope she isn't ill."

"As do I." He came up behind her in the stall and wrapped an arm around her. "Are you all right, love?"

"I will be."

"What can I do for you?"

"I need to clean up and a drink of water would help."

"I'll go get it for you. Will you be all right for a few minutes?"

Maeve nodded. She needed time to herself to collect her thoughts and find her composure.

Aubrey kissed her forehead. "Stay here. I'll be right back."

After he left the room, Maeve sat at the vanity, easing into the chair carefully in deference to the stomach pains that were continuing to make her sweaty and uncomfortable. She had no idea how long she sat there, breathing through the pain, when the door opened and closed, the snick of the lock sliding into place jolting her.

She spun around to find her mother-in-law glaring at her. "We need to talk."

Eliza Nelson was the last person on earth Maeve wished to speak to, but Eliza had bided her time, and now she had Maeve right where she wanted her—locked in a room with no way for Aubrey or his illustrious friends to help her.

"You may not be aware of this, but the man you married is brilliant," Eliza said.

"I know that."

"Shut up and listen."

Maeve was horrified by the crimson creep that came from her chest to her face, hating that it gave away feelings she'd much prefer to keep hidden from the other woman.

"He's *brilliant*. He's been on the front lines of using refrigeration in railcars and has helped to revolutionize the way food is transported in this country, putting the Nelson name on par with the Vanderbilts, Astors and Russells. Anderson and Alfie are competent businessmen. Aubrey is the genius. He doesn't know it yet, but when his father passes away, he will be named the new chairman of Nelson Industrial."

Maeve listened to what Eliza said with a growing sense of dread. Why was Eliza telling her these things?

"Under no circumstances can he have an Irish wife who was once in service to the family. He needs a wife who will understand the demands of his new role and who can adequately support him as he takes the company to even greater heights. That wife will *not* be you."

Maeve had known it was coming, but the words sliced through her like a knife to the chest nonetheless.

"What's it going to take to get rid of you?"

"P-pardon?"

"You heard me. How much do you want?"

Maeve stared at her in disbelief. What was she saying?

"Have you gone deaf and dumb now? Don't pretend you don't know what I'm asking you or that it's not exactly what you hoped to gain by marrying my son."

"I . . . I don't want your money."

"*Please*," Eliza said, scoffing. "Don't insult my intelligence. Name your price and hurry up about it. I don't have all night. I have far better things to do with my time than deal with the likes of you."

"I have no price."

"*Everyone* has a price."

"I don't." She forced herself to look the other woman dead in the eye. "I love Aubrey. He loves me. That's all I want."

Eliza laughed. "That's rich. He doesn't *love* you. He loves *fucking* you. Are you too stupid to know the difference between love and lust?"

Shocked to her core and horrified by the vulgar term, Maeve could only stare at Eliza and wonder how a mother could be so callous toward her own son.

"What will people say when they find out you murdered your former husband?"

How did *she* know that? Maeve's mind raced with horror at the implications of Eliza knowing about her past. "I didn't murder him. I defended myself—"

"Save the theatrics. If word gets out that you killed a man, you'll be shunned by everyone who matters—and so will Aubrey. Is that what you want for him?"

"How would the word get out?"

Eliza waved away the question with a sweep of her hand. "Let me put it to you this way—if you don't leave him, immediately, he'll be passed over for the opportunity of a lifetime. Serving as chairman of Nelson Industrial will cement his rightful place as a titan of business and society. He'll make history. You say you love him. Would you deny him such an opportunity?"

Maeve's heart broke in two, the searing pain leaving her breathless.

"Well? Would you deny him that?"

"No," Maeve said softly. She would deny him nothing.

"Then you'll leave immediately. Tonight."

Maeve pressed a hand to her chest where she'd tucked Mr. Farthington's money in anticipation of a moment just like this.

Eliza stepped forward, her hand extended.

Maeve recoiled, wishing there was anywhere she could go to escape the woman.

"Take this." Eliza held out a stack of bills. "Go back to Ireland where you belong."

Maeve eyed the cash and then looked up at Eliza. "You have nothing I want or need."

"Suit yourself." Eliza curled her hand around the wad of cash. "But if I ever see you again, I'll ruin him. And just for good measure, I'll make sure everyone who matters here and in New York knows how your first marriage ended. If you think I won't do it, try me."

"I have no doubt you'd do it as you're probably the most heartless human being I've ever met, and I've met some rather heartless people in my day."

Eliza's lips turned white, and her face flushed with fury. "Our business is concluded. Take your leave and don't come back. Or else." With that, she unlocked the door and left the room.

As Maeve watched her go, devastation set in. She would never see Aubrey again. She would never wake up to his beautiful face on the pillow next to hers. She would never again experience the pure joy of joining her body with his, of kissing his lips or sleeping with his arms around her, keeping her safe and protected.

A sob escaped from her tightly clenched jaw as she forced those thoughts to the back of her mind—for now. There would be a lifetime to mourn what she'd lost. She had to go before he returned and made it impossible for her to leave.

The crush of people standing between Aubrey and the refreshment table frustrated and irritated him. Anxious to get back to Maeve, he excused himself a hundred times before he gave up and began throwing an elbow or two to get through the crowd.

An *oomph* from next to him had him looking over to apologize to the owner of the gut he'd assaulted. "Mutt! So sorry, chap."

Matthew rubbed the sore spot on his abdomen. "That's a rather lethal elbow you've got there, Aubrey."

"My wife is unwell, and I'm trying to get her a glass of water, which is a seemingly impossible mission in this maelstrom."

"I'm glad I ran into you. I've been meaning to come by."

Matthew's words were somewhat slurred, his puffy face indicative of a protracted bender.

"But I've been a little busy. I do need to speak to you somewhat urgently."

Aubrey cast a glance over his shoulder, noting that the retiring room where he'd left Maeve was now out of sight. "About what?"

Matthew curled a hand around Aubrey's arm and guided him out of the fray into a dark hallway.

Aubrey wanted to shake off his friend so he could return to Maeve, but Matthew's tight grip had him staying put. "Whatever it is, Matthew, spit it out. I need to get back to my wife."

"It's about her."

"What is?"

"There was something I didn't tell you after you sent me to pay off Tornquist. I was going to tell you, but you seemed so . . . happy with her."

"I am happy with her, and I already know what happened with her former husband. I'm not sure how much you've had to drink that you don't remember—"

"It's not that. It's something else."

A sense of foreboding overtook Aubrey as he noticed Matthew's speech had lost the slur and his eyes were intently focused.

"Another man who courted her turned up dead, reportedly from poisoning, a year before she married Farthington."

Aubrey stared at his friend, wondering if he'd heard him correctly.

"I didn't want to tell you because you were happy, but then I started to worry about something happening to you and how guilty I'd feel if it did."

"You . . . you think I'm unsafe with her?"

"Men seem to die in her presence, Aubrey. You'd be wise to practice all due vigilance."

"With my wife? Whom I love and who loves me? I don't need to be vigilant with her. She's no threat to me."

"Two men are dead, Aubrey. You can't allow love to blind you to the possibility—"

Aubrey held up his hand to stop the man. "Enough. Your conscience is now clear, and I must get back to my wife. Enjoy your evening."

"Aubrey . . ."

Whatever else Matthew had to say, Aubrey wasn't listening. If another man in Maeve's past had died prematurely, he had no reason to believe she'd been involved in any way. And he knew, without a shadow of a doubt, she was incapable of harming anyone unless her own life was in peril. He thanked the good lord above every day that she'd fended off Farthington's attack and managed to escape to America. That chain of events had led her to him, and for that, he would always be grateful.

Making his way toward the refreshment table, he encountered Derek and Catherine.

"Ah, there you are," Derek said. "This is like the first ball of the London Season when everyone wants to be seen."

"It's ridiculous." Aubrey finally poured a glass of water from one of the iced pitchers on the table. "Maeve is not feeling well, and I've been trying to get her a drink of water for fifteen minutes now."

"Where is she?"

"In the ladies' retiring room."

"Allow us to help clear a path for you," Derek said.

"I would appreciate that very much."

With Derek and Catherine leading the way, the crowd parted to allow the duke and duchess to pass. Aubrey made it back to the room where he'd left Maeve in half the time it would've taken without their assistance.

"It certainly does help to have friends in high places," Aubrey said.

Derek laughed. "Whatever I can do for you, my friend."

"Do you mind if I stay to make sure Maeve is all right?" Catherine asked as they approached the closed door.

"Of course not. Give me just a minute to get her." Aubrey knocked on the door and stepped inside the room where he found two women he didn't recognize and no sign of his wife. "I'm looking for my wife."

"The Irish woman?"

"Yes," Aubrey said through gritted teeth. "Have you seen her? She was here a few minutes ago."

"I saw her heading for the main door as I came in. My friend commented on her lovely gown and how the right clothing can make anyone seem elegant."

The rude comment raised his hackles, but he had no time to give the woman a dressing down when he had far greater concerns. He turned and left the room, still carrying the glass of water and bringing a growing feeling of desperation with him. Where would she have gone?

Derek and Catherine waited for him outside the room.

"She's gone," he told them.

"Gone where?" Derek asked, brows furrowed.

"I don't know. One of the women said they saw her heading for the main door."

"Let's go," Catherine said, gathering her skirts and taking off toward the front of the house.

Derek and Aubrey followed her.

Aubrey's heart beat so fast, he worried he'd pass out from the overabundance of blood beating through his system. He just needed to find her and everything would be all right again. That's all it would take. As they walked briskly through the crowd that had thinned somewhat now that everyone was in the ballroom, he scanned the landscape in front of him, seeking his wife's distinctive shade of reddish-brown hair.

But he didn't see her anywhere, and with every minute that passed, his concern intensified. She had felt ill when he left her. Had her condition worsened to the point that she had decided to leave? And why would she leave without telling him?

They rushed through the main door, and the footmen hopped to when they saw the duke and duchess.

"How may we assist you, Your Grace?" one of them asked.

"We are looking for Mr. Nelson's wife, Maeve," Derek said. "We heard she headed in this direction."

"Mrs. Nelson departed about ten minutes ago."

"*Departed?*" Aubrey asked, incredulous. "Where did she go?"

"I'm sorry, sir, but she didn't say."

"Did she take the carriage?"

"No, sir, she left on foot."

The words were no sooner out of the other man's mouth when Aubrey took off running, dropping the glass of water in the driveway in his haste to catch up to her.

"We'll meet you back at the house," Derek called after him.

Aubrey raised an arm in acknowledgment but didn't slow down as he cleared the gates to the Russell estate and ran toward home as fast as he could. Thankfully, only half a mile separated the two estates, so it didn't take him long to cover the distance. Wiggie and Kaiser came out of the house when they saw him coming.

"Mr. Nelson, is everything all right?" Wiggie asked.

"Is Mrs. Nelson here?"

"Neither Mrs. Nelson is in residence at the moment," Kaiser said.

If he hadn't been out of his mind with worry about where Maeve had gone, he would've been impressed with the politely worded response from the footman, who'd clearly been paying attention to the training Plumber had been doling out to the new staff.

Aubrey put his hands on his hips, attempting to catch his breath as he contemplated his next move.

"Will you have my horse brought around, please?"

"Of course, sir," Wiggie said, taking off for the stables.

"Is everything all right, sir?" Kaiser asked.

"No." Aubrey ran a hand through his hair as frustration and concern held him in their grip. "It's not all right." And if he couldn't find her, nothing would ever be all right again.

Chapter Twenty-Two

Like she had the last time she ran for her life, Maeve headed for the docks, hoping to book passage to somewhere far from Newport. Being on an island made it difficult to go anywhere other than the port. If she'd been on the mainland, she could've hopped aboard a train and headed west.

Here, she had but one option, and at this hour, the harbor was largely deserted, much to her dismay. What would she do if she couldn't find a boat leaving tonight?

"What's a fancy piece like yerself doing in these parts alone at night?" The raspy voice had her spinning to find the owner, a man hunched against a large brick building.

"I'm looking for a boat leaving tonight. Do you know of any?"

"Anyone going is already long gone."

Filled with despair, Maeve studied her surroundings, looking for an answer amid the brick buildings mired in fog rolling in off the harbor. A chill ran through her as a cramp seized her midsection.

"Help ya with somethin', sis?" The raspy voice came from her right, and when she turned to look at the man, she immediately wished she hadn't.

The man wore rags and leered at her with yellowy eyes, and when she caught a whiff of his foul breath, she nearly fainted. Stepping backward, she stumbled over a rock. Another man appeared out of the fog and stopped her from falling with a hand on her arm.

"Get out of here, Leon," the second man said in a growl that sent goose bumps down her arms. "Can't you see she's quality?"

"She's *Irish*," the man named Leon said, sneering.

"She's someone's wife, and he'll gut you if you so much as look at her."

"And you're so much better?"

"Get out of here, or I'll gut you myself."

Maeve wasn't sure if the second man was an improvement over the first, but at least he didn't smell like death warmed over.

"Are you all right, miss?" he asked after Leon slunk off into the mist.

"I . . . I don't know." The pain in her midsection required almost all of her attention as it intensified, coming and going in waves that left her feeling sweaty and nauseated.

"What're you doing down here by yourself?"

"I was hoping to book passage to Boston or New York." She could always go to the captain's wife who'd been so kind to her when she first arrived in America.

"There's nothing leaving tonight. You should go home before something terrible happens."

"I can't go home." She thought of Aubrey, wondered if he was worried about her, and blinked back the tears that filled her eyes.

"You can't stay here. You won't survive the night." He released a deep sigh. "Come with me."

"Where?"

"Away from here. I live with my sister. We can put you up for the night. You will be safe with us. I promise."

Since she had no alternative, and the pain in her abdomen

was worsening with every passing minute, she decided to trust this man who had protected her and offered her shelter. If she was wrong about him, she would find a way to escape. She'd done it before, and she'd probably have to do it again.

She yearned for Aubrey, who had made her feel so safe. Knowing she would never see him again broke her heart, but it was for the best. His mother would never back down, and Maeve loved him too much to deny him the opportunity to run his family's business. He'd be a brilliant, innovative, forward-looking leader.

Theirs had been a short but beautiful time together that she would carry with her for the rest of her life. She would never forget him, and she would always love him. A sob escaped from her tightly clenched jaw. An intense pain, sharper than the others, bent her in half, and a rush of wetness between her legs brought her to her knees.

"Miss! Whatever is the matter?"

Maeve heard the man's voice but couldn't form words or even breathe over the brutal pain that ripped her apart. Darkness swirled around her, dragging her under. Her last conscious thought was of Aubrey's handsome face and kind eyes.

Where could she possibly be? Aubrey had personally searched the neighborhood on horseback while the staff had searched every inch of the house. Back at the house, Aubrey paced from one end of the foyer to the other, feeling impotent as he waited for news.

"I need to go back out to look for her myself," he said to Derek and Simon, who were keeping him company.

"You have people fanned out all over town," Derek said. "They will find her."

Aubrey wished he could be so certain.

"I hate to ask . . ."

Aubrey glanced at Simon, who seemed exquisitely uncomfortable. "Ask what?"

"What if she doesn't want to be found?"

"Why wouldn't she?"

"Perhaps something happened that sent her into hiding?"

Before Aubrey could respond, his mother, sisters and brothers-in-law returned from the ball, stopping short when they found Aubrey, Derek and Simon in the foyer, still dressed in their formal attire.

"How could you leave so early?" Eliza's eyes flashed with rage. "Dora Russell was *mortified* that the duke and duchess left before dinner! She was in tears, the poor dear."

"We can't find Maeve."

"Regardless, you can't just *leave* the social event of the Season before dinner."

Aubrey stared at her, flabbergasted. "*Regardless?* Did you actually say *regardless* when I told you my *wife* is *missing*?"

"Watch your tone with me, young man." Her haughty British accent made him want to scream.

"My wife is missing, Mother. Until I find her, you'll have to pardon me if I don't give a shit about the social event of the Season."

Eliza was about to snap back at him, when Alora intervened. "Aubrey is right, Mother. Maeve's safety is the only thing that matters."

Eliza made a face that indicated how little she cared about Maeve's safety.

An uncomfortable suspicion took root deep within him, causing him to take a closer look at his mother. "Have you done something?" he asked, his tone low as his heart rate slowed to a crawl.

"Whatever do you mean?" Eliza asked haughtily.

"I mean—have you said or done something that caused my wife to run away?"

She scowled as her face flushed and her eyes narrowed. "I barely know the woman. What could I possibly say to her?"

"Oh, I don't know, maybe something like the things you said to last year's staff that led them to vandalize the house?"

"That again. You've become tedious like your father, Aubrey."

"Watch yourself, Mother. Your snide comments about Father aren't welcome with me." All at once, his father's warning resurfaced. He'd told Aubrey to be vigilant—and he hadn't heeded his father's alarming words. "*What did you do to her?*" Now, he was certain she'd done something. The only thing was—what was it and how much damage had been done as a result? Aubrey took her by the shoulders and gave her a vicious shake. "Tell me!"

"Aubrey," Adele said, a note of warning in the way she said his name.

"I swear to God, Mother, I'll choke the life right out of you if you don't start talking right *now*!"

Even as his sisters gasped with shock, his mother's face went totally white with fright. Good. She ought to be afraid. If she'd done something to drive Maeve away, there wouldn't be a safe place for her to hide from his rage.

"I merely mentioned that you will become the new chairman of Nelson Industrial when your father passes away, and it will become ever more important for you to have the *right* wife."

"*I have the right wife!*" Aubrey's vision went red with fury, and he had to force himself not to make good on his threat to strangle her.

His brothers-in-law pulled him off Eliza.

"Get her out of my sight. Before I actually kill her."

"Aubrey," Eliza cried, tearful now. "You don't understand!"

"I understand perfectly, Mother. But you should understand this—I'll never spend another day working for Nelson Industrial, and as soon as I locate my wife, I'll never see you again, either."

"Don't say things you don't mean!"

"I have never said anything I didn't mean, and you, Mother dearest, are dead to me." To his sisters, he said, "Please get her out of here before I make good on the overwhelming desire to end her."

His tearful sisters dragged Eliza, shrieking and flailing, from the room.

Only after she was gone did Aubrey realize his hands were shaking. "I have to find Maeve."

"We'll go with you," Derek said as Simon nodded in agreement.

Plumber went to alert the stables that three fresh horses would be needed immediately, and the men set out ten minutes later—every one of those ten minutes feeling like a year to Aubrey.

"I'm sorry you had to witness such ugliness," Aubrey said to his friends.

"Oh, please," Simon said. "Have you heard the stories about my father and what he did?"

"I have."

"We know ugly," Derek said. "All too well, unfortunately. Please don't think a thing of it, Aubrey. Every family has their problems."

"I've always known my mother to be an exacting, difficult, hard-to-please woman who held her children to nearly impossible standards. But I never for the life of me imagined she would deliberately sabotage my marriage."

"Didn't you, though?" Derek asked. "Didn't you know she'd be furious when you married Maeve, and didn't you do it anyway?"

"Yes." Aubrey slumped in his saddle. "I knew she'd be furious, and I did it anyway."

"Which to me is indicative of the depth of your feelings for Maeve," Simon said.

"I love her to the ends of the earth." Aubrey spoke nothing less than the truth.

"That is apparent to anyone who has spent even five minutes with the two of you," Derek said, "including your mother."

"She knows you truly love Maeve, and that's why she's so threatened by her," Simon said.

"I hate that she's more concerned about her standing in society than she is about her own son's happiness," Aubrey said.

"You can't understand that because you weren't raised amid the British aristocracy where your standing in society is *everything*," Derek said.

"It's more important than your own children?" As he rode and talked with his friends, Aubrey scanned every nook and cranny on every street they traversed, eyes peeled for the distinctive color of his wife's hair. *Liquid fire.* Recalling her telling him that her mother had called it that made him ache for her.

"At times," Simon said. "My own father would've gladly traded me for the opportunity to be the duke. He would've done it without hesitation."

"Your father has no idea what he missed out on by disregarding you all of your life," Derek said emphatically.

"That is kind of you to say, dear cousin."

"I mean it. You know I do. I'd be lost without you, so you can't ever let his opinion matter more than mine does."

"I would never make that mistake," Simon said, grinning at Derek.

The conversation helped to keep Aubrey from going mad as he prayed for Maeve's safety. She could be anywhere by now, a thought that had his heart sinking. How could she have let his mother convince her to run? Did she have so little faith in him, in what they'd shared, that she'd think he'd choose the business over her?

"What're you thinking, Aubrey?" Derek asked.

"That I can't believe she'd run rather than come to me."

"Don't fault her for that. She was probably frightened after her encounter with your mother and acted before she thought it through."

"Perhaps, but still . . . I wish she'd put more faith in me." Another thought occurred to him, stealing the breath from his lungs. "What if I never see her again?"

"Don't think that way," Simon said.

"We won't give up until we find her," Derek added.

"Thank you for being such good friends. I've never had better friends than you two and Justin."

"Likewise," Derek said as Simon nodded in agreement.

They rode for hours, traversing every street in Newport. Dawn was breaking when they reached the waterfront, which bustled with early-morning activity.

Aubrey asked everyone they encountered if they had seen Maeve. He described her down to the last detail, including the plum-colored gown she'd been wearing the last time he'd seen her.

"Plum, you say?" The filthy man had yellowy eyes and three rotten teeth.

Aubrey's stomach plummeted at the thought of Maeve encountering such a character. "Have you seen her?"

"Possibly."

"Tell me what you know. Immediately."

Derek tempered Aubrey's harsh words with a softer approach. "Please, sir. My friend's wife is missing, and we are very eager to find her."

The man took in Derek's fine clothing and regal bearing. "How eager are you?"

Derek reached into his pocket, removed some bills and pressed them into the man's hand.

His rheumy eyes lit up with unfettered glee. "Scroogey took her home with him."

A sharp pain lanced Aubrey's chest, making him fear he was having a heart episode. "She . . . went home with a strange man?"

"Scroogey ain't strange. He's good people. Lives with his sister on Grafton Street."

Aubrey touched the spurs to the horse's side and took off toward Grafton, which was off Lower Thames. The pounding of hooves let him know Derek and Simon were behind him. If this Scroogey character had done anything to hurt Maeve, Aubrey wouldn't be responsible for his actions.

Upon reaching Grafton Street, Aubrey dismounted, tied his horse to an iron rail at the bottom of the street and began knocking on doors with no concern whatsoever for the early hour. "Where is Scroogey's house?" he asked the first sleep-rumpled woman who answered the door.

"Second house from the top. Left side."

Aubrey took off running, charging up the hill, his arms pumping and his gaze fixed on the white clapboard house the woman had identified. He ran up the stone steps and pounded on the door with a closed fist. When no one answered, he pounded some more and was about to bust down the door when it finally opened.

The man's hair stood on end as his blue eyes narrowed in annoyance. "Whatya want?"

"I'm looking for my wife. I was told you brought her home with you."

"Who's your wife?"

Aubrey forced himself to remain calm when he wanted to beat the man to a pulp to get him out of the way. "Maeve Nelson. She was wearing a plum ball gown."

"Your Maeve was quite upset when I came upon her last night. Was that your doing?"

"No." Aubrey gestured to his friends. "Ask them. They can attest it was most definitely *not* my doing."

"I'm Derek Eagan, the Duke of Westwood, and I can assure you that my friend is telling you the truth. He is not to blame for his wife's distress."

"She is unwell," Scroogey said.

Aubrey gasped. "Please let me see her. I love her with all my heart."

Scroogey took a long measuring look at Aubrey before stepping aside. "Upstairs. First door on the right."

Aubrey rushed past the man and took the stairs three at a time, bursting into the room to find Maeve being tended to by another woman, who startled at Aubrey's sudden appearance. "I'm her husband. What is wrong?" The first thing he noticed was how ghostly pale Maeve's face was.

"I believe she lost the babe she was carrying."

A knife through the chest wouldn't have hurt more than that news did. He would never forgive his mother for this.

Aubrey fell to his knees at Maeve's bedside and reached out to stroke her sweet face. He was alarmed by the heat radiating from her. "Maeve, sweetheart. It's me, Aubrey. I'm here. I'm right here, and I love you."

Her low moan went straight to his broken heart.

"She lost a lot of blood," the other woman said. "It went on most of the night."

Aubrey noted the crumpled plum gown on the floor and

the plain cotton nightgown Maeve wore that must belong to the woman who'd tended to her. He would see that the siblings were well compensated for the aid they'd rendered. "Is she . . . Will she . . ." He couldn't get the words past the pervasive panic that gripped him.

"She needs a doctor," Scroogey said from the hallway. "Wouldn't let us get him last night."

Aubrey glanced at Derek and Simon in the doorway.

"We'll find him," Derek said.

"He's on Spring Street," Scroogey said, rattling off the address.

"Hurry." Aubrey returned his attention to the woman who had changed his life in every possible way. "Please hurry."

Their pounding footsteps on the stairs echoed through the small house.

While he waited for them to return, Aubrey bathed her face with cool cloths that Scroogey's sister handed him and prayed for Maeve to open her eyes and talk to him. He would give anything to hear her lovely voice. Every minute he had spent with her raced through his mind, beginning with the day he'd found her in the midst of a nightmare with a giant feather duster in hand. He recalled their first picnic at the shore, catching her when she fell off the ladder, their wedding day, the first time they made love and every beautiful, joyful moment that had made up the best weeks of his life. If he lost her now, he would never survive.

A sob erupted from the deepest part of him. He rested his head on her chest. "Please come back to me, Maeve. Please don't leave me. I need you more than anything." He would give up everything he had for one more day with her.

He had no idea how long Derek and Simon had been

gone when they returned with a doctor in tow, a white-haired man with wise brown eyes that provided immediate comfort to a distraught Aubrey.

"You have to help her," he told the doctor. "She's my whole world."

"I'll do everything I can. Please give me a few minutes to examine her."

Derek took Aubrey by the arm and gave a gentle tug. "Come on, Aubrey. Let the doctor help her."

Aubrey feared that if he left her, even for a minute, she would leave him and never return.

Only Derek's insistence got him to move into the hallway.

While Aubrey waited, he felt like a caged animal with no room to pace or rage against the fates that had brought him to the precipice of disaster.

"She's young and strong and endlessly capable," Simon said. "It'll take more than a little blood loss to get the better of our indefatigable Maeve."

Comforted by his friend's kind words, Aubrey glommed on to the reminder that his Maeve was indeed indefatigable. She had escaped certain death with Farthington to run for her life to America. She'd survived terrible illness after her journey and found her way to Newport where she'd single-handedly confronted the disaster she found at the Nelson home, proving nothing could defeat her.

He only hoped their luck would hold a little while longer to get her through this latest catastrophe.

"What is taking so long?" Aubrey asked after what seemed like hours.

"It's only been fifteen minutes," Derek said.

"How is that possible?" Aubrey ran his hands through his hair again and again until it probably stood on end, not that he cared in the least. He would start pulling it out of his head if he didn't get word of her condition soon.

"What can we do for you, Aubrey?" Simon asked.

He thought about that for a long moment before he knew exactly what he needed. "I want you to go back to the house and instruct my sisters to remove my mother from the premises. If she puts up any sort of fuss, let her know that you'll call in the authorities, who will see to it that she's charged with a crime for what she has done to Maeve. Tell her I'll stop at nothing to see her ruined if she does not depart immediately. As soon as she is gone, bring the carriage so we can transport Maeve home where she belongs to recover. And if you would, take my horse with you. I'll ride home with her."

"Consider it done." The two men took off to see to his wishes. When all of this was over, he would owe them a debt of gratitude he would never be able to repay. With his father so gravely ill, Aubrey refused to be pushed out of the house. No, his mother was the one who needed to go, and his only regret was that he wouldn't be there to see her ejected from the property.

She would be enraged. He hoped she would know she had only herself to blame. With his arms propped over his head, he clung to the door frame outside his wife's room, whispering prayers for her recovery and offering anything and everything God chose to take from him to ensure her survival. He could live without anything except her.

By the time the door opened, he was on the verge of a complete breakdown. "Is she all right?"

"She will be," the doctor said. "In time."

Aubrey was so relieved, his legs refused to support him. He fell to his knees and dropped his head into his hands as sobs wracked his body.

"Aubrey."

One word from her was all it took to send his heart soaring. He raised his head, saw her looking at him and crawled around the doctor to join her on the bed, taking her into his arms even as his body continued to shake with uncontrollable sobs.

"Shhh."

She was comforting *him*? That would never do.

"I'm so sorry, Maeve. You'll never have to see her again. Whatever she said to you, it doesn't matter. There's nothing in this world I want more than you and a life with you. Please don't ever leave me again. I wouldn't survive without you." He kissed the tears that slid down her pale face. "I love you more than life itself. You must believe me when I tell you that."

"I do." Though her voice was barely a whisper, the music of Ireland he heard in her words buoyed his battered heart.

As he clung to her, he didn't care that they were surrounded by strangers. He didn't care about anything but her and making sure she had everything she needed to regain her health.

He held her while she slept, soothed her when she moaned and later, when Derek and Simon arrived with the carriage, he carried her downstairs after expressing their heartfelt thanks to Scroogey and his sister, Eileen. Aubrey snuggled Maeve into his arms for the ride up the hill to Paradis Trouvé where the entire staff rushed out to greet them.

He refused to hand her over to anyone, preferring to carry her into the house and up the stairs himself. Only when she was settled in their bed, where she belonged, did he release the deep breath he'd been holding for hours by then.

Derek and Simon came to the door, along with Catherine and Madeleine.

"How is she?" Catherine asked, her eyes red from lack of sleep and tears on behalf of her friend.

"She is exhausted and in need of a long rest to regain her strength," Aubrey told them. "But the doctor assured me she will make a full recovery."

"And will she be able to have other children?" Madeleine asked.

"He said there was no reason to believe otherwise."

"Thank God," Derek said for all of them.

"And my mother . . ."

"You needn't concern yourself with her again," Derek said. "We made it very clear that we would ruin her on this side of the Atlantic and on our side if she ever bothered you or Maeve again. Your sisters were so upset by what she did to Maeve that they encouraged her to leave before she made things worse."

"Thank you," Aubrey said. "I can never thank you enough for everything you've done for me and for Maeve."

"You both are family to us," Derek said. "And family takes care of family."

"We'll leave you to get some rest," Catherine said, squeezing Aubrey's arm. "Everything is all right now."

Aubrey glanced back at Maeve, asleep in their bed. As long as he had her, he had everything. "Yes, it is."

Epilogue

September 1904
Essex, England

Riding in a chauffeured motorcar from the train station to Westwood Hall, Derek and Catherine's country home, Aubrey held his squirming six-month-old son on his lap while Maeve sat next to them, watching with amusement as he struggled to contain the baby's boundless energy.

He got that from his mother, who had bounced back quickly from losing their first child, even if they both continued to mourn the baby that had been lost on that long-ago terrible night.

"He's going to get the better of you," Maeve said, her lilting accent even more pronounced after spending a joyous week in Dingle with her family.

"It's a good thing the ride is brief." From the day of his birth, Maximilian Sullivan Nelson had had a mind of his own. When Aubrey and Maeve had discovered they each had a great-grandfather with the distinctive name, they'd never considered naming their firstborn anything else. Max or Maxi, as they called him, had filled their lives with indescribable joy that had helped to temper Aubrey's grief over the loss of his father the previous fall.

Per his edict to his mother, he had declined the chairmanship of Nelson Industrial and had gone into business with Derek and Simon, overseeing their interests in the United States while branching out into areas that interested him, including investing in manned flight after Wilbur and Orville Wright had finally succeeded in flying an airplane and returning it safely to the ground the previous December.

He and his friends from England believed the future of aviation was limitless, and they were determined to be on the leading edge of innovation. They worked well together, had similar sensibilities and trusted each other implicitly. While Aubrey missed working with his brothers in the family business, it had been the right thing to branch out on his own. In a time of tremendous innovation and advancement, he enjoyed having the freedom to pursue projects that interested him. Not to mention, his new arrangement allowed him to work from his home office in New York, where he could be close to Maeve and Maxi during the day.

When they had first returned to the city, they had kept largely to themselves. The last thing Aubrey had wanted, after the disastrous summer in Newport, was to expose his beautiful wife to any more discrimination or social nonsense. A funny thing had happened, however. The more they avoided society, the more invitations they received, due in no small part to their friendship with the duke and duchess, who had bought a home on New York's Fifth Avenue so they could spend more time in America.

"Are you ready to see Uncle Derek and Aunt Catherine again?" Aubrey asked his son.

He received baby chatter in response and wiped the drool from the little guy's chin. Teething made for messy business, Aubrey had discovered. He reveled in everything the baby did and quite feared he would spoil him rotten if Maeve were not there to keep that from happening.

"He wants to see Gracie."

Their son and the Eagans' daughter had taken an immediate shine to each other, sparking talk of future marriages and other such nonsense.

"I can't wait to meet Robert and Isabel," Aubrey said of Derek and Catherine's newborn son and Simon and Madeleine's four-month-old daughter.

Anchoring his son with one arm, Aubrey rested his other hand on the small but growing bump under Maeve's dress. "I can't wait to meet this little person," he said, leaning in to kiss her.

"Five more months."

"I don't know how I'll stand to wait that long."

"Patience is definitely *not* your best quality."

"You've known that about me from the start."

"Indeed, I have." Her smile lit up her face and made his life worth living. There was nothing he wouldn't do to make her smile.

After that terrible night last summer, he had shared with her the information Mutt had passed along to him and had heard the tragic story of her friend Padraig's death and how much it haunted her to this day. Aubrey had known men in school who had seemed to favor other men over women and had witnessed their suffering firsthand.

The driver took a right turn into the gates at Westwood Hall, and Aubrey experienced a profound feeling of homecoming, knowing he would soon see his closest friends and business partners. It'd been almost two months since they'd last seen each other in New York, and he'd looked forward to this reunion for weeks.

Derek, Catherine, Simon, Madeleine and the entire

household awaited their arrival outside the main entrance. Derek, Catherine and Madeleine all had babies in their arms, so Simon helped Maeve from the car and hugged her warmly. Aubrey would never have the words to properly thank his beautiful friends for the way they had welcomed Maeve into their group.

He gasped with surprise when Justin came ambling out of the house, drink in hand. Aubrey and Maeve hadn't seen him since he left Newport the previous summer and hadn't been told he'd be there when they arrived. They had learned that his father and brother had been killed when they rode into a live electrical line that had fallen in a windstorm the day before the accident. In the past year, Justin had done his best to step into his formidable new role as the earl, but his burden was obvious to anyone who'd known him before disaster struck.

Aubrey handed the baby to Maeve and hugged Justin. "What a delightful surprise this is, my lord."

Justin scowled at him, just as Aubrey had expected him to when he used Justin's title. "Drop the formality, Nelson. I'm off duty for a blessed few days."

Laughing at Justin's comical facial expression, Aubrey and Maeve hugged the others and together they went inside to settle the babies with governesses, so their weary parents could enjoy luncheon with their friends. He and Maeve had chosen to travel without a governess, preferring to take care of Maxi themselves.

"Will they tell us if he's a bear?" Aubrey asked Catherine, eyeing the stairs.

"Of course they will." Catherine patted his arm. "Enjoy a little respite while you can."

Aubrey allowed her to direct him toward the veranda on the back of the house where the housekeeper, Mrs. Langingham, supervised the kitchen staff as they put out an informal picnic lunch on a long table. She let out a happy cry when she saw Aubrey, giving him a welcoming hug. Since he and Justin had assisted in caring for Derek after he was felled by influenza, Mrs. Langingham had treated him like a long-lost son.

Was it any wonder that he loved visiting Westwood Hall so much? "Mrs. Langingham, I'm pleased to introduce you to my wife, Maeve."

Mrs. Langingham hugged her, too. "I'm delighted to meet you, my dear. By all accounts, you have made our Aubrey very happy."

Maeve's face heated with the blush he loved so much as she glanced at him. "He has done the same for me."

"Come, everyone," the housekeeper said. "Luncheon is served."

The meal was presented buffet style, meats and cheeses and bread and fruit. Wine flowed along with conversation and laughter that made for a perfect afternoon with some of his favorite people. Despite the residual tension in the family after Aubrey's blowup with their mother, he had remained close to his siblings as well as his nieces and nephews. Though the others remained in touch with their mother, Aubrey did not, and thankfully the others respected his wishes where she was concerned. He would not have welcomed a rift with his siblings and was grateful every day for their support of him—and Maeve.

Hours later, when he noticed Maeve suppressing a yawn, Aubrey stood, stretched and extended a hand to his wife. "Let's have a rest before dinner, love."

"A rest before dinner," Simon said, eyeing his own wife. "That sounds like a capital idea."

"Couldn't agree more," Derek said.

Their wives rolled their eyes in unison, setting off a wave of laughter.

"I assume we're in my usual room?" Aubrey asked.

"You assume correctly," Catherine said. "And Maxi is in the nursery on the third floor, but I knew you'd want him with you at night, so there's a cradle for him in your room."

"Thank you for thinking of that," Maeve said.

"Our home is your home," Catherine said. "Whatever you need, you only have to ask."

As they walked upstairs, Aubrey kept an arm around Maeve and pointed out the portrait of Derek's parents that occupied a prominent spot at the top of the grand staircase.

"He looks just like his father," Maeve said.

"Yes, he really does. He was only six when he lost them to murder, orchestrated by his power-hungry uncle."

"I can't imagine such a thing."

"I can't either. It's hard to believe that he's been a duke since the tender age of six."

"If anything were to happen to us, I'd want them to raise Maxi."

"You would?"

"I can't think of anyone better prepared to guide an orphaned child to adulthood than someone who has survived a similar ordeal and gone on to have such a successful life."

"You make a very good point, my love. I'll ask him if they'd be willing, although I have no doubt that they would love him like their own." He ushered her into the room that had become familiar to him from previous visits, and closed the door behind him, sliding the lock into place to ensure they wouldn't be disturbed. "However, I don't wish to discuss the possibility of our premature demise on such a fine and perfect day."

"What would you rather discuss instead?" she asked, with the coy smile that made his blood boil. He'd expected his desire for her to wane somewhat over time, but the opposite had occurred. The more he had of her, the more he wanted.

He went to her, turned her to face away from him and began to unbutton the shirtwaist she had worn for traveling. "I'd like to discuss my lovely, sweet, delectable wife and how much I love her."

"I like that topic. Please proceed."

Smiling, he kissed the curve of her neck that had held him in thrall from the day they met. Knowing that glorious neck and every other part of her belonged to him and him alone was the best thing in his life. "I love her more than anything in this entire world, except for our glorious Maxi, whom I love equally."

"I'll allow that. Continue."

Aubrey laughed at her witty reply. "I love her gorgeous neck and her creamy white skin." One garment at a time, he revealed her to his hungry gaze. "I love her bountiful breasts and the way they get larger when she's carrying my child." He cupped her breasts and ran his thumbs over the sensitive tips, reveling in her gasp. "I love sleeping with her, making love with her, having babies with her, laughing with her, arguing with her, kissing her."

She wound her arms around his neck and returned his kiss with the enthusiasm he'd come to expect from her.

"I love everything with her." Backing her up to the bed, he freed his cock from his trousers and pushed into her in one smooth stroke.

When her back arched off the mattress, he marveled at how she was always ready for him.

"Aubrey," she whispered.

"Hmmm?"

"I love everything with you, too." With her hand on his face, she gazed into his eyes, staring straight into the very heart of him as only she could. "I'll never forget the way you protected me when I was at my lowest moment. I don't know what would've become of me if you hadn't found me in the ruins of your family's summer home and made up your mind that we were meant to be."

"I found my whole life amid those ruins, and I'll always be thankful that you agreed to be mine."

"Best thing I've ever done was agree to be yours."

"I couldn't agree more, my love."

Author's Note

Thank you for reading *Deceived by Desire*! I hope you loved Aubrey and Maeve as much as I enjoyed writing them and visiting again with Derek, Catherine, Simon, Madeleine and Justin from *Duchess by Deception*. Join the Deceived by Desire Reader Group at facebook.com/groups/DeceivedbyDesire to discuss Aubrey and Maeve's story with spoilers allowed, and the Gilded Series Group at facebook.com/groups/GildedSeries for updates on the series.

This second book in my Gilded Series took me on an exciting journey through the historical past of my beloved hometown of Newport, Rhode Island. For years, I have wanted to write about Newport's storied Gilded Age history and the glorious summer "cottages" that are managed today by the Preservation Society of Newport County. I recommend a visit to the society's website at newportmansions.org to experience the grandeur for yourself. I love all the amazing houses, but The Breakers is my favorite. Several of the houses referred to in this book were given fictional names, such as the Nelson and Russell homes, which didn't actually exist.

If you're ever in the area, I recommend spending a day in Newport touring the mansions as well as other historically significant sites such as the Newport Casino, which is home now to the International Tennis Hall of Fame. Also of historical interest are the Redwood Library, Trinity Church, Touro Synagogue and St. Mary's Roman Catholic

Church, where President and Mrs. Kennedy—as well as Mr. and Mrs. Force—were married. Newport, the longtime host of the America's Cup races, is also known as the "sailing capital of the world," and is home to amazing shopping, restaurants and world-class beaches.

My late father, George Brown Sullivan, was raised in Newport's Fifth Ward, where many Irish people resided. It's still known as the Irish end of town. In his younger days, my father lived on Grafton Street and worked for TJ Brown Landscaping, founded by his grandfather, Timothy J. Brown, in 1901, and run by his uncles, William "Wiggie" Brown and Timothy J. "Kaiser" Brown, during my dad's time with the company. My paternal grandmother, Margaret Mary Pauline Brown Sullivan, was their sister and kept the books for the company for many years. TJ Brown is one of Newport's oldest businesses and is still in existence today with fourth-generation proprietors that include Wiggie's grandson, TJ Brown. As an aside, my twenty-three-year-old daughter, Emily, bears a striking resemblance to my grandmother Margaret. Side-by-side pictures of the two as young girls are quite remarkable!

My dad's father, who died when my father was only nineteen, was known as "Scroogey" in the Fifth Ward after playing the role of Scrooge in a school production of *A Christmas Carol*. By all accounts, he was a kind and generous man who was loved by all who knew him, unlike his namesake. My father's beloved cousin, Wiggie's daughter Eileen Brown, was a constant presence in our lives as kids. Eileen's mother was an Irishwoman named Bridget, who was known to all as Bridie. Bridie married Wiggie after they met while working at Newport's John Nicholas Brown estate, owned by the family that founded Brown University—not the Browns I was related to! Wiggie and Kaiser had a niece named Kathleen, who was known as Heine, the name her siblings gave her when they couldn't pronounce Kathleen.

My dad told stories about working on the grounds of all of Newport's illustrious homes and had tall tales to tell about the colorful characters who occupied them. He was well acquainted with the homes that provided generous noontime meals for the help, even the guy who cut the grass—and he cut a lot of grass before he was drafted into the army at the end of the Korean conflict and found his life's work as an aviation mechanic. He talked of driving Cadillacs to Florida for the millionaires he worked for from the time he was nineteen. He delighted in the fact that he parked cars at the Kennedy wedding at Newport's Hammersmith Farm, the family home of Jacqueline Kennedy's stepfather, Hugh D. Auchincloss. Hammersmith Farm became known as the "Summer White House" while Kennedy was president, and his yacht, the *Honey Fitz*, was often docked in front of the home.

I had great fun bringing my family's interesting history—and their colorful nicknames—into this book as well as featuring the Brown and Sullivan family names with Maeve's character. I intended it to be a love letter of sorts to the place where I was raised and to the people who came before me.

I relied on several books about Newport to help frame the story told in this book, particularly *To Marry an English Lord: Tales of Wealth and Marriage, Sex and Snobbery*, by Gail MacColl and Carol McD. Wallace, and *Gilded: How Newport Became America's Richest Resort*, by Deborah Davis. Both offered interesting and illuminating details of Newport's colorful past. To find more information about the Fall River Line that connected New York and Boston and served as a central transportation component for turn-of-the-century travelers to Newport, go to cruiselinehistory.com/the-old-fall-river-line-everyone-from-presidents-to-swindlers-sailed-the-sound-on-mammoth-palace-steamers-in-the-heyday-of-the-side-wheelers.

This book was due a few short months after I lost my beloved dad, in the summer of 2018, and I wish to express my heartfelt thanks to my Kensington Books editor, Martin Biro, and the entire Kensington team for giving me a much-needed extension on my deadline to deliver this book. I appreciate their kindness and understanding during a difficult time in my life.

Many thanks as always to the team that supports me behind the scenes, giving me the freedom to spend my days in made-up worlds with the fictional characters that live inside my overactive imagination—my husband, Dan, as well as Julie Cupp, Lisa Cafferty, Holly Sullivan, Isabel Sullivan, Nikki Colquhoun and Jessica Estep. Thank you also to my beta readers, Anne Woodall and Kara Conrad, for always making time for me when I need you! You're the best! Finally, to my cousin Sydney Mello, who majored in history in college and is a Newport history buff, thank you for braving my saucy romance novel to fact-check me!

Last but certainly not least, thank you to my faithful readers who come along for the ride, no matter where my imagination takes me, even to Gilded Age Newport. Thank you for your support of me and my books. You will never know how much each of you means to me.

Much love,
Marie

See how Catherine and Derek's story began
in the first book in Marie Force's Gilded series,

DUCHESS BY DECEPTION

Derek Eagan, the dashing Duke of Westwood, is well
aware of his looming deadline. But weary of tiresome
debutantes, he seeks a respite at his country home in
Essex—and encounters a man digging on his property.
Except he's not a man. He's a very lovely woman.
Who suddenly faints at his feet.

Catherine McCabe's disdain for the aristocracy has
already led her to flee an arranged marriage with a
boorish viscount. The last thing she wants is to be
waylaid in a duke's home. Yet, she is compelled
to stay by the handsome, thoughtful man who
introduces himself as the duke's estate manager.

Derek realizes two things immediately: he is
captivated by her delicate beauty, and to figure out
what she was up to, Catherine must not know he is
the duke. But as they fall passionately in love,
Derek's lie spins out of control. Will their bond
survive his deception, not to mention the scorned
viscount's pursuit? Most important, can Catherine
fall in love all over again—this time with the duke?

Keeping reading for a special look!

A Zebra mass-market paperback and eBook on sale now.

London, May 5, 1902

"I cannot bear another minute of this charade," Derek Eagan, the seventh Duke of Westwood, declared to his cohorts as they watched a simpering group of debutantes work the gilded ballroom. He tugged impatiently at his starched attachable collar and wished he could remove it and the tie that choked him without sending yet another tedious scandal rippling through the *ton*.

"What charade?" asked Justin Enderly, his smile dripping with the charm that had endeared him to many a mother. "Watching nubile young things flit about with love and marriage on their minds?" As the second son of an earl, Enderly was much less desirable to the simpering debs than Derek, once again considered the Season's top prize— and Enderly knew it, of course.

"All of it." Derek gestured to the glittering scene before them in the Earl of Chadwick's enormous ballroom. Surely half the aristocracy was in attendance at one of the Season's most anticipated balls. Women in frothy gowns made of the finest silks and satins, dripping in exquisite gems. Men in their most dashing evening wear. "The balls, the gowns, the dance cards, the ludicrous conversations, the desperate mothers. I've grown so weary of it, I could spit."

Aubrey Nelson, the American-born industrialist who'd humored his English-born mother with a second Season, nodded in agreement. "The pomp, the ceremony, the *rules*." He shook his head. "I'll be back in New York—or banished from polite society—long before I master them all."

Unlike Nelson, Derek had been raised for the charade, but many of the rules escaped him, as well. "Utter drivel," Derek murmured. "I've half a mind to compromise a willing young maiden and be done with the whole nightmare."

"What's stopping you?" Enderly asked, crooking a wicked eyebrow.

"I'd have to attempt to converse with her for the rest of my days," Derek grumbled. His friends and the hangers-on surrounding them howled with laughter. "I've talked to every one of them and haven't found one who interests me enough to pursue anything further."

"Same as last year," Enderly said.

"And the year before, and the year before that," Derek said, the despair creeping in once again. It wasn't that he didn't *want* to find a wife. He would love nothing more than to have one person in the world who belonged only to him and vice versa. Not to mention he *needed* a wife, albeit for altogether different reasons. Yet he wasn't willing to settle.

Each year he approached the Season with a new sense of hope, and each year, as the young women got younger and he got older, the disappointment afterward became more intense and longer lasting. This year, however, the bloody *deadline* loomed large, coloring his view of the Season's limited options.

"This year's group seems particularly *young*," Enderly noted.

"Or perhaps we're just getting particularly old," Derek said morosely.

"No doubt," Enderly said. As a second son he was under much less pressure to marry than Derek and enjoyed his bachelor life far too much to give it up before he absolutely had to. For that matter, *everyone* was under less pressure to marry than Derek, thanks to the damned deadline.

"Is there one among them who cares about something other than her hair or her gown or her slippers?" Derek asked. Was there one among them, he wanted to ask, who looked at him and saw anything other than his title, his rank, his wealth *or* the looming deadline that had filled the betting books all over town?

"They *all* care about their dance cards," Nelson said dryly.

"Too true," Derek concurred. "Speaking only for myself, I've had enough. I'm returning to Westwood Hall in the morning."

"But the Season still has weeks left to go," Enderly said in obvious distress. "You can't go yet, Your Grace. What of your deadline? What will Lord Anthony say?"

"He would hardly care. He's practically salivating, *hoping* I fail to marry in time."

"Whatever could your ancestor have been thinking, putting such an utterly daft provision in his will?" Nelson asked. "Enter into a 'suitable state of matrimony'—whatever that is—by thirty or abdicate your title? I've never heard of such a thing."

Of course, he hadn't, Derek mused. The colonists had left such barbaric practices behind in England. "I suppose he was out to ensure the bloodline. Instead, he placed a matrimonial pox upon each succeeding generation."

"Is it even legal?" Justin asked.

"Probably not, but the previous dukes married young, so it was never an issue for them, and I chose not to contest it with Anthony waiting in the wings drooling all over the duchy."

"What happens if you don't marry in time?" Nelson asked.

"The title and all accompanying holdings transfer to my uncle and then later to Simon, who, as the heir, would also be required to marry *posthaste. That* would truly be a travesty." If anyone was less suited to a life of marriage, responsibility and duty, it was Derek's happy-go-lucky first cousin and dear friend.

"Have any of your ancestors missed the deadline?" Nelson asked, seeming genuinely intrigued by the drama of it all whereas Derek was just weary—from thinking about it, dreading it and from imagining being married to a nameless, faceless woman just to preserve his title. He shuddered at the thought of shackles and chains.

"Not so far, and I have no desire to be the first. However, I refuse to pick just anyone in order to keep my title." His ancestor's efforts to ensure the dukedom had put Derek in a serious quandary. His thirtieth birthday was now mere days away without a female prospect in sight who sparked anything in him other than utter apathy, not to mention *despair* at the idea of having to actually talk to her for the rest of his life.

Naturally, the entire *haute ton* was captivated by Derek's plight, but not a one of them gave a fig about his happiness or well-being. He would almost prefer to surrender the title than be shackled for life to a "suitable" woman who did nothing else for him but ensure his place in the aristocracy.

Almost.

With his deadline the talk of the Season, every available young maiden had been marched before him—more than once. Judging his prospects by what he'd seen of the Season's available crop, he was in no danger of imminent betrothal. "What's the point of hanging around when I already know that none of them suit me?"

"They don't have to suit you, Your Grace," Enderly reminded him. "You only need one with the proper equipment to provide an heir—and a spare if you're feeling particularly randy."

"And you need her to say, 'I do,' by the sixteenth of May," Nelson added with a wry grin.

"Don't remind me," Derek grumbled. Was it just him, or was it exceedingly warm tonight? Or was it the reminder of his coming birthday that had him sweating? Perhaps it was the rampant wagering that had him on edge. He'd lost track of whom among his so-called peers and "friends" was betting for or against the likelihood of his securing a suitable marriage before his birthday.

Derek never would've chosen the title he'd inherited at the tender age of six when his parents were killed in a carriage accident. Over the years since his majority, however, he'd grown into his role as one of the most powerful and influential men in England. He didn't relish the idea of turning over his title and holdings to an arrogant, greedy, overly ambitious uncle who would care far more about how he was judged in polite society than he ever would about ensuring that their tenants had adequate roofs over their heads. Nor did Derek wish to see his cousin constrained by a life he had no interest in. Too many people depended on the dukedom to see it end up in the hands of someone who couldn't care less about it.

A vexing debate for sure, especially since Derek often dreamed of shedding his responsibilities and taking off to see the world as he'd always wanted to do. But then he thought, as he often did, of his late parents. Since their deaths, he'd aimed to live his life in a manner and fashion that would've made them proud. Losing his title, especially to an uncle his father had despised, would not make them proud, so Derek would do what was expected of him because that was what he'd always done—no matter what it might've cost him.

"What of all your meetings?" Enderly asked.

"I had the last of them today with the Newcastle upon Tyne Electric Supply Company to pump some capital into their Neptune Bank Power Station. They're doing some intriguing work with three-phase electrical power distribution." The blank looks on the faces of his friends tampered his enthusiasm. Where he would absorb such information with obsessive attention to detail, he'd come to realize that others were less interested in the *how* of electrical lighting and other innovations. They were, however, more than content to fully luxuriate in modern conveniences without bothering themselves with the details. Electricity was making its way into wealthy homes and public buildings in town, but it would be a while yet before it reached the country.

"Wasn't there another one?" Justin asked. "Something with brothers?"

Derek nodded. "I'll be providing emergency financing to the brothers from America who believe they've found the secret to manned flight."

"You can't be serious," Nelson said. "The Wright brothers?"

Derek nodded, used to his peers finding his investment decisions questionable at best. They couldn't, however, argue with his results.

"Has everyone in America finally said no to them?" Nelson asked.

"I didn't ask that. I simply wish to be a part of what they're doing. I believe they will attain success, perhaps before the end of the decade."

Nelson rolled his eyes. "It's your money to throw away."

"What's next?" Enderly asked, his tone tinged with sarcasm. "Motorcars?"

"As a matter of fact, due to my involvement in Wolseley Tool and Motor Car Company, I was asked to back a venture with Lord Austin and his brother that will bring production of motorcars to England in the foreseeable future."

"Why am I not surprised?" Enderly asked with a smile.

One of the most annoying of that year's debutantes, Lady Charlotte something or other, flashed Derek a suggestive smile full of invitation. As he'd learned early in his first Season, he didn't make eye contact unless he wished to encourage attention, which he most assuredly did not.

"All you'd have to do is snap your fingers, and Lady Charlotte would say 'I do,'" Enderly said.

Derek could have been mistaken, but it seemed as if his friend was enjoying baiting him. "If I'm going to shackle myself to a woman for life, she's got to have more than the proper plumbing." Derek tugged again on the collar that poked at his neck and the strangling tie. His valet Gregory had been rather rigid in his knot tying that night, as if he too were out to constrain Derek to his husbandly fate.

"What is it exactly that you seek, Your Grace?" Nelson asked with a kind smile.

"Damned if I know. I just hope I'll recognize it when I see it, and I hope I'll see it soon." She was out there somewhere. He had no doubt of that. If only he knew where to look.

"You're holding out for a love match then?" Enderly asked.

"I don't necessarily yearn for the mess that accompanies a love match, but is it too much to hope for some intelligent conversation with my after-dinner port?" The utter despair of his situation came crashing down as he viewed the gay scene before him. "What in the world would I *talk* about to any of them?"

Apparently, neither of his friends could supply a satisfactory answer.

Enderly shifted with discomfort from one foot to the other. "What are your plans, Westy?" he asked softly, reverting to Derek's nickname from their years together at Eton.

"I need to spend some time riding Hercules and thinking. I can't think here. Just a few days, and then I'll come back and bite the proverbial bullet." He'd have no other option but to choose one of the young women flitting before him unless he wanted everything he had to slip through his fingers to an uncle who didn't deserve it. But the thought of being stuck with a wife who didn't suit him made him ill.

"You'll be the talk of the *ton*," Enderly declared, scandalized.

"Let them talk. I won't hear it in Essex."

"But it won't be any fun without you, Your Grace," Nelson said mournfully.

Enderly nodded in agreement. "Nor will the ladies flock about us with quite the same . . ."

"*Desperation?*" Derek asked with a grin. His friends laughed. As usual, they had kept this dreadful experience from being a total loss.

"Lady Patience will wish to visit," Enderly said with an evil grin. "She's apt to follow you to the country."

"She won't gain an audience with me even if she does give chase," Derek said of the Duke of Devonshire's daughter, who had pursued him with relentless determination. "She holds even less appeal than the others."

"Why is that?" Nelson asked.

"She brays like a donkey when she laughs."

"Ouch," Enderly said, chuckling.

"I quite fear that no woman will meet the discriminating requirements of our dear, distinguished friend," Nelson said to Enderly.

"That's just fine with me," Derek said, happier than he'd been in weeks now that a decision had been made. "I'd rather be a lonely commoner than be shackled for life to a 'suitable' braying donkey."

Lord Anthony Eagan, son of a duke, brother of a duke and uncle to the current duke, reclined on a red velvet chaise and took a sip from his glass of port. Always on the outside looking in, just barely on the fringes of tremendous wealth and power. Thankfully, all three dukes had provided handsomely for him, allowing him the freedom to pursue his own interests.

But what interested Anthony, what *seduced* him more than anything else ever could, was the *power* of the title. When the Duke of Westwood entered a room, people noticed. Society noticed. No one paid much heed, on the other hand, to the duke's second son, his brother, or his uncle. In the fifteen years he'd served as his nephew's guardian, he had sampled a generous helping of power. Having to cede it to a boy just barely out of leading strings had been demoralizing, to say the least. The subsequent years had reduced Anthony once again to the fringes. He didn't much care for the fringes, and he never had.

While Derek had stepped nobly and with infuriating independence into the position he'd been born to, Anthony had been relegated to watching and seething and planning. Now, on the eve of Derek's thirtieth birthday, came opportunity. If Derek failed to marry by the sixteenth of May, the title would revert to Anthony, and he would finally be the Duke of Westwood. The way it always should have been.

And while he had come to grudgingly respect his nephew's acumen with finance and his bearing among the *haute ton*, he disdained the boy's inner softness. That softness, Anthony mused, would be his downfall, just as it had been his father's. Perhaps it was because Derek had lost his parents at such a tender age or maybe it was the guilt that came from being the twin who'd survived the journey into this world. Regardless of the cause, Derek lacked the inner fortitude that Anthony possessed in spades.

Anthony wasn't afraid to use that fortitude to gain what should've been his all along. Derek was supposed to have been in that carriage the night his parents had been killed. They had planned to dine as a family at a neighboring estate. No one had bothered to tell Anthony that the boy had been left behind in the nursery when he showed signs of fever.

No one had told him until it was far too late, until he'd been saddled with an orphaned young nephew and vast holdings to "oversee" until that nephew gained his majority.

The holdings were supposed to have been *his*. Instead, he became the steward rather than the duke. Instead, it was left to him to nurse his grief-stricken nephew through those dreadful months after "the accident." Since another "accident" so soon after the first would've raised suspicions, he had nursed when he'd wanted to strangle. He'd mentored when he wanted to stab. If only the boy had been where he was supposed to be, Anthony would've had what was rightfully his for all this time.

Soon, Anthony mused. That softness within Derek

wouldn't permit him to marry for the sake of his title. Like the fool he was, Derek wanted *more*. The softness would be his downfall. Anthony was betting on it and breathing a bit easier after realizing that none of the Season's debutantes had caught his discerning nephew's eye.

Lucy Dexter, one of London's most accomplished courtesans, crawled from the foot of the chaise to envelop him in soft curves and sweet scent. Silky dark hair cascaded invitingly over his chest.

"What troubles you tonight, my lord?"

"Nothing of any consequence."

"You ponder the fate of your nephew and the duchy you covet."

Anthony raised an imperious brow. "It is rather impertinent for you to speak so boldly of things that are none of your concern."

Lucy's husky laugh caught the attention of his recently satisfied libido. "How can you say such things are none of my concern when you've made them my concern by *unburdening* yourself to me quite regularly?"

The double entendre wasn't lost on Anthony. Through the silk dressing gown he had given her, he cupped a bountiful breast and pinched the nipple roughly between his fingers, drawing a surprised gasp from her bow-shaped mouth. "If you speak of my concerns with anyone else, madam, you will quickly discover my less-than-amiable side, which I usually prefer to keep hidden from the fairer sex."

Her blue eyes hardened with displeasure. "I believe I have proven my allegiance time and again over these many years, my lord. There is no need for threats nor less-than-subtle attempts at intimidation."

She could quite ruin him. She knew it. He knew it.

Power. He had given her far too much, he realized, and that was something he might, at some point, need to contend with. But certainly not right now, not when she was pushing his dressing gown aside to drop soft, openmouthed kisses on his chest.

Anthony sighed with satisfaction, placed the empty glass on a table and buried his fingers in silky tresses. When she took his cock into the velvety warmth of her mouth, he closed his eyes and let his head fall back in surrender.

Power—the only commodity that truly counted. As she sucked and licked him to explosive fulfillment, it hardly mattered that he had ceded some of his to her for the time being. Before long, he'd have more than he knew what to do with. It was only a matter of time.